MIDNIGHT BOND

MIDNIGHT BOND

WOLVES OF MIDNIGHT

BECKY MOYNIHAN

BROKEN
BOOKS

Published by Broken Books
www.beckymoynihan.com

ISBN-13: 979-8-9883737-5-9

Cover design by Becky Moynihan
Cover model by www.depositphotos.com

To all the readers who fell in love with this series . . .

You're my pack.

CHAPTER 1

BRIELLE

I squirmed in my seat, resisting the urge to fan my flushed skin.

It was almost that time of month again, the time I dreaded most in the world.

No, not shark week. This was much, much worse. Something I'd been living with for over a year now.

I was getting better at catching the signs earlier on—the random hot flashes, the agitation and restlessness, the need to be outdoors. Thankfully, the desire for raw meat hadn't hit yet. Still, I'd take my period any day over this incessant itch under my skin. Hell, I'd take *menopause*.

Despite the chill in the late November air, I felt another drop of sweat slither down my spine beneath my magenta-colored dress. I'd thought the symptoms had been warning me of something else at first. I'd nearly jumped out of my chair when the hot flashes had hit, convinced that I'd finally—*finally*—gone into heat.

My relief had faded a moment later when my body did nothing else but sweat. I'd been around enough female werewolves to know that I'd be doing a *lot* more than sweating right now if I were in heat. For one, I'd probably be rubbing my lady bits against the plastic chair in hopes of getting off.

The fact that I was at a *wedding* wouldn't matter. Orgasms would be the only thing on my mind.

Sadly, I had no such urges. Even when the priest loudly proclaimed for all to hear, "You may now kiss the bride," the only rush I felt was another hot flash.

As the groom eagerly swept his blushing bride into his arms to kiss her, excited cheers rose into the air. I stood from my seat with the rest of the crowd, fixing my lips into a smile while I clapped.

This was the second wedding I'd attended in the past couple of months. The first was Griff and Vi's, and now it was Reid and Desirae's turn. Both couples had experienced a whirlwind romance before quickly tying the knot. Apparently, werewolves didn't do long engagements. Once they'd claimed each other, they were as good as married anyway.

Then there was the *breeding*.

While Reid continued to kiss his mate with heated passion, I peeked at the females on either side of me. Namely, their bellies. Both were over halfway along in their pregnancies and clearly showing. My fiery-haired best friend, Nora, was a little rounder, but that was because she'd already done this a couple times.

Three pregnancies in one year, *sheesh*.

I'd quickly learned that werewolves had a tendency to hump like jackrabbits. My poor sensitive ears could attest to that—on a daily basis. It seemed like everyone was mating and having babies these days, and if Reid pursued Desirae with that same passion later on tonight, they would no doubt have a little one in a handful of months too. A handful, because the werewolf gestational period was around four months. I still couldn't wrap my head around that.

The dark-haired female on my other side laughed as her new husband whooped and hollered at the top of his lungs, urging Reid to give his bride a little tongue. I glanced at Vi and Griff, noting how happy they looked. Even though Vi had been dating Reid only a few short months ago, there was no lingering animosity or tension

2

between the couples. Both had found their true mates, and they were equally happy for each other.

Still, it had been a surprise when Reid and Desirae had invited us to their wedding in Maine. She would soon be initiated into his pack and stand by his side as he became the new alpha in a few months. Although Midnight Pack and Lunar Falls Pack were now close allies, wolves from different packs didn't casually intermingle like this very often.

If werewolves could be summed up in one word, it would probably be territorial. Too many dominant males in one location was usually a recipe for disaster, especially if they were unmated.

I glanced to the left again, but my eyes went straight past Nora and her mate to the male quietly standing on the end. The glance was brief. Barely a glance at all. But in that split second, I found his gaze already on me.

The breath stalled in my lungs as his intense blue-gray eyes met mine.

I quickly looked away, hating that my body had reacted so viscerally. *Again.* Annoyed, I faced forward and joined Griff in loudly whooping for the newlyweds, hoping no one would notice how strained my voice sounded. I normally loved attending weddings. Several of my high school and college friends had recently become married, and I was truly happy for them, especially for my best friend who'd *literally* found her soulmate. But lately, I'd felt . . .

Restless.

For months, I'd blamed the feeling on my recently-acquired werewolf instincts, but as more and more of the people in my life found their happily ever afters, I could no longer deny the real reason for my restless spirit.

I wanted what they had.

I wanted to find my true mate. I wanted a whirlwind romance. I wanted to fall madly in love, get married, and have lots of babies.

I wanted that for myself so badly that it was starting to hurt. And being around so much love and happiness all the time made it harder and harder to pretend that I wasn't downright miserable. I hadn't even gone into *heat* yet.

A lone tear slid down my cheek before I could stop it, and I paused in my clapping to hurriedly brush it away. Just when I thought no one had noticed, the feeling of being watched heightened my awareness. I would have ignored the feeling if it weren't for the fact that I'd felt it countless times before.

Him.

He was watching me.

He was *always* watching me.

Refusing to look his way again, I kept my gaze firmly glued on the newlyweds who were now making their way down the aisle. Another wave of heat swept over me, but I continued to clap instead of wipe away the sweat beading my forehead. Only a few more minutes and I could get some much-needed fresh air. The wedding was outside, but with the press of bodies all around and love practically oozing from their happy pores, I desperately needed space.

Which was odd for me, even at this time of month.

"You okay?"

I glanced at Nora, surprised to find her aqua blue eyes worriedly fixed on me. As soon as she said the words, her husband's attention went to me as well. Always the vigilant alpha, he took me in, his dark amber gaze probably seeing far more than I wanted it to.

"Of course," I quickly reassured, all too aware that a pair of blue-gray eyes were still watching me. "Just a little warm."

Nora's brows lifted.

4

"Not *that*," I said, smirking despite my discomfort. "The moon's just extra bright tonight."

"Oh," my best friend exclaimed, glancing up at the evening sky. "Maybe we should—"

"Don't even finish that sentence," I interrupted, waving off her concern. "I've got two whole days before I need to wolf out. You know I'm just extra sensitive this time of month."

Despite my words, I could feel the blue-gray eyes still watching me. Another drop of sweat slid down my spine.

Nora glanced at her dark-haired husband, no doubt sharing a quick telepathic conversation with him. Sure enough, Kolton looked down at her and nodded, as if agreeing with whatever she'd just said.

Smiling at him, she turned back to me and said, "Well, don't feel the need to push yourself. We're fine with heading home early. I haven't been away from Luca and Lillian this long before and already miss them."

"Yeah, and Vi is feeling horny," a voice from my right chimed in, followed by a loud "*Ooph!*" as his wife no doubt elbowed him.

"Griffin Hayes," she hissed under her breath, but his only response was an unapologetic chuckle.

Normally, I appreciated their banter and often joined in, but I suddenly felt stifled. The restless itch beneath my skin grew unbearable, and I muttered a quick response before excusing myself. Thankfully, the other guests were starting to leave their seats as well, so no one thought it odd when I hurried from the scene and out into the starry night.

Well, maybe no one but the male whose eyes were pinned on my back as I left. The male who'd been watching me for over a year now. The male who'd helped me transition into a wolf for the first time after I'd almost died. Who'd cradled my body tenderly and watched over me throughout the entire agonizing process.

Who'd barely spoken to me ever since, let alone touched me.

More heat flushed my face, but this time, it didn't have anything to do with the wolf stirring inside me, desperate to be let out. The heat was pure hurt. No. *Anger.*

The emotion was irrational, I knew that. But I couldn't stop myself from feeling it. From *obsessing* over it.

We'd lived in the same house for over a year. A *year.*

But despite my unmated status—and despite the way he constantly watched me . . .

Jagger Montgomery wanted nothing to do with me.

His loss, I told myself for the umpteenth time, expertly navigating the uneven ground in my high heels. A cool breeze stirred my hair, plastering a few of the wavy honey-brown strands onto my red lipstick. As I impatiently tugged the strands free, the gold bangles on my wrists loudly clinked together.

This stupid obsession with Midnight Pack's second in command needed to end and *fast.* It was clear he wasn't interested in me. If he was, he would have pursued me by now. I'd been pursued plenty of times in my twenty-three years of life. Boys had taken an interest in me at an early age, drawn to my flamboyant personality. I'd dated dozens of males. *Dozens.* Sometimes two at a time.

Everywhere I went, heads turned. Guys tripped all over themselves to get my attention. I'd never needed to pursue a relationship because it always came to *me.* Hooking up with a guy was easy, even if it always ended the same way. I hadn't wanted more back then, but now that I did, I could only focus on one male.

An unavailable one who had absolutely *no* intention of pursuing me.

How infuriating was that?

6

As I neared the edge of the clearing where the ceremony and reception were being held, the feeling of being watched swept over me once more. I tensed, knowing that he'd only followed me because I was an unmated female, alone and far from pack territory. It was his duty to keep me safe. He had no intention of *speaking* to me, so I planned to do the same.

But before I could flounce off and pretend he wasn't there, a male voice that wasn't his said, "Care for a drink?"

Startled, I whirled to face the stranger.

"Sorry," he said, giving me a sheepish look. The flickering sconces from the wedding didn't illuminate his face this far away, but I easily picked out his features with my night vision. He was handsome in a boy scout sort of way, his expression open and his smile casually confident. Gesturing to one of the drinks he held, he added, "I couldn't help but notice that you looked flushed during the ceremony, so I thought you might want a drink. And some company."

Heh. Definitely confident. I'd met his type countless times before. After a little charm and gallantry, he expected to be in my panties by the end of the night. Human and werewolf males weren't all that different when it came to sex.

I was about to turn him down when a dark shadow several yards off shifted in my peripheral vision. A split-second glance confirmed what I already knew. Jagger had followed me. Of *course* he had. His dark suit, closely-shaven black hair, and light brown skin blended into the night, but one of the diamond studs in his ears caught the moonlight. As it winked at me, *taunted* me, I refocused on the boy scout and replied, "I'd love a drink and company. My name's Brielle, by the way."

His smile widened as he handed me a drink. "Theo. You must be pretty special if you travel with the infamous Alpha Rivers."

I shrugged with a small laugh before taking a sip of my drink. Alcohol. He *definitely* wanted inside my panties. "Nah, I'm just the alpha female's best friend."

His brows rose in interest. "Hybrid?"

"Nope. Turned last year."

Disappointment flashed in his brown eyes. Ouch. Guess that meant I wasn't *mate* material—not that I expected him to pursue me in that way. He clearly only wanted a quickie, and despite how cheap that made me feel, I was tempted to give it to him.

Ever since I'd moved into the Rivers' mansion, I'd been in a dry spell. Becoming a werewolf might have a little to do with it, but several of the unmated males from Midnight Pack had shown an interest in me over the past year.

I was off my game, and maybe a little romp with a perfect stranger was just what I needed to feel like myself again. Or at least distract me from the male lurking in the shadows.

So, I decided to flirt with the horny boy scout, laughing at his jokes and coyly fluttering my lashes at him. It worked like a charm. Half an hour later, he boldly asked me, "Want to get out of here? I have much better booze at my place."

Unoriginal, but I could roll with it.

Downing the last of my drink, I opened my mouth to accept his blatant sex invitation.

"Brielle."

At the sound of Jagger's voice, I stiffened. So did Theo. He'd obviously known Jagger had been watching us but hadn't mentioned it. Unable to ignore him any longer, Theo turned to the male with a tight-lipped smile.

"You're Jagger Montgomery, Midnight Pack's second in command, right? Don't worry about Brielle. I can have her back before they cut the wedding cake."

At that, Jagger's blue-gray eyes flashed a bright yellow. Theo stiffened even more, no doubt intimidated by the sight. As a regular werewolf like me, he didn't stand a chance if Jagger decided to shift right now and challenge him.

I was surprised yet not surprised by Jagger's reaction. Theo was making his intention toward me more than clear, but it was bordering on disrespectful.

As if he'd just realized this, Theo placatingly said, "I meant no disrespect, man. I didn't scent a claim on her and assumed she was available. If she's not—"

"I am," I interjected, popping a hand onto my hip. "Jagger was just leaving."

Jagger's yellow eyes slowly fixed on me. I stood my ground, even as a few more drops of sweat slithered down my spine. When he wouldn't look away, it became hard to breathe. He didn't say a single word, but I knew *exactly* what he was thinking.

"You wouldn't dare," I said in a deathly quiet whisper.

He continued to stare at me, his gaze unwavering. Then, "You're not leaving with him."

I clenched my jaw, stubbornly glaring back, but it was no use. As a frustrated tear threatened to spill over, I whirled and headed back toward the wedding. Theo made a sound of protest, but I didn't bother to apologize. I was too *furious.*

Jagger outranked me by far, but I still wasn't used to obeying pack hierarchy. I'd been raised to be independent, to make my own decisions—even if they were poor ones. If I wanted to have sex with a complete stranger, that should be *my* decision. My wolf practically howled inside my chest, wholeheartedly agreeing.

This wasn't the first time Jagger had robbed me of a choice. He clearly thought he had the right to dominate me, and I was sick of it. Sick of the looks. The constant monitoring. The broody attitude. The *silence*. I wanted *more* out of life, and he was preventing me from having it.

But maybe with him around, I couldn't have the life I dreamed of. Maybe the only way to have it was to run far, far away from him.

To *forget* about him.

And that meant leaving Midnight Pack.

CHAPTER 2

BRIELLE

"It's only for one day. I'll be *fine*."

"But it's so close to the full moon," Nora worriedly said, even as she handed me my makeup bag. "And this is your first visit in over a year. Are you sure you want to go alone?"

I paused in my packing to give my best friend a firm yet adoring look. "I love you to death, Nora Bora, but it's time I stand on my own two feet again. My parents were devastated when I didn't come home for the holidays last year. This is my chance to repair the rift between us. Besides, they still think you dragged me into a cult, so arriving alone will help prove to them that your billionaire husband isn't keeping me in a harem."

Nora made a face at me, and I flashed her my dimples.

"This time tomorrow," I went on, "I'll be back. Promise. With all the people you'll be hosting this year, you won't even miss me."

"Not true," she replied with a frown. "You're family, Brie. We're *all* going to miss you."

I gave her a grateful smile, then reached over and pulled her into a hug. It was on the tip of my tongue to tell her that not *everyone* would miss me, but I swallowed the words. Ever since our time together as roommates in college, Nora and I had shared practically everything with each other. She'd even told me about the supernatural world while I was still a human.

But when it came to talking about Jagger, I always froze.

What was there to say, anyway? I thought he was smoking hot and was inexplicably drawn to him, but we'd been living under the same roof for over a year and had barely spoken two words to each other. Not exactly my finest piece of gossip. In fact, it was downright embarrassing.

I knew she was aware of the constant tension between me and the infuriating male, though. It often felt like she was holding her breath and waiting for something to happen. When nothing did, she'd sigh and move on.

Well, it was way past time for *me* to sigh and move on, too.

I was done waiting for something, *anything* to happen. If I wanted to find my forever mate and start a family, I'd have to look elsewhere.

"You'll call the instant you feel the urge to wolf out?" Nora said, pulling back to give me a stern look.

"Yes, Alpha," I replied, earning myself an eye roll.

"I mean it, Brielle. You'll be in a heavily populated area surrounded by humans. Someone could get hurt, including you."

I sobered at that, all too aware of what could go wrong. Even after a year of shifting every full moon, I still struggled to control my wolf. I couldn't talk to her like Nora could with her wolf. She wasn't a separate entity like Storm was. She was *me*. Well, a brown-furred, feisty, somewhat feral version of me that walked on four legs. I hadn't even named her because, well, she was me.

After I'd been scratched and infected with werewolf toxin, I'd actually been excited to turn into a wolf. Living among supernaturals was way more thrilling than working nine-to-five at my accountant job and going home every night to an empty apartment. I'd never been the outdoorsy type, but I'd been looking forward to experiencing a new adventure alongside my best friend and the family she'd married into.

And then my body had rejected the werewolf toxin.

Just like that, my rose-colored dream of becoming a supernatural had turned into a terrifying nightmare. If it wasn't for Nora's powerful healing ability, I'd be long dead.

Shaking off the painful memory, I hugged Nora again and murmured, "I promise to call at the first sign. I won't take any chances."

"Thank you," she replied with a relieved sigh. "Oh!"

"What is it?" I pulled back, immediately concerned when she reached down to rub her belly.

"The baby kicked. Here." She grabbed my hand and placed it on her round stomach. A moment later, it sharply moved beneath my palm.

I sucked in a soft gasp, lifting my eyes to beam at her. "That was a strong kick. I bet it's a boy."

"Kolton thinks so too, and he was right about Luca and Lily."

A sudden ache throbbed in my chest, and I gently pulled my hand away to resume packing. "I still can't believe you're about to become a mother of three. Remember in college when you just wanted to be a normal werewolf so you could leave home and live a simple life of your choosing?"

She chuckled. "If I'd been told back then that I would become a hybrid alpha female, marry the most powerful alpha in America, live in a mansion, and conceive three babies in one year, I never would have believed it. Life has a tendency to surprise you that way, and I couldn't be happier with the outcome."

"You've definitely been blessed." I smiled at her, but it didn't quite reach my eyes—the annoying downside to having a heart-on-your-sleeve personality type.

Not surprisingly, she noticed right away. "You okay? You've

seemed a bit down lately."

Knowing there was no point in denying it, I let my smile fade. "It's stupid, really. I've just been pining for something I don't have."

"Like what?"

At the sincere look on her face, I finally caved and admitted, "A family of my own. You know: husband, kids, the whole shebang. I'm not jealous of you. I'm actually very happy for you and the life you now have. I just . . . I want it too and can't seem to get it out of my head."

Her expression fell. "Oh, Brie, I'm so sorry. I didn't realize."

"It's okay. I didn't realize either until recently. Now that everyone is getting married and having babies, my biological clock started ticking or something. But I'm not even dating anyone, and Jagger is being so—"

I slammed my mouth shut, realizing too late what I'd just done.

Pathetic. I was so *pathetic*.

But there was no undoing my slip, and Nora was searching my face far too intently to let it go.

Sure enough, she quietly said, "What did he do?"

Ugh, she was definitely going to think less of me after this. Grimacing, I flipped my suitcase shut and zipped it closed before confessing, "He's always *watching* me. Remember when Buck used to visit? I know he's interested in me, but I think Jagger scared him off with his silent glares. And then last night when I was about to hook up with some guy I met at the wedding—" Nora's brows flew up in surprise. "Hey, I haven't had sex in eighteen months. I'm horny and lonely, okay?"

She held up her hands, not quite able to hide a smirk. "Not judging."

"Anyway, Jagger wouldn't let me leave with him. I mean, what is his *deal?* It's not like I was in any danger. It's just sex. For a guy who barely speaks to me, he sure tells me what to do a lot. I know he's the pack's second in command and feels duty-bound to protect me, but he acts like my babysitter or something. What? What's that face? Ugh, sorry. I sound like a whiny brat. Just ignore me."

Nora huffed a laugh. "Slow down, Brie. You don't sound like a whiny brat. You're frustrated and understandably so." She paused for a moment, then said, "You know, I think this trip will actually be good for you."

I frowned, a tad suspicious at the way she said it. "How so?"

With a shrug, she grabbed my suitcase and hoisted it off my bed. "I just have a feeling. Jeez, Brielle, how many pairs of shoes did you pack in here?"

I hurried over to help her, but she'd already placed the suitcase on the floor and was rolling it toward my bedroom door at a rather fast clip. I bustled after her, grabbing my purse and phone before replying, "Just six. I wanted to be prepared in case it snowed."

As she opened the door and rolled my suitcase out into the hallway with an amused snort, a little body covered in blue tulle bounded toward her.

"Where are you going? Can I come this time? Pretty pleeeease?"

"Sorry, Mellie," Nora replied to her husband's youngest sister. The energetic seven-year-old was bouncing up and down in her newest princess dress, hugging the daylights out of the stuffed blue unicorn she took with her everywhere. "This trip is only for Brielle. She's going to visit her family for Thanksgiving."

The girl stopped bouncing to stare at me in confusion. "But *we* are your family. Right, Brie?"

I smiled down at her little cherub face as I closed the bedroom door behind me. "Of course you are, but I also have a human family, and they haven't seen me in a long time."

Her nose scrunched up. "But you're a werewolf now. What if you're tempted to eat them?"

A barked laugh, followed by a familiar head of spiky blond hair, rose up the stairs. "Like how you were tempted to eat Brielle when she was still human?" Griff teased the little brunette, earning himself an indignant pout.

"That was Blue," Melanie said, stamping her foot. "And she's better now. When she needs to chase something, she tells me."

Yet another reminder of why I needed to master my instincts. Even a *seven-year-old* had more control over her wolf than me.

"Well, I'm better now too," I replied, hating how untrue the words sounded. "I can handle one day out in the world by myself."

I *needed* to. And then maybe one day could become two, which could become three, then four, then five. The more independence I regained, the stronger my chances were of finding the future I dreamt about.

"And you're sure Jagger will be okay with this little trip?" Griff delivered the question casually, but I saw the pointed look he gave Nora as he took the suitcase from her and slung it over his shoulder.

Before Nora could answer, I snipped, "It's not up to him. Nora and Kolton are okay with it, and that's all that matters."

Griff turned to head back downstairs with the suitcase, but I didn't miss the amused smirk on his face at my words. Whatever. They all could sense the tension between me and Jagger, but I didn't feel like laughing about it. The sooner I could put some distance between us, the better. It wasn't like me to be this cranky, especially over a guy.

Man, I *really* needed to get laid. Maybe I'd bump into one of my exes while I was in Albany. I'd dated all throughout high school and at least a few of them probably still lived in the area. So long as they were still single. I did *not* hit up married men.

It would be just my luck if they were all happily married, I grumbled to myself. Someone should really make a dating app for supernaturals.

By the time we made it downstairs, the rest of the household had filtered into the foyer to wish me farewell.

Except Jagger.

I'd intentionally chosen this time of day to leave when I knew he'd be out on his morning run. Despite my resolve to put space between us, I knew it would be harder to leave if he was standing there watching me. I didn't know *why*. I just knew that it would.

"Here's a ham sandwich for the road in case you get hungry, dear," Nora's mother-in-law said, handing me the food wrapped in cellophane while she held her squirming seven-month-old granddaughter. "I know how starved I get right before the full moon."

At the reminder, heat flushed up my spine. One and a half days. I could act like a normal human being for the next thirty-six hours— give or take an hour or two.

"B! B!" a little voice exclaimed, and I quickly placed the sandwich in my purse so I could scoop up the nearly one-year-old boy toddling toward me. He squealed as I spun him around, and that same ache I'd felt in my chest earlier returned. Unable to resist, I breathed in Luca's intoxicating baby scent before placing a kiss on his chubby cheek.

"I'll be back soon, little man," I told him, my voice noticeably tight with emotion. One of his little hands snagged my hoop earring, and Nora swooped in to disentangle his fingers before he could rip it off.

As I handed him over to her, she took one look at my pinched face and softly whispered, "Sure you want to do this?"

All too aware that everyone was watching me, including my alpha who could force me to stay with a single word, I swallowed the emotion and cheerily replied, "Of course. Just make sure you guys save me a piece of pumpkin pie. And don't eat all the ice cream."

From beside her brother, Vi made a small guilty noise.

"Really, babe? *Again?*" Griff groaned. When she fluttered her dark lashes at him, he rolled over like the golden retriever he was and added, "I'll pick up some more ice cream this afternoon."

"And pickles."

He stared at his wife like she'd grown two heads.

She just shrugged and said, "I can't control what this baby craves."

When his gaze dropped to her distended stomach and lovingly caressed it, the itch to leave became unbearable.

"Okay, time to go," I rushed to say, grabbing the suitcase from Griff's shoulder. "Love you all. Don't have too much fun without me."

With my ovaries about to explode from all the gooey love and baby talk, I booked it toward the front door. Just as I reached for the handle, the door swung open, and I stopped dead in my tracks.

The instant I saw Jagger's broad frame fill the doorway, dread filled me. But something else did too. Butterflies. It was like an explosion of wings in my stomach, and the sensation punched all the air from my lungs.

As he quickly took in the situation, I couldn't help but let my own eyes wander down his front. His light brown skin was slick with sweat, making his well-defined muscles stand out even more. Both arms were covered in dark tattoos, the most prominent of them a big black snake coiled around his right forearm. He was naked from the waist up, and the sight was almost more than my poor eyes could handle.

I looked further down, but that was a huge mistake. He was

wearing black sweatpants, and they hung dangerously low on his hips. A dark trail of hair under his navel caught my eye, and I followed the path downward until—

"Where is she going?"

The demanding question was like a slap of reality to the face. My head snapped back, and I yanked my eyes up to glare at him.

"*She* is visiting her family. Now please step aside so I can leave."

When he refused to budge, my glare turned menacing. God, why did he have to *smell* so good? It was really hard to look mad when my senses were drowning in his earthy cedarwood musk. The wolf within me stirred, urging me to breathe him in a little deeper.

Ignoring me completely, Jagger looked over my head and focused on his alpha. "Why wasn't I informed of this?"

"Because where I go and what I do isn't up to you," I spoke for myself despite his rudeness—maybe a tad snidely.

His eyes finally slammed into mine. I almost took a step back, overwhelmed by the intensity. He was definitely more dominant than me, and at the moment, I hated it. Hated that he was wielding it like a weapon to put me in my place.

As the need to submit pulsed through me, I clenched my teeth, refusing to give in this time. I was leaving. I *had* to. And he wasn't going to stop me.

Just when my gaze started to waver under the weight of his dominance, a voice from behind me rumbled, "Stand down, Jagger. Let her go."

Jagger went still as stone. It didn't even look like he was breathing. The only things that moved were his nostrils, which flared slightly at Kolton's command.

After a tense moment, he said in a deathly quiet voice, "She's not ready."

"That isn't your decision to make," Kolton calmly replied, yet there was no mistaking his firm tone. He expected to be obeyed, not questioned.

A muscle feathered in Jagger's chiseled jaw as he ground his teeth together. For a split second, it looked like he was going to challenge his alpha's orders, but in the next instant, he slowly stepped out of the doorway to let me pass.

Too relieved to speak, I exited the house without a word, hurrying down the porch steps to reach my car already parked in the roundabout. Only after I'd placed my suitcase in the back and slid into the driver seat did I dare look toward the house.

Everyone was on the porch to watch me leave. Everyone but Jagger.

Feeling a tightness build in my chest, I waved goodbye and started the engine.

Then, before I could change my mind, I did something terrifying.

For the first time since becoming a werewolf . . .

I left my pack and struck out on my own.

CHAPTER 3

JAGGER

Never in my life had I come so close to disobeying a direct order from my alpha.

There had been times when I'd needed to become Kolton's voice of reason, but I'd never been tempted to challenge his command without just cause.

Until today.

I'd nearly lost my cool in front of everyone when Brielle had swept by me with her rainbow-colored suitcase in hand. Unable to watch her leave, I'd gone to my room to take a shower. Half an hour later, I was clean, dressed in my usual black garb, and practically crawling out of my skin.

Get mate, a deep gravelly voice growled inside my mind. When I ignored him, my wolf familiar growled more forcefully, *GET MATE.*

No, I growled back with equal intensity, swiftly putting Onyx in his place before he made me do something stupid.

Like go after her.

The demonic spirit that had turned me into a hybrid snarled quietly at my command. I tensed in the middle of my bedroom, ready to fight if he tried to wrestle control from me. He'd tried to at the wedding and had almost won, nearly losing his mind when that arrogant male from Lunar Falls Pack had made it clear he'd wanted Brielle for sex.

I waited for Onyx to challenge me, but when he chose to settle back down with a disgruntled huff, I relaxed my stance and strode for the door. Sensing someone on the other side, I tensed again as I opened it.

When Kolton's broad form greeted me, I had the sudden urge to puff out my chest. Quickly shoving the feeling down, I made sure my emotions were carefully in check before saying, "You should have warned me. I had a right to know."

He searched my face in that unflappable way of his before replying, "I know how you're feeling. I was in your shoes not long ago. But if you've chosen to reject the bond, the kindest thing you can do for Brielle right now is give her space so she can move on."

Onyx reared up again, his howl of protest exploding through our telepathic connection.

I barely flinched, more than prepared for his outburst after an entire year of enduring them. Hearing Kolton mention the bond felt strange, though. He and Nora had been there during Brielle's first shift when I'd let slip that she was my soulmate, but we hadn't spoken of it since. I'd asked them not to tell Brielle about the bond, but without her here, Kolton probably felt it was time to give me "the talk." Only I had no intention of letting him do so.

As soon as Onyx's howls started to fade, I said to Kolton, "This isn't about the bond. She hasn't been surrounded by humans on her own before, and the full moon is less than two days away. You know she still struggles to control her wolf, especially when her emotions are heightened. She'll be stressed about seeing her parents after the way she left them last year, and her instincts will be amplified. For her safety and theirs, she shouldn't have been allowed to leave."

Kolton studied me for a long moment, no doubt picking up on my uneven pulse. I'd tried to remain calm, but the thought of her out there all by herself was messing with my instincts.

Just when my patience started to wear thin, Kolton replied, "She's a free spirit, Jag. Keeping her here against her will would only foster resentment."

"I don't care. At least she'll be *safe*."

The words were out before I could stop them. Kolton's dark amber irises flashed in warning, but he calmly said, "I'm not calling her back. If Brielle needs us, she'll let us know."

It took all of my restraint not to reply. Staring at my alpha a moment longer, I finally relented with a curt nod. He studied me for another beat, then nodded in return and stepped back.

"We need a few last-minute items for Thanksgiving dinner before the stores close. I told Griff that you'd join him on an errand run."

I nodded again, all too aware that his goal was to distract me. As a male who'd found his own fated mate, Kolton understood better than anyone why I was so agitated. It didn't matter that I'd kept Brielle at arm's length this past year. The pull to be near her was relentless, and it had only grown stronger over the last several months. Knowing that I wouldn't see her for a full twenty-four hours was maddening.

As the day wore on, though, no amount of distraction could keep my agitation at bay. Even when Nora's parents joined us for Thanksgiving dinner and the celebrations were underway, I couldn't relax. With my meal practically untouched and my mood darker than ever, I made my excuses and retreated to my bedroom.

Hours later, as the house settled into slumber, something terrible happened. Something I never let happen. Something that would fill me with regret the moment I was thinking clearly again.

I gave in to my instincts.

Jumping from my bed, I grabbed the keys to my Porsche and strode from the room. Onyx sat up in excitement, encouraging me onward. I left the house without telling a soul, consequences be damned.

All I could focus on was the need pounding through my body. The instinct that only cared about one thing.

Bringing my mate back home where she belonged.

CHAPTER 4

BRIELLE

I didn't expect my *brothers* to be here.

Neither of them lived in Albany anymore and hadn't been home for Thanksgiving in years. Mom and Dad must have told them I was coming shortly after I'd called last night.

Sawyer was the first to greet me, answering the front door before I could even knock.

"Ellie!" he exclaimed, sweeping me into a bear hug.

I froze in his arms, my senses firing off on all cylinders. I'd never paid attention to his scent before. Not the smell of cologne or shampoo, but the scent that was distinct only to him. As it washed over me, the wolf trapped beneath my skin perked up in a way that made me stiffen even more in alarm.

Prey.

He smelled like *prey*.

And my wolf wanted nothing more than to take a bite out of him.

I squeezed my eyes shut and stopped breathing, willing the urge to fade away. After what felt like an eternity, Sawyer finally released me, only for my eldest brother to take his place.

The more serious of the two, Zeke hugged me more formally, patting my back almost awkwardly. I hadn't seen either of them since I'd graduated college, and we didn't have a super close relationship like Kolton did with his sisters. Still barely breathing, I tentatively hugged him back, relieved when he released me only a few seconds later.

"See? You guys worried for nothing. She looks perfectly normal," Sawyer said before reaching a hand up toward my mouth.

I jerked my head back and slapped his hand away. "What are you doing, weirdo?"

"Seeing if you have fangs."

"Dude, I told you not to do that," Zeke muttered with a disapproving frown.

"Well, *someone* had to."

"All right, leave your sister alone," a feminine voice scolded, and a lump formed in my throat when a middle-aged woman with honey-brown hair similar to mine squeezed past my brothers.

"Hi, Mom," I managed to say, my voice strained.

She looked thinner since the last time I'd seen her, the age lines on her face more pronounced. As she took me in, her emerald green eyes filled with tears. Mine did the same until I could barely make out her familiar features.

"Can I . . ." she croaked, then cleared her throat and tried again. "Can I hug you?"

A laugh that sounded a lot like a sob left me, and I nodded my head.

She immediately stepped forward and enveloped me in her arms, making the tears spill down my cheeks. I hugged her back fiercely, trying not to burst into uncontrollable sobs. I'd missed my family terribly this past year, but I hadn't realized how much until now.

"Praise Jesus, you've finally come home," she whispered with a shaky exhale, sniffing back her own tears. "I told your father again and again that you would. He didn't believe me, but now that you're here . . ."

As I sensed another body join us in the crowded doorway of

26

my suburban childhood home, I reopened my eyes and spotted my dad. His hair was dark and wavy like my brothers', but it had grayed considerably over the past year. Certain that I'd been the cause of it, guilt hit me hard.

"Daddy," I said. His back went ramrod straight, as if the sound of my voice had struck him like a bullet. Before I could say more, he stiffly turned and disappeared back inside the house.

Shocked, I stared at the spot he'd vacated, trying to grasp what had just happened.

"It'll be okay," my mom quietly reassured before releasing me. "Your dad is happy you're here. He's just . . ."

"Hurt," Sawyer finished for her.

Mom frowned at him.

Sawyer shrugged. "What? You raised us to speak our minds. Brielle should know how her actions this past year have hurt this family. Dad especially."

"N-no. I know," I said, wiping the tears from my face. "I've hurt you all with my absence, and I'm sorry."

Mom turned back to me with a sympathetic look. "I'm just glad you're here, sweetheart. Your dad will come around, and we'll all be back to normal in no time. Let's head inside now. It's *freezing*."

She shivered, reminding me that things wouldn't be going back to normal, as much as I wanted them to. I hadn't even felt the cold.

Zeke carried my suitcase up to my old bedroom on the second floor, and I allowed myself a nostalgic moment in my childhood room before heading back down again. Everything in the house looked the same. Even my brothers' rooms still held their old trophies and hockey paraphernalia from when they'd played in high school.

My clothing, purses, shoes, and wide array of accessories had gone with me to college, but I'd left behind my cat figurine collection.

I'd been obsessed with cats from a young age but had never owned one on account of my mom's allergies. I'd been about to adopt one after graduating college—since living in an apartment by myself was kind of lonely—but I'd become a werewolf before I could.

Now, my obsession with cats was more on a primal level. As in, I wanted to chase and *eat* them. Probably not a good idea to adopt one.

A shout caught my attention as I finished descending the stairs, and I turned the corner to see my dad and brothers in the living room, glued to a football game. Thankfully, Reid's team wasn't playing today. Desirae deserved a few uninterrupted days with her famous quarterback husband. I paused behind the couch to watch the game, but when all three men shifted in their seats as if suddenly uncomfortable, embarrassment flushed my face.

They could sense me. They could sense that a predator was near.

Not consciously, of course. They still didn't believe I was a werewolf.

But when my dad glanced over his shoulder and saw me standing there, only to frown and look away, I suddenly felt like a stranger in my own home. An *unwanted* one. Tears stung my eyes, and I quickly left the living room before anyone could see.

I couldn't really blame him for his reaction. I was no longer his precious little girl who could do no wrong. I'd hurt him. I'd *left* him. In his eyes, I'd turned my back on my family. Still, I'd tried to keep in touch with my parents the only way I could, faithfully calling them every week for the past year. The only one who'd ever picked up though was my mom.

Unprepared for how painful my dad's rejection felt, I stumbled into the kitchen on autopilot, not noticing I wasn't alone until I nearly ran into my mom.

"Oh!" she exclaimed, placing a hand over her heart as she turned to me with wide eyes. "You scared me, Brielle."

I opened my mouth to apologize, then froze when I heard her heart skip several beats. Seconds later, a scent hit me. An unmistakable one that excited me as much as it filled me with dread.

Fear. I'd *actually* scared my mom.

As her heart continued to nervously flutter, heat flushed through my insides, a reaction that instantly made me feel sick to my stomach. Intrigued, my inner wolf eagerly sat up, anticipating what would happen next.

I immediately knew what she was waiting for. She wanted my mom to turn tail and *run*.

For the first time since making the decision to come here, it hit me how dangerous this situation was.

I was a *predator*. A wild animal lived inside me now. Her instincts were to hunt and kill prey, and at the moment, her sights were set on my family, on the people who'd loved and protected me my entire life. But she didn't see them that way, and if she managed to slip past my control, God only knew what she'd do to them.

Even if I kept her from attacking them, I knew just how easily werewolf toxin could infect a human. One little scratch was all it would take.

Suddenly terrified of the danger I'd put my family in, I backed away from my mom.

"Brielle?" She took a step toward me, concern replacing her fear when she saw my expression.

I shook my head and continued to back away. "I just . . . I-I need some fresh air."

Without another word, I whirled and left the kitchen, hurrying through the living room and out the front door before anyone could stop me.

"Brielle, your coat!" my mom shouted after me, but I scurried down the sidewalk without a backward glance, my heart about to explode from my chest.

Chase, chase, chase, my inner wolf chanted, still hyped up on my mom's fear. I took off running, barely aware of the snow that had begun to fall.

Away. I needed to get far, far away. But where would I go? There was nowhere left for me to flee.

I was alone. *Lost* in a way I'd never felt before.

I couldn't move forward, and I couldn't move backward, so where did that leave me?

I didn't know, but I did know one thing for certain.

I needed to *run.*

Hours later, when the sun had begun to set and my wolf was firmly under control again, I returned home. The second I opened the front door, though, I could sense something had changed.

Mom jumped up from her wingback chair in the living room, the lines on her face deeply etched in worry. But when she came toward me, my dad stopped her with one word.

"Elaine."

She glanced at her husband who'd risen from his spot on the couch, then back at me, her expression growing pained. "But, Michael . . . it's *Brielle.*"

My brothers had risen as well, quietly looking on as Dad crossed his arms over his chest, a hard glint of suspicion entering his eyes. "Something's off about her. She's different. We all know Brielle doesn't go out in the cold unless absolutely necessary. Yet, despite the freezing temperature and snow, she was outside for hours without a coat. And look at her now. She's not even shivering."

I swallowed with difficulty, saddened that he was still in denial about who I was. Not knowing what else to do, I said, "It's because I'm a werewolf, Dad. My blood runs hot, and I don't get cold anymore."

Sawyer swore under his breath.

Dad's eyes hardened even more. "Brielle Victoria Lacroix, I will not tolerate this fantasy any longer."

"It's not a fantasy, Dad. It's *real*. I was infected with werewolf toxin and transform into a wolf every month. Why won't you believe me?"

"Because it's a *lie*," he snapped, so vehemently that I blinked at him in shock. This wasn't the man who'd raised me. The man who'd raised me hardly *ever* raised his voice, even when one of his children did something stupid. When I didn't respond to his accusation, he went on, "I have been *very* patient with you this past year, Brielle, but you refuse to get the help you need. As a father, it is my duty to look after my children's welfare, even when they don't want it. Zeke. Sawyer. Escort your sister up to her room."

I gaped at him like he'd lost his mind. "Seriously? You're *grounding* me? I'm twenty-three-years old, Dad. I don't even live here anymore."

My dad's expression didn't change. "Boys, do what I told you. And make sure you confiscate any electronics she brought with her."

"Michael!"

"Dad!"

My mom's cry of protest and mine melded together, but my dad ignored them, staring at his sons until they moved forward to do his bidding.

As they approached me, I stiffened, my fight or flight instincts kicking in. Both were around six feet tall and outweighed me by far, but I wasn't a frail little human anymore. If I fought them, I'd probably win. Still, the thought of hurting them kept me from bursting into action.

I glanced back at the door, hating the idea of fleeing my family again, but what other choice did I have?

"Don't do it, Brie," Zeke quietly said, and I turned back to him. His words were imploring, and he almost looked afraid. Not of me, I noted in surprise. More like afraid he'd never see me again if I left this time.

I hesitated, stuck between love for my family and my own self-preservation.

"We'll get through this, Ellie," Sawyer said, his expression one of sympathy. "Together."

I hesitated a moment longer, and they reached me before I could listen to my instincts screaming at me to run. Boxing me in, they both placed a hand on my back and guided me toward the stairs. I allowed them to nudge me forward but not before giving my dad a pleading look. "Daddy, please. Don't do this."

His expression wavered, and for a split second, I was certain he saw his little girl again. But in the next instant, he turned away and gave me the cold shoulder.

My heart splintered, and I struggled to draw in air past the pain.

A small sob left my mom, and she weakly whispered, "It's okay, sweetheart. E-everything will be okay."

But as my brothers escorted me to my bedroom, making sure to secure my phone before shutting me inside, I knew that was the furthest thing from the truth.

It wasn't okay. And I didn't think it ever would be again.

CHAPTER 5

BRIELLE

I paced my bedroom, feeling the way my wolf probably felt ninety percent of the time.

Trapped.

I could easily leave the house if I wanted to, either through the front door or out my window. A fall from the second floor wouldn't even faze me, but I didn't want to leave my family that way. Nora had been forced to leave her family when she'd been unable to shift, and the strain it had put on them had nearly broken their relationship.

I'd never thought something like that would happen to my family, yet here I was, struggling to fix what had started to break.

They didn't believe me. They couldn't *accept* this new version of me.

So what now?

I couldn't stay here much longer. I had one more day left before the full moon forced me to shift, and the stress of my current situation wasn't helping matters. As the evening bled into night and I sensed the moon climb high into the sky, more and more symptoms racked my body. I was *starved*, and it felt like an oven in here. I'd stripped down to my white tank top hours ago and was now contemplating removing my pants.

Even if my family had a sudden change of heart and sought to repair the growing rift between us, I doubted I'd be lucid enough to hold a conversation.

It was just so *hot*, and my hunger for red meat was starting to take over my every thought. Thanksgiving dinner had come and gone hours ago, and I didn't even think my family had eaten. I could hear them down below, quietly arguing amongst themselves about me. At one point, Dad had raised his voice, and I'd clearly heard two words.

Mental institution.

The rest of the family had sounded shocked by the words, including me. Did he really think I was mentally insane?

Coming here had been a terrible idea. I hated to admit it, but maybe Jagger had been right.

I wasn't ready to be on my own.

At the thought of him, my wolf pushed even closer to the surface, making my skin feel too tight. She was used to being around him this time of month. Used to drawing strength from his quiet presence as we made the slow painful shift from human to animal. Every time my inner wolf emerged, either he or Onyx was there to greet us. To greet *me*. The wolf version of me.

I'd never been away from him this close to the full moon before, and I keenly felt the weight of his absence.

Shaking my head, I tried to banish him from my thoughts. Thinking about him only reminded me of how lonely I'd felt lately. Then again, I was feeling pretty lonely right about now, with or without him. A whine pushed at my throat, but I forced it back down.

This wasn't the time to feel sorry for myself. I needed to convince my human family that I was still me—still *Brielle*—before I turned into a wolf.

Yeah, right. Even *I* wasn't convinced.

It was around midnight when I heard a vehicle stop in front of the house. Before I could peek through my curtains to see who it was, the voices downstairs suddenly rose in volume. Both of my brothers started shouting, but I could only make out a few words here and there. I tilted my head to better hear them and caught the tail end of something Sawyer said.

". . . not crazy, Dad!"

Okay, they were definitely talking about me.

A knock came at the front door, and the voices quieted. Seconds later, I heard a new voice, then another. Both male. Neither of them sounded familiar.

"Michael, this isn't necessary," my mom said, panic evident in her tone.

"She's upstairs. First door on the left," Dad said, clearly speaking to the newcomers.

When I heard heavy footsteps start up the stairs, all the hair on my body stood on end.

He didn't.

He *wouldn't* have.

In a state of disbelief, I waited for the two individuals to reach my room. The entire time, I prayed I was wrong. I *had* to be wrong. The man who'd raised me couldn't *possibly* have done this. I was his only daughter. His little *girl*.

I had to be wrong. There was no way he would do this to me.

The footsteps reached the top of the stairs and turned left toward my bedroom. Seconds later, someone knocked on the door.

"Miss Lacroix?"

I didn't answer, frozen in place like an ice sculpture.

"Miss Lacroix, we're here to help you. Don't be alarmed."

Yeah, right. I was *seriously* freaking out right now.

Please, please, please, I chanted, squeezing my eyes shut and willing the two strangers to disappear. Maybe this was all just a hallucination. That had to be it. I was so hot and hungry that I'd conjured them into existence.

But the doorknob suddenly rattled, and I yanked my eyes back open just as the door swung inward. One look at the two burly men dressed in white uniforms and my heart completely shattered.

"Miss Lacroix," one of them began, taking a slow step into my room, "we're with the Albany Psychiatric Center, and—"

"Mom! Dad!" I cried, desperation making my voice crack. "Please!"

"Call them off, Dad," I heard Sawyer say from downstairs. "Ellie's not crazy!"

The man who'd entered my room took another step, and a low growl rumbled in my throat before I could stop it.

His posture abruptly changed, taking on a more defensive stance. "Easy now," he said, taking another step. "If you come freely, there will be no need for restraints."

Restraints? Like a *straight jacket?*

Heat flooded my body, my wolf going wild at the thought of being subdued in such a manner. As she swiftly rose up, my control over her slipped, and she bared her teeth at the men—*my* teeth—before loosing a vicious snarl.

The men froze for a split second. Then came at me like linebackers.

It happened so fast that I had no choice but to let my survival instincts take over. The first male tried to grab me in a bear hug, but before he could wrap me in his beefy arms, I shoved him. *Hard.* He flew back and crashed into my bed, breaking the frame as he went down in an inglorious heap. The heavy fall loosened the shelves over my bed, and every single one of my ceramic cat figurines crashed to the floor.

As I stared in shock at the man and my broken figurines, his partner barreled into me.

I hit the ground with a resounding thud, stunned when all two-hundred-fifty pounds of him flattened me to the floor. Before I could shove him off, he grabbed one of my arms and yanked it behind me so forcefully that I cried out in pain. Even though he was human, he was made entirely of muscle and definitely knew more about wrestling than I did. I tried to twist free, but he managed to yank my other arm behind me and slap something around my wrists.

As I felt the cold metal touch my overheated skin, I assumed he'd handcuffed me. No problem. I could easily break free of them with my supernatural strength and planned to do so the second he lifted off me.

But a moment later, a burning sensation stung the skin around my wrists. It was tolerable at first, but as the seconds passed, the heat intensified—until I was pretty sure my wrists were on *fire*.

Frantic to stop the pain, I pulled on my restraints, but they wouldn't budge. With each pull, the heat grew and grew. When it felt like my very *blood* had started to boil, I threw my head back and screamed in agony.

"Let her go!" I heard a familiar voice bellow over my screams. The man on top of me suddenly disappeared, and through my tears, I saw Sawyer shove him back. The man stumbled but quickly recovered, and then did the unthinkable. I cried out again as he lurched forward and punched my brother, so hard that blood spurted through the air.

"You bastard!" another voice roared. Zeke was suddenly there, coming to Sawyer's aid. Drowning in pain, I helplessly looked on as my eldest brother lit into the man fifty pounds heavier than him.

My brothers had gotten into their fair share of fights over the years, especially during their time as hockey players, but the orderlies wouldn't go down easily. Sure enough, the one I'd shoved into my bed had recovered and was now striding toward Zeke with a wicked gleam in his beady eyes.

Who *were* these men? I was pretty sure psychiatric orderlies weren't this violent. At least, I certainly hoped not.

"Zeke!" I cried out in warning, struggling to keep up with the fight as the fire consumed my entire body.

Just in the nick of time, Zeke ducked under a fist aimed at his temple. Before he could straighten, the other orderly lashed out and caught him square in the jaw. As his head violently snapped back, Sawyer jumped back into the fray.

The fight seemed to go on forever, but in reality, it only lasted seconds. I tried to get up several times, but every time I did, a debilitating weakness stole over me and I'd crash back down to the floor. My brothers fought valiantly, but the two orderlies overpowered them with brute strength. As Sawyer went down for the second time, the male closest to me turned and picked me off the floor like I weighed nothing. Tossing me over his shoulder, he strode for the door.

I twisted and flailed, trying to break free, but his arm around my thighs was like a steel cable. At the top of the stairs, he abruptly stopped.

"I changed my mind. You can't have her," my dad said, blocking the man from descending. "Release my daughter, or I'll call the police."

The man stood motionless for a moment, then lashed a foot out, kicking my father square in the chest.

"No!" I wailed as my dad fell back and tumbled down the stairs.

"Michael!" my mom screamed, bursting into sobs when her husband hit the ground hard. Terrified that he broke his neck in the fall, I thrashed in my captor's grip for all I was worth, desperate to break loose.

As his grip on me weakened, he grunted in annoyance and turned sharply. My head thwacked against the wall, making me see stars. Before I could recover, he was down the stairs and stepping over my dad on his way toward the door.

"You're not taking her!" my mom shrieked, stumbling forward to beat at the man with her small fists. Barely pausing, he swept an arm out and knocked her back. I screamed as she fell hard and hit the back of her head.

The front door suddenly exploded open, banging sharply against the wall. Still staring at my mom's prone form, I didn't see who it was. But as the burly orderly stiffened, I caught a scent, one that immediately made my body light up in recognition.

"Let her go. Now."

At the sound of Jagger's deep voice, goosebumps erupted over my flesh.

The male's hold on me tightened even more. "Step aside, sir. She's none of your concern."

"Oh, she most definitely is," Jagger said, his tone deathly quiet. "You have two choices. Release her and face a swift death, or defy me and die painfully."

Despite the excruciating pain I was in, I blinked in surprise at his words. Whatever the orderly decided, he was dead meat.

A loud commotion from upstairs interrupted the tense moment, the second orderly and my brothers bringing the fight into the hallway. The man holding me took advantage of the distraction and burst into action.

One second, he was barreling toward Jagger, and the next, stopping dead in his tracks. I slammed into his back and nearly slipped from his shoulder, confused when he started to rise into the air. The awful choking noises he made clued me in to what was happening. Jagger had him by the throat and was lifting him into the air. Rather, *both* of us.

As the burly male flailed in Jagger's grip, he finally let go of me. The action tipped me sideways, and I began to fall, my shackled arms unable to brace me. Before I could hit the floor, a strong arm snagged my waist and set me upright.

Still flailing, the orderly tried to grab me again. Jagger caught his hand and savagely twisted it. A sharp *crack* cleaved the air, and the man screamed in agony. Struggling to stand, I stumbled sideways, and the other orderly made his move. He lumbered down the stairs far faster than a man his size should be capable of, beelining for the front door.

And me.

I tried to lurch out of the way, but my legs buckled beneath me. With Jagger preoccupied with the other male, there was no one stopping the orderly from scooping me up and running out the door. Expecting that very thing to happen, I blinked in surprise when he suddenly went flying. About to be bowled over by him, I dropped to the ground just as he soared over me and crashed into the wall.

Two figures were suddenly surrounding me, forming a protective wall between me and the violent orderlies. Sawyer crouched down and tried to free my wrists, but it only made the pain ten times worse. The second a scream burst from me, an unearthly roar clapped the air.

Sawyer suddenly went airborne. He flew backward and struck the stair railing, crashing through the wooden slats like they were toothpicks. Jagger turned to Zeke next, his eyes blazing bright yellow.

"No!" I cried. "He's my brother. Don't hurt him!"

Confusion flitted across Jagger's face. He paused to glance down at me, and the orderly he'd let go burst into action. Not to escape, but to attack Jagger from behind. Something in my eyes must have warned Jagger, because he whirled around and snapped the male's thick neck in a dizzying blur.

As the light left his eyes and he crumpled to the floor, his companion picked himself up and charged out the door. Both Jagger and Zeke looked ready to storm after him, but when a pained whimper escaped my lips, their attention shot back to me. Seconds later, tires squealed as a vehicle peeled away from the curb.

Zeke started to kneel by my side, but Jagger barked, "Don't touch her."

My brother straightened, narrowing his eyes at Jagger suspiciously.

"It's okay, Zeke," I managed to say, blinking away dark spots from my vision. "Jagger is . . . a friend. Go check on Mom and Dad."

He continued to eye Jagger suspiciously but didn't stop him from approaching me.

"I think . . . it's silver," I gasped out as he crouched low to inspect my bound wrists. The adrenaline high from the fight was already wearing off, making the pain feel like a raging inferno in my veins. My vision tunneled even more, and I knew unconsciousness wasn't far off. "You sh-should probably—"

He grasped the shackles with his bare hands and yanked them apart, freeing one of my wrists, then the other. The second the metal fell away, the fire in my veins began to cool. A relieved sob burst from me.

As I brought my tender wrists around to inspect them, he stood to his feet and offered me a hand. When I saw the angry blisters on his palm from his brief contact with the silver, I hesitated for a moment, then placed my hand in his and let him help me up.

Once on my feet, my knees immediately threatened to buckle, my body still embarrassingly weak. The second Jagger dropped my hand, I swayed, my vision completely flickering out this time. When I came to again, I was in someone's arms.

In *Jagger's* arms.

Without a word, he strode from the house and out into the night.

"Wait," I faintly said, struggling to regain consciousness. "My parents . . ."

"Your parents are fine. Their heartbeats are strong."

"But . . . that man. We can't leave him here."

"I'll call Buck to take care of him. You're my priority right now."

Priority . . .

"Hey! Where are you taking her?" I heard Sawyer shout.

As feet pounded after us, Jagger whirled to face my brothers. "Home," was all he said.

I didn't understand why, but that one word loosened something in my chest. Looking at their faces lined in worry, I found myself saying to my brothers, "I'll be fine. Just don't call the police. Please. We'll send someone to take care of everything."

As Jagger started to turn again, Zeke called out, "I'm sorry." Jagger paused, allowing me to see my brother's crestfallen expression. He took a step toward us and pulled out my phone from his back pocket. "You're my little sister, and I should have better protected you. I'm sorry I let this happen."

Jagger stiffened but didn't stop him from handing me my phone. The second it was in my grasp, though, he whirled and left my brothers behind before I could respond.

"Jagger."

Silence.

"My stuff . . ."

"I'll send someone to collect your things tomorrow," he replied in a clipped tone. "You're never stepping foot in that house again."

My mouth slowly fell open. Did he just . . . ? No way. He wouldn't *dare*. But it suddenly dawned on me why he was here right now. He'd come to *collect* me. To drag me back to the Rivers' estate—kicking and screaming if he had to. If it weren't for my recent injuries, I'd probably be over his shoulder. This wasn't any different from what that *orderly* had tried to do.

Realizing that this wasn't a rescue at all but an *abduction*, anger sizzled through me. Clenching my teeth, I ground out, "Put me down."

"No."

Heat practically shot from my eyes as I gave him my best death glare. "Jagger, if you don't put me down, I swear I'm going to—"

His arm beneath my legs abruptly dropped so that my feet hit the ground. Surprised that he'd listened to me, I didn't react right away. Before I could collect myself, he opened the passenger side door of his gray Porsche and pushed me inside. It was a light push, but I tumbled inside all the same.

"Hey!" I protested, but he shut the door in my face.

Rage ignited inside me. My body all but burst into flames, raging hotter and hotter and *hotter*. When he opened the driver side door and claimed the seat, I was ready to tear him a new one. Just as I opened my mouth to give him a tongue lashing worthy of an Oscar, pain streaked through my body. A pain I knew all too well.

Terror gripped me, and all that emerged from my mouth was a little squeak.

Jagger glanced over and immediately spotted the fear on my face. He tensed, looking around as if he expected an attack. "What's wrong?"

"I . . ."

His eyes focused on me again, and when I saw them flicker

yellow, fresh pain ripped through my insides, stealing the breath from my lungs.

"Brielle."

"I . . ."

"Brielle, *speak* to me. I can't protect you if I don't know what's wrong."

That did it. The dominant tone. The faint worry line between his dark brows. The slightest hint of panic in his words . . .

"I . . . I think I'm starting to *shift*."

CHAPTER 6

JAGGER

She let out another low moan, her back arching off the seat.

I tried to stay focused on the road, but her mounting pain made it nearly impossible to drive. Even with the AC blasted, her skin was damp with sweat. I could feel the heat pulsing off her in waves, and I could only imagine the agony she was in. As a hybrid, my ability to shift at will had spared me from the slow, torturous transformation that regular werewolves endured every month. Natural-born werewolves learned to cope with the pain at an early age, but humans who were infected with toxin later on in life struggled the most.

Brielle's body had initially rejected the toxin, and the fear I'd felt watching her slowly die an excruciating death came back to haunt me now as she writhed in the seat beside me. Regular werewolves could only shift when the moon was full. She shouldn't be experiencing these symptoms right now. She *couldn't* experience them. If she started to shift early, her body might fail again, overwhelmed by the shock.

She tried to roll down her window for the third time, but it was still locked. "*Please*, Jagger," she whimpered. "I need fresh air."

Ignoring the way her plea tugged at me, I firmly replied, "Fresh air will only encourage the shift more. I already told you why transitioning early can't happen."

"Because I'll probably die again, blah blah. But you don't know that for sure. Just a few minutes. *Please*. I can barely breathe."

When her voice wobbled, I nearly broke. Onyx wasn't making it any easier, restlessly pacing inside me as he sensed how close her wolf was to the surface. I counted on him to protect her while she was in wolf form, but he didn't fully grasp how dangerous it would be if she transitioned right now.

Needing a subject change before I caved, I asked her, "When's the last time you ate?"

She moaned again, gripping the armrest as more heat pulsed through her. "This . . . this morning."

Alarm shot through me. This *morning*? No wonder she was in so much pain. The stress, combined with hunger and close proximity to the full moon, was a cocktail she wasn't equipped to handle. Her body was literally in survival mode right now, and with the added component of silver exposure, it was starting to shut down.

She needed sustenance. *Now*. But stores were closed this time of night, and home was still two hours away.

Pulling out my phone, I searched for the nearest butcher shop. It was closed, of course, but I didn't care about that right now.

"Hold on," I said and stepped on the gas. The Porsche eagerly shot forward, and I spent the next several miles keeping an eye out for cops as we clocked one hundred down the freeway. The entire time, Brielle gripped the door handle and kept her eyes tightly squeezed shut.

Fifteen minutes later, I swerved into the shop's empty parking lot and slammed on the brakes.

"Stay here," I told Brielle and swiftly exited, making sure to close the door firmly behind me. My phone chose that moment to ring, and I bit back a curse before quickly answering it, already knowing who it was. "Brielle's in trouble."

Kolton immediately focused on the problem at hand. "Do you

46

need backup?"

"No, but her wolf is trying to force the change."

Kolton was silent for a beat before saying, "That can't happen. It's too early."

"I know. I'm getting her some meat now, so hopefully that will help calm her wolf. But you'll need to contact Darin, because I'm about to break-and-enter."

It was moments like this that made having a pack member in the NYPD very useful.

"No problem. Anything else?"

"You'll need to call Buck too. There's a body at the Lacroix household. Human male."

Kolton went silent again, probably so he could take a calming breath. It's what made him such a good alpha, especially during moments of crisis. I strived to emulate him at all times, but that often required a control I didn't possess. After another beat, he asked, "What happened?"

"I don't know the full story yet," I replied, bypassing the shop's front entrance and heading around toward the back, "but two men in white scrubs were trying to take Brielle away. I killed one, but the other escaped. Brielle's family was hurt pretty bad too, and that's the odd part. It wasn't a forced entry."

"You think her family allowed the two men inside their home?"

"Possibly. And she was bound in cuffs when I arrived. *Silver* ones meant to subdue a werewolf or vampire."

Kolton's tone changed. "That's serious. They might be supernatural hunters. Get back here as quickly as you can."

"I will, boss."

"And, Jagger?"

"Yes?"

"We need to have a talk about your actions."

A grimace pulled at my mouth. "I know."

"Call if you need me. Keep Brielle safe."

Always. The word was on the tip of my tongue, but I kept it to myself.

Ending the call, I quickly scanned the building's exterior for any cameras before reaching the back door. With one sharp twist, I broke the lock on the handle and slipped inside. Minutes later, I emerged with a juicy slab of steak that I'd pilfered from the back refrigerator. I hadn't even bothered to wrap it, knowing that Brielle would want to devour the whole thing raw the second I handed it to her.

As I rounded the building and made for the parking lot, the urge to ease Brielle's suffering made me pick up speed. But when the Porsche came into view, I slowed, my stomach filling with dread.

The passenger side door was wide open, and Brielle was no longer inside.

CHAPTER 7

BRIELLE

"Brielle!"

I could barely hear the booming voice calling out my name. As soon as Jagger had opened the car door to leave, the blast of fresh air had sent me into a frenzy of need. The second he was out of sight, I had stumbled out of the car and across the parking lot, desperate to reach the woods on the other side of the road.

When I'd reached them, a howl had threatened to burst from my lungs. The moon was high above, and my wolf ached to feel its glow on her rich brown fur. Responding to her desperation, I'd stripped the last of the clothing from my body and taken off naked into the forest.

I hadn't gotten far, though. Every step was agony, and the more I moved, the hotter I became. Flurries of snow swirled around me, melting the instant they touched my boiling skin. Finally, the pull became too strong, and I dropped to all fours. Panting rapidly, my heart thundering like a runaway horse, I crouched on the forest floor and waited for the first bone to crack.

"Brielle!"

Jagger's clear desperation called to my own, and a pitiful whine burst from me. But it was too late. Digging my nails into the frozen earth, I shut my eyes and surrendered to the powerful need to shift.

"No! Stop. STOP!" Jagger roared, rushing toward me.

My body shook uncontrollably, and I felt my claws shoot from my nailbeds. Just as my canines elongated, setting my gums on fire, Jagger crashed to his knees and yanked me back against him. The contact startled my wolf, and she went wild. With a savage snarl, she thrashed in his grip, swinging her head—*my* head—back and forth to bite him. When he evaded her teeth, she dug her claws into any flesh she could find, scratching and gouging like a feral beast.

A breath later, powerful arms snaked around me and bound my flailing limbs tightly against my chest. Unable to bite, scratch, or even kick, I was rendered helpless, just like when I'd been subdued by those silver cuffs. Sudden terror gripped me, and I belted out a scream that echoed through the trees.

"Brielle, you're safe," Jagger tried to reason with me, but the terror was too great.

I screamed and screamed and screamed until my screams became howls. Unable to break loose of Jagger's hold, my wolf surged upward even more, and brown fur erupted over my skin.

"Brielle, *stop.*"

My wolf pushed and pushed, making several of my bones groan in protest. My howls intensified, filling with agony as every bone in my body vibrated, on the verge of snapping.

Just as the first bone began to break, a voice thundered, "ENOUGH!"

The word was like a slap to the face, dominant and demanding. The timbre was deeper than usual, and my wolf froze. Although she'd never heard him speak aloud before, she instinctively knew who the voice belonged to.

Onyx.

"Settle, pup," he rumbled into the sudden stillness, his voice scraping over my sensitive nerves in a way that was somehow soothing. "Not time."

The words were rough and halting as if he wasn't used to speaking.

Unhappy about being told what to do, my inner wolf released a low growl. Before she could resume her struggle, I felt a sharp nip on my shoulder.

I gasped at the unexpected sting and glanced down at the patch of skin.

"You . . . you *bit* me," I accused, the words garbled as my elongated canines got in the way.

"It was a nip, not a bite. If I'd bitten you, there would be blood."

At the sound of *Jagger's* voice, my eyes widened. I'd thought Onyx had bitten me, not *him*. Shocked by the discovery, a shudder rocked my body. Jagger's arms tightened around me, and I suddenly realized how close he was. His powerful thighs were bracketing mine from behind, and I could feel the hard muscles of his chest and stomach pressing into my spine. My *bare* spine.

Crap. I was naked, and he was *holding* me. The hold wasn't sensual or even comforting, though. It was meant to keep me together in my human form so I couldn't shift, nothing more.

Such a *Jagger* thing to do, dictating what I could and couldn't do. Even my wolf wasn't safe from him.

She started to squirm again but for a very different reason this time. She wanted to rub against him. To *play* with him. To break down his stringent walls and convince him to have a little fun.

Oh, girl, that is such a bad idea, I told her. Told *myself*.

But the animal trapped inside me had a mind of her own. As she pushed at my bones once more, another gasp left me, this one pained. Wave after wave of heat pulsed through my insides, and I began to shake again.

"She really . . . *really* wants out," I moaned, arching my neck back. My head fell against Jagger's shoulder, but I was in too much pain to move it.

He was silent for a long moment, holding me steady as I writhed against him. And then he said, "Think about something else."

An incredulous laugh burst from me. "Like what?"

Another beat of silence. Then, "I didn't know you had two brothers."

I scoffed this time. "That's because we barely speak to each other. This is the most we've spoken in over a year." When he didn't respond, I added between pained gasps, "Zeke's twenty-six and works in construction. Sawyer's twenty-five and a mechanic. They both moved closer to The Big Apple for better job opportunities, and I don't see them much anymore."

"But they know you're a werewolf?"

"Yes."

The lines of Jagger's body grew even more rigid. "Were they responsible for what happened at the house earlier?"

"No. No, it wasn't them. It was . . ." I bit my lip as another painful shudder rattled my frame. "My dad . . . tried to have me committed."

Admitting the words out loud was like a punch to the gut. A small sob left me before I could catch it, and tears came unbidden to my eyes.

"I can't believe he would do that to me," I said in a strained whisper. "My own dad thinks I'm insane."

As my heart splintered all over again, Jagger didn't say a word. But something about having him this close made the pain hurt less. Or maybe I was just too exhausted to feel any more pain.

Either way, my racing pulse and jagged breaths gradually slowed. Heat still simmered in my veins, but even that dimmed.

"You should eat," Jagger said after a lengthy moment of silence. "It'll help calm your wolf."

At the mention of food, my wolf didn't perk up like I thought she would. As soon as I'd brought up my dad's betrayal, she'd curled into a ball like a kicked puppy.

I weakly shook my head, realizing that it was still resting on Jagger's shoulder. "Not hungry."

"Too bad. You need to eat, and we're not going anywhere until you do."

I bristled at his bossy tone but was too tired to sass back. Instead, I shut my eyes and let my body go limp against him.

"Brielle." He lightly shook me. "*Brielle.*"

Silence.

Sighing through his nose, he abruptly let go of me and stood. With a startled squawk, I fell backward and landed in the snow with a soft thump.

"Here. Eat this." He picked something up and thrust what looked like a slab of raw steak at me. I sat up to take it, noting with surprise that my fingers were no longer tipped in claws and my skin was free of fur. My elongated canines had receded as well. The second I accepted the meat, Jagger pivoted on his heel and took off.

"Wh-where are you going?" I sputtered, confused and a bit alarmed by his swift departure.

"To get your clothes," he muttered, then said more loudly, "We're not leaving until you eat that entire steak, so hurry up."

I gaped after him, struggling to decipher what had just happened. One minute, he'd been wrapped around me, and the next—*poof.* Gone.

Shaking my head, I gave up trying to understand him and focused on the steak. It looked wholly unappetizing, but the moment I caught a whiff of it, a loud growl vibrated my stomach. One tiny bite later and I was ravenously scarfing it down like the feral wolf I was.

By the time Jagger returned, the steak was gone and I was feeling a little more like myself. As I dressed, I was all too aware that he'd angled himself away from me. Now that the danger was over, he was back to his distant self, acting as if the moment between us had never happened.

Pain tightened my chest, but this time, it had nothing to do with my wolf. I finished dressing, and we left the woods in tense silence.

CHAPTER 8

BRIELLE

I was surrounded on all sides. Faces peered down at me. Familiar ones.

They watched as my body began to shift, transforming from the girl they knew into a feral wolf.

I tried to warn them away. Tried to scream at them to run. But all that came out was a growl.

My wolf shook off the shift and focused on my family members. Mom. Dad. Zeke. Sawyer.

I begged her to leave them alone, but she blatantly ignored me as if I no longer existed.

She sprang toward them with her jaws opened wide, but before she could touch them, a large cage slammed down, trapping her inside.

She threw herself at the bars, only to cringe back in pain.

Silver. The cage was encased in silver.

I looked up at my family in disbelief, but they were no longer there. Strangers had taken their place. Burly men in white scrubs.

"Don't be alarmed, Miss Lacroix," they said in unison. "You're safe here."

My wolf went wild, fighting to break free of the cage. Pain lit up our body, but she wouldn't stop.

The men stared and stared as my wolf fought and fought.

Hours turned into days, but the cage held fast.

The entire time, the men simply stared at us.

Stared and stared as if I was nothing more than a wild animal.

I bolted upright in bed, a scream of terror lodged in my throat. Wildly glancing around the room, I forced it back down.

Just a dream.

I was alone in my bedroom at the Rivers' estate, no burly men in sight.

It had been over three days since the incident, but the nightmares were only growing stronger. After returning to the estate, we'd looked into the Albany Psychiatric Center, but according to them, the two men who'd arrived at my parents' house weren't a part of their staff.

All research had led to dead ends, and no one had any idea where they'd come from. But they'd definitely known that I wasn't human.

With a new unknown threat lingering in the air, the males of the household were acting extra vigilant—especially Jagger. He'd watched me like a hawk all weekend, yet had somehow managed to keep his distance without uttering more than a handful of words to me.

When I'd shifted with the full moon on Friday night, he'd overseen the entire transformation as if making sure I didn't die in the process. The next evening, it had been the same thing.

Thankfully, I'd managed to shift both nights without a hitch. The change had been more painful than usual, though, my mind and body extra resistant to giving my wolf control.

"Your body is still fighting the werewolf toxin and maybe always will," Kolton had said as an explanation for why I'd nearly shifted before I was supposed to.

The werewolf toxin had almost killed me a year ago. It *had* killed me. Maybe that meant I was living on borrowed time. I'd cheated death, and it wanted me back.

The past few days had definitely been a wakeup call. Ever since becoming a werewolf, I'd been letting everyone else control my life. That needed to stop, and now. I needed to take charge of the time I had left on this Earth before it ran out. Death could come for me tomorrow, for all I knew.

With that sobering thought in mind, I flung back my covers and stood from the bed. It was earlier than I normally got up, but I wanted a jump-start on the day. Plus, I'd only have more nightmares if I fell back asleep.

Five minutes later, I was dressed in a magenta sports bra and black running shorts with my wavy hair swept into a high ponytail. I briefly picked up my phone to check the time, then set it back down, ignoring the dozens of texts and phone calls from my parents and brothers. I still hadn't talked to them. I wasn't ready, even with my new outlook on life.

Everything had changed, and I didn't have the courage to face it yet.

Hence my reason for getting up before the crack of dawn like a crazy person. It was time for me to adjust, to make some changes of my own. And the first thing on my list was a long run to burn off the excess energy simmering in my veins.

It was always like this after the full moon. My body felt supercharged, practically crackling with electricity after bathing in the moon's powerful glow for two nights in a row. Everything was heightened, which probably explained why my nightmares were heightened as well.

For the past year, I'd ignored my body's symptoms, focused on living life like I had as a human. Work. Socialize. Eat. Sleep. But maybe I needed more than that now. Maybe the key to better controlling my werewolf nature was to embrace it more fully.

So, despite the fact that my human self despised running—

especially outdoors—I slipped on my sneakers and out my bedroom door. It was eerily quiet as I descended the stairs and exited the house. The holiday weekend was over, and we were all prepared to go back to work, but not even *Jagger* was up this early.

Which was a good thing. I could take the trail he ran in the mornings without running into him.

Ever since Thanksgiving, things had been extra tense between us. Although we'd shared with the others what had happened that day, neither of us had discussed it with each other. He'd saved me. *Twice.* But other than staring at me like he always did, he was more aloof toward me than ever.

"You'd think rescuing a girl would mean something, but no," I grumbled under my breath as I left the porch and veered toward the wooded path behind the garage.

Then again, I couldn't forget that he'd driven to my parents' house to *retrieve* me. In his eyes, I was just a wayward pack member. A *weak* one who wasn't worth his time, apparently.

I tried not to let his distant attitude bother me, but I'd always been great at making people warm up to me. Maybe I was slipping. Maybe I wasn't as approachable as I used to be.

Frustrated that I kept letting Jagger get under my skin, I broke into a jog, doing my best to empty my mind. The sooner I learned to embrace all aspects of my werewolf nature, the sooner I could strike out on my own again. Thanksgiving had been an epic fail, but I would do better next time.

Focusing on the trail so I couldn't think about that disastrous day, I picked up speed, losing myself to the sights, sounds, and smells surrounding me. The air was crisp, and it fled my lungs in visible white puffs as I steadily breathed in and out. As a math nerd, I'd never made exercising a priority. I was usually at a desk with my nose glued to a screen, not working up a sweat at the gym or out in nature. As a result, I was embarrassingly out of shape. Good thing I'd inherited supernatural strength when I'd become a werewolf. Otherwise, I'd already be huffing and puffing.

Still, those two burly orderlies—or whatever they were—had trussed me up like a turkey way too easily. If I wanted to prove to my pack that I was ready to stand on my own, then I needed to learn a thing or two about protecting myself. With that thought in mind, I ran even faster, my shoes crunching in the thin layer of snow that dusted the wooded trail.

The land surrounding the Rivers' estate was vast, and I ran for several miles before slowing at a stream to take a quick water break. Any bacteria in the water wouldn't affect me like it would a human, yet another perk of being a werewolf. My stomach was practically made out of steel, and I could eat whatever I wanted. Knowing I wouldn't have to worry about getting fat later on in life was definitely a positive—if I lived that long.

With a sigh, I finished drinking the cold water cupped in my hands and straightened from my crouched position. As I did, I heard a twig snap behind me. My heart immediately leapt into my throat, and I whirled around with a startled yelp.

Before my fight or flight instincts could fully kick in, I recognized the tall form standing a few yards off. Relief weakened my knees, but annoyance quickly followed. "You scared the crap out of me. What are you doing here?"

Jagger stared at me for a long moment, no doubt taking in my flushed skin and agitated state. His gaze dipped below my chin but swiftly returned to my face. I did the same, noting that he was bare from the waist up—and his skin was far less sweaty than mine. Finally, he crossed his arms over his chest and said, "You shouldn't be out here by yourself."

"So you *followed* me?"

He was silent for another beat before replying, "You weren't aware?"

That gave me pause. Ah, hell. He'd been following me this entire time, and I hadn't even *known?*

Embarrassment flushed my face even more, and I quickly snapped back, "Of *course* I was aware. I'm not clueless, you know."

Except that I was, and I was absolutely mortified.

Jagger didn't say anything, but he didn't have to. He and I both knew that I'd had no clue he was following me. The need to run trembled through me, along with a wretched vulnerable feeling.

What if it hadn't been *him* following me? Kolton thought the orderlies had actually been supernatural hunters who'd tapped into the psychiatric center's phone lines in order to find leads. They knew where I used to live and, although it wasn't public knowledge, could find out where I currently lived.

Realizing how stupid I'd been to come out here alone, I inwardly deflated like a balloon. It was on the tip of my tongue to apologize to Jagger for snapping at him, but what came out was, "I want to be trained."

He blinked at me like he'd heard wrong, and I owlishly blinked back.

Where the hell had *that* come from?

Before he could say anything, I added, "I need to learn how to protect myself. I can't do that on my own."

There. I'd admitted the truth. Mostly.

I closely watched his expression and saw the moment he'd made his decision. As he opened his mouth to reject me, I dug my heels in and blurted, "If you won't train me, I'll ask someone else. I'm sure

Buck could teach me a thing or two."

Jagger's eyes flashed bright yellow, and my breath caught. Wow. I hadn't expected him to react like *that*.

He blinked, and the yellow winked out, making me wonder if I'd only imagined it. Expecting him to deny me, I was startled when he abruptly said, "I'll train you on one condition."

Excitement zipped through me, but I managed to calmly say, "And what's that?"

"You don't go anywhere without my approval."

My mouth slowly fell open. What. The. Hell? Did he just . . . ? No way. No one was *that* full of themselves. But as I stared at him, it became *very* clear that he was dead serious. Biting back a few choice words, I said through clenched teeth, "For how long?"

"Until I think you can handle yourself in the real world."

Why, you controlling, egotistical— I forced the words down, grinding my teeth together until my jaw hurt. Jagger just stared at me, his expression impassive. I nearly gave him the finger and stormed off, unwilling to let him control me any more than he already did. But I paused, slowly realizing that it was actually the other way around. I could end our training whenever I wanted. He would be under *my* control, giving me his time and attention whether he wanted to or not.

Not to mention, he wouldn't be able to keep his usual distance from me.

Something about that arrangement pleased me immensely, and a little smile formed on my lips.

"Deal," I said, struggling to contain a full-blown grin. "We'll start right now."

CHAPTER 9

JAGGER

"I told you not to wear earrings. They're a safety hazard."

Brielle scowled at my reprimand, barely avoiding my fist aimed at her cheek.

"See? My knuckle could have caught one and torn it out."

"*You're* wearing earrings," she rebutted, tossing her ponytail back indignantly.

"They're studs. You're wearing several sets of hoops."

"Potato, po-tah-to. I avoid Luca's grabby little fingers every day. This is no different."

Deciding to nip this debate in the bud, I said, "Regardless, don't wear them tomorrow. Now focus."

"I *am* focused," Brielle growled before taking a swing at me.

To prove just how unfocused she was, I slipped past the weak jab and locked her into a chokehold from behind. Instead of using the techniques I taught her, she panicked and tried to pry my arms from around her neck.

As she struggled against me, my own focus started to slip. This close, I couldn't help but breathe in her tantalizing tropical aroma. The scent completely invaded my senses, tempting me to bury my face in her soft honey-brown hair. It sure as hell didn't help that she kept wearing a sports bra and tight shorts that left little to the imagination.

We'd spent every morning this week training beside the creek, and each session grew more and more unbearable. Being this close to her for hours on end was the definition of hell, but the thought of her training with another male made me see red.

Even though the sparring sessions were anything but sensual, having her locked against my body and wholly at my mercy was awakening a part of me that I'd shut down years ago—and for good reason. But Onyx didn't care about those reasons. As Brielle continued to struggle against my hold, her physical strength so much weaker than mine, I could feel his excitement. The feeling quickly became mine, and blood rushed to my groin.

Brielle's backside brushed against my hardening dick, and just like that, I lost all focus.

Dominate mate, Onyx purred, a command he'd given me countless times this week. Every time I'd wrestle Brielle into a submissive hold during one of our training sessions, Onyx's reaction was the same.

Subdue her.

Mark her.

Mate her.

His one-track mind was messing with my head, making it nearly impossible to think straight. Brielle was my soulmate, even if she didn't know it. My instincts screamed at me to claim what was mine, to seal the bond so that any male who came near her would know who she belonged to.

But I'd already given in to my instincts once this week and risked my alpha's disapproval. He'd forgiven my transgression—considering the outcome to my actions had saved Brielle—but I hadn't yet forgiven myself. As Midnight Pack's second in command, my position always needed to come first. Kolton relied on me to be level-headed at all times, and chasing after Brielle was anything but.

It shouldn't matter that she was my soulmate. My duty to Kolton came above all else.

That reminder was exactly what I needed to regain my focus and common sense. Ignoring the throbbing appendage between my legs, I curtly said to Brielle, "Use your feet and elbows. We've been over this several times. My arms are stronger than yours, and you won't be able to—"

She stomped on my foot. *Hard.* Hard enough that I stopped talking. In that moment of pause, she jabbed an elbow into my ribs, and I couldn't hold in a pained grunt. Onyx quietly observed, but I could feel how pleased he was by her swift recovery. I shared the feeling, glad that she'd overcome her initial panic and remembered the moves I'd taught her.

Compared to me, she was small, almost delicate. But what she lacked in size and strength, she made up for with a feisty spirit and plucky attitude. Being incapacitated by those two human males had frightened her, but she was dealing with it and moving on.

The same couldn't be said about me.

I couldn't get over how close they'd come to taking her. One minute more and she would have been lost to me. I'd spent the past week trying to learn the humans' true identities, but there wasn't much to find. Even the van they'd driven had fake plates and couldn't be tracked. If Kolton was right about them being supernatural hunters, they'd been careful to mask their trail. I didn't regret killing one of them, but in hindsight, I wished I'd taken the time to secure the other one for questioning. *Painful* questioning.

Human supernatural hunters often formed groups, all too aware that there was safety in numbers when going up against a much stronger supernatural. The groups were usually home-based and not a huge threat to the supernatural populace. The human world saw them as fanatics and didn't take them seriously, but we'd shut more than one group down over the years before they could grow too large.

I'd been sloppy that night, though. One look at the agony on Brielle's face and I'd chosen to free her of the silver cuffs over securing the other male. I hadn't been able to bear seeing her in pain—although the exposure to silver had probably kept her from fully shifting that night.

Almost losing her twice in one night had triggered something deep inside me, and ever since then, I'd been warring with my instincts to keep her close. If it wasn't for my pack responsibilities, she wouldn't be out of my sight for a second. Training her for the fifth morning in a row helped soothe that protective instinct, but at the same time, I knew how dangerous these sessions were. Despite my attempts to remain professional, the constant contact was doing things to me.

I usually avoided physical touch at all costs, but the pull to be near her—to *touch* her—was growing, which could only mean one thing.

Our bond was growing stronger.

Distracted by my thoughts, I wasn't prepared for Brielle's next move. My upper body had curled forward after her rib jab, and she used the opportunity to whip her head back. I heard a sickening *crack* as her skull connected with my nose, and before I could fully realize that she'd just broken it, she pounded a fist into my groin.

All the air fled me at once, and I let out an involuntary groan. Pain splintered my vision, and by the time I blinked it away, she'd broken free of my chokehold and had turned to face me.

"Oh God, I'm *so* sorry," she exclaimed.

Through the uncontrollable tears filling my eyes, I saw her reach for my face. Before she could touch me, I shot a hand out and caught her wrist. She froze, her emerald green eyes widening as I reached up with my other hand and—*snap!*—reset the broken bone.

Her face immediately paled, and she twisted free of my grip to retch into a bush. With my nose and dick still painfully throbbing, I looked on, unsure what to do.

"Sorry," she murmured after a moment, straightening to cast me a sheepish look. "I don't do well with broken bones and stuff. Which is stupid, I know, coming from a werewolf who shifts every month."

Comfort mate, Onyx urged me.

Watching her for a moment more, I said, "You didn't hesitate to inflict pain this time. You're improving."

Onyx growled in exasperation.

"Um, thanks," Brielle slowly replied as if uncertain how to take my compliment. After another beat, she focused on my nose with a frown.

"What?" I questioned, wondering if I hadn't set it right.

"It's just . . . You've got a little . . ." With a sigh, she strode back up to me. "Hold still."

As she lifted a hand toward my face again, I went stiff as a board. The instinct to pull away trembled through my bones, a feeling that I almost always listened to. It was rare that I let others touch me, and most knew better than to try.

But Brielle wasn't waiting for my permission, and before I could stop her, she swept her thumb under my nose. The edge of her nail caught my upper lip, and a thrill went through me. I sucked in a quiet breath and tried to ease my head back, but she doggedly followed the motion with a cluck of disapproval.

"I'm almost done, you big baby. Just one more . . ." She swiped just above my lip again, setting the skin on fire. "There."

With a satisfied look, she turned to wash my blood off her fingers in the cold stream. I watched her, the skin she'd touched still burning with heightened awareness. When she stood from her crouched position, I was suddenly beside her. I hadn't meant to. Hadn't even realized that I'd moved. But when she turned and found me so close to her, she jerked back with a startled yelp and lost her footing on a slippery rock.

As she started to fall, I reached around her without thought and pulled her to me. It happened in an instant. One split-second decision and her perfect body was flush against mine. At the feel of her soft curves pressed against my hard muscles and her small hands resting on my bare chest, my mind emptied and another instinct took over.

An instinct that I'd kept locked away for years. An instinct that immediately took advantage of the moment and initiated further contact.

A gasp left Brielle as I firmly gripped the nape of her neck. Not hard enough to hurt, but with enough force to make her eyes widen.

Onyx went wild with excitement, his feral instincts further heightening mine.

Take, take, take, he chanted inside my head as my gaze lowered to her luscious lips. They were slightly parted, and I felt a sudden ache to thrust my tongue between them.

As the ache swiftly built, making my breath quicken and my heart pound out of control, I almost lost it. Almost took what I couldn't give back.

At the last second, the resolve that had kept me sane for the past several years kicked back in, and I wrenched myself away from her with a sharp hiss.

Onyx went ballistic at the loss of contact. He immediately began to rage inside me, fighting to take over. I barked at him to back down, but he was in no mood to listen. Seconds later, black fur rippled up my arms and sharp claws shot from my fingertips.

"Jagger."

Brielle took a step toward me, and I jerked my head up to snap, "Stay back."

Her eyes widened to saucers as she no doubt saw Onyx in my wild gaze. She unconsciously took a step back, and Onyx surged upward, nearly breaking through my control.

"*Brielle*," I snapped again, my voice little more than a growl. "Don't. Move."

She froze, and I quickly squeezed my eyes shut, unwilling to watch her expression fill with fear. Fear of *me*.

After a long moment, I finally regained control of my wolf familiar, making sure he was securely locked down before reopening my eyes. Noting that the black fur and claws had receded, I slowly lifted my gaze to Brielle. Her mouth was open, her shock more than clear, but . . .

I blinked. Blinked again.

She didn't look frightened.

We stared at each other for a solid minute, neither of us saying a word. Then . . .

"What the hell was *that*?" Brielle blurted rather loudly.

Something about the way she spoke sent relief barreling through me, but instead of relaxing, I straightened and stiffly replied, "Training is over. Time to head back."

When she just gawked at me like I'd lost my mind, I turned and headed back the way we'd come.

A beat later, I heard her follow. "Wait, permanently?" she said, catching up to walk beside me.

Onyx stirred again, and I lengthened my strides to put much-needed space between us.

When I didn't respond, she said more forcefully while following in my wake, "I thought we were past this silent broody thing, Jagger. You agreed to *help* me. I still have so much to learn."

I continued in silence for several more moments, then muttered under my breath, "I never should have agreed to train you."

She sucked in a quiet gasp, letting me know that she'd heard. Guilt immediately filled me, but I wouldn't take back the words.

Dangerous. Being close to her was *dangerous*. Better that I push her away now before she realized it too, before it was too late and I irreparably hurt her. I'd almost lost control, but that was the last time.

As she started to slow, I forced myself to speed up. Every step away from her grew harder and harder, until I thought my body would give out on me.

But I kept going. Kept widening the distance between us until it felt like my skin was being stripped from my flesh. But the pain would fade. And the longer I maintained my distance, so would our bond.

CHAPTER 10

BRIELLE

That tight feeling in my chest was back.

I was starting to call it the biological-clock feeling. After a full day of celebrating not only Kolton's twenty-seventh birthday but his son's first, I was extra emotional. Time was flying by so quickly. It felt like everything and everyone was changing around me while I stood still.

A tug on my hair drew my attention downward, and I smiled at the adorable redhead in my lap. Although Lillian wasn't mobile yet, it was only a matter of time before she joined her brother in zipping down the halls. Good thing they had a built-in grandma, plus several aunts and uncles to keep them out of trouble. Their poor mother could barely keep up the closer she got to her due date. She had at least one more month to go, but she tended to deliver early.

"I'm *exhausted*," Kolton's sister moaned, and I looked up as Vi joined me on the couch with a theatrical flounce. Well, as much as a very pregnant female could flounce. "I feel like I've been pregnant forever."

I snorted. "At least you're not human."

"True. I can't believe human females have to carry babies for a whole nine months. Bet you're glad you dodged *that* bullet."

"Yeah," I said, but my smile faltered. Before I could recover, Nora caught my expression as she joined us in the sitting room with a tray of refreshments.

At the sympathetic look she gave me, I fought back the sudden urge to cry.

"Whoa, what did I miss?" Vi asked, straightening from her slumped position to stare at us suspiciously.

"Nothing," my best friend quickly replied before setting the tray on the coffee table and sitting on my other side. Her daughter immediately let go of my hair and squirmed toward her mother. Nora picked her up, and the little girl snuggled against her chest, a sure sign that she was hungry.

"It's okay," I said, watching Nora adjust her top to feed her child before looking away. "I've just been wanting a family of my own lately, and it's making me super emotional."

Vi's mouth formed a large O. She flicked a glance at Nora, so fast that I almost missed it. Focusing on me again, she said, "Is that why you've been so restless lately?"

I glanced out the sitting room windows. The guys were still in the front yard with Luca and Melanie, attempting to bring them down from their birthday cake sugar highs. I could hear the children's delighted shrieks as they pelted the males with snowballs—even Jagger. It had stormed a few days ago, blanketing the world in white, but that wasn't the reason why I'd stopped running in the mornings.

Jagger suddenly charged Melanie and, in one fell swoop, tossed her over his shoulder. As he spun her around, her peals of laughter echoing across the white clearing, my chest tightened to the point of pain. Wrenching my gaze away, I answered Vi, "Mostly. But what happened at Thanksgiving and the fallout with my family has been weighing on me a lot too."

Not to mention what had happened between me and Jagger a few days ago, but I wasn't ready to face that debacle, let alone talk about it. I still didn't even understand what had gone wrong.

"I'm so sorry, Brie," Nora said. "I never should have encouraged you to go."

Hearing the guilt in her voice, I turned to her with a stern look. "Girl, we've already been over this. Stop apologizing for what happened. It's not your fault. Even if you'd told me not to go, I probably would have anyway."

"True," she muttered with an eye roll, and I flashed her my dimples impishly.

"Good thing Jagger was there," Vi casually remarked. *Too* casually. I narrowed my eyes at her, but her gaze was studiously glued out the windows as she gently rubbed her round belly. "The close call with those human hunters was bad enough, but we were all terrified when Kolton told us your wolf was trying to emerge early."

"And yet I haven't gone into heat *once* in the fifteen months since becoming a werewolf," I groaned and grabbed a pillow to cover my face. "I'm broken."

"You're not broken," Nora said. "Just different."

At that, I couldn't help but feel a little better. If there was anyone who knew how it felt to be broken, it was my best friend. She hadn't been able to shift her whole life until coming to the Rivers' estate.

"And don't forget that the first heat for a turned werewolf is unpredictable," Vi added. "Sometimes it comes right away, and sometimes it takes a while. But if you're looking to jumpstart it, there's always the annual Mate Gala. With all those eligible bachelors around, your hormones are sure to burst awake."

"Vi," Nora said with a note of warning, but I was too fixated on Vi's words to give it much thought.

Lowering the pillow, I glared at them both accusingly. "And why am I just *now* hearing about this?"

Nora shook her head with a quiet exhale. "Because the event can be dangerous. Everyone who attends is single, looking for a mate, and from different packs. Hormones are high, and that many unmated males in one location often results in multiple fights and even a few deaths."

"But I hear the orgies are incredible," Vi said with a wistful sigh. When we both raised our eyebrows at her, she added with a shrug, "If you're into that sort of thing."

Still digesting that shocking bit of information, I asked, "If it's so dangerous, why do they keep holding the event?"

"To prevent pack inbreeding," Vi explained with another shrug. "The Mate Gala helps keep the werewolf genepool strong."

"That, and it keeps dominant unmated males in check," Nora said. "Even if they don't find their mate at the event, most spend the entire weekend having sex, which helps cool off their raging hormones. That way, they have a better chance of not getting kicked out of their pack for unruliness."

Oh my.

As shocking as their explanations were, humans weren't all that different in their mating rituals. I'd been to my fair share of nightclubs and had even dabbled in a few one-night stands.

Which was why I blurted without thinking twice about it, "When's the next event?"

A calculating light entered Vi's purple irises. "This coming weekend, actually. It's at a remote campsite in northern Pennsylvania. Neutral territory, of course."

"Brie," Nora said, that warning tone now directed at me. "I know what you're thinking, and I don't think it's a good idea. This isn't like the nightclubs you attended in college. Plus, after what happened to you on Thanksgiving, I doubt Kolton will allow you to go."

"Not to mention Jagger," Vi said with a snicker, which quickly morphed into a cough when I gave her the stink eye.

"Jagger hasn't spoken or even looked at me in three days, so I doubt he'll care," I firmly replied, not quite able to keep the bitterness from my voice. "And convincing Kolton to let me go will be easy."

Vi leaned forward to grab a glass of ice water from the tray. "Well, I know how my brother feels about the gala. He's all for letting *males* in our pack attend, but females? Not so much. They get fought over a lot and oftentimes become injured. If you're going to convince him, it'll have to be good."

"Oh, it is," I confidently said, smirking when both females lifted an eyebrow at me. "It's simple. I'll tell him my reason for going is to find my soulmate."

Vi spewed the sip of water she just took all over the coffee table, and Nora went abnormally still.

"What? The notion isn't *that* inconceivable," I said, a bit annoyed by their reactions. "Nora bumped into her fated mate at a nightclub, so chances are, mine's out there too. But I won't find him if I stay in this house all the time."

Both were *way* too quiet after that, but Vi eventually said, "Nora, I think we should—"

"No, Brielle is right," Nora interrupted before she could finish. "She wants a family of her own, and I know Kolton will understand that."

"True, but letting Brielle go by herself is a risk."

"But I wouldn't be alone," I felt the need to point out. "I'll be surrounded by werewolves all weekend."

"Yes, but those supernatural hunters are still out there," Vi reminded me.

"There's only one now, and he's not even a supernatural."

"Don't underestimate humans, especially ones who know about

supernaturals and their weaknesses," Vi said in all seriousness. "The Supernatural Containment Agency consists mostly of humans."

I swallowed with difficulty. "Do you think the SCA sent those two men to my parents' house because they thought I was a danger to my family?"

Seeing the worry on my face, Vi's expression softened. "We already contacted the SCA to make sure it wasn't them, Brielle. Besides, they would never treat humans the way those two men treated your family."

I nodded, some of my worry fading. After a beat of silence, I quietly said, "The last thing I want to do is put myself in danger, but this gala could change everything for me. Please. I really, *really* want to go."

Nora and Vi exchanged looks, then, with a weighty sigh, Nora said, "I'll talk to Kolton about it tonight before bed. I'm sure I can convince him."

A small grin twitched my lips. "With sex, you mean. You'll convince him with sex."

I watched as color slowly painted her cheeks red. It didn't matter that I heard the two of them humping like jackrabbits almost every night. She still blushed when I teased her about it.

"Aaand on that note, I'm out of here," Vi said, grumbling under her breath about knowing too much about her brother's sex life. "I swear this baby is murdering my bladder. I can barely go two hours without needing to pee."

As she stood from the couch, a random thought popped into my head and out of my mouth before I could stop it. "Does Jagger struggle to control his wolf?"

She paused with a hand on her belly and blinked down at me owlishly. "Uh, not that I'm aware of. Why?"

I waved the question away, and yet found myself saying, "He just seems so pent-up all the time, like he has a stick permanently wedged up his butt. The guy seriously needs to get laid or something."

She blinked down at me for another moment, then burst out laughing. "Oh, man," she wheezed out, clutching her belly. "I think I just peed a little."

When she waddled from the room in a rush, still snorting on laughter, I turned to Nora with an exasperated look. "What did I say?"

Nora unlatched Lillian from her nipple and switched her over to the other breast before replying, "We all know that Jagger is a very private male. Even Kolton doesn't know everything about him. He once told me the story of how his parents and pack rejected him at the age of five, but I don't know much more than that about his past. If you want to know more, maybe you should ask him."

"Well, *that's* never happening," I muttered, unable to keep the bitterness from my voice yet again.

Nora looked up from her daughter to search my face intently. "Did something happen between you two? I know those morning training sessions were helping you deal with everything that happened on Thanksgiving, but you haven't left the house for a few days now."

I shrugged and began to fidget with the chunky gold bangles on my wrists. "We decided to take a break. No biggie."

Her stare turned pointed. "I know you, Brielle. You're an open book, and the past few days, you haven't been yourself. Usually when you're stressed, you eat your weight in junk food, but I noticed you didn't even touch the birthday cake and ice cream earlier. What's going on?"

I tried to play off her concern, but my emotions betrayed me and I burst out, "He stopped training me, and I don't know why. One minute, everything was fine, and the next, he was . . . I seriously thought he was going to *kiss* me, Nora. Which is delusional, I know. He's been ignoring me ever since, and it's just . . . it's really bugging me. I thought he'd *finally* started warming up to me."

Nora's expression fell. "Oh, Brie, I'm so sorry."

I gave her a sad smile. "It's okay. Apparently, my charm doesn't work on broody males or family members who think I've gone crazy."

"I could talk to them, and I could ask Kolton to talk to Jagger."

"I love you, bestie," I quickly replied, "but don't you dare. These are my problems, and I need to figure them out. But first, I want to go to that Mate Gala this weekend. You're right that I haven't been myself, and maybe this is just what I need to snap me out of my funk. Do me one huge favor, though."

A worry line bisected her brows, but after a moment, she nodded for me to go on.

Taking a deep breath, I said, "Jagger can't know that I'm planning to go. Please ask Kolton not to tell him."

"Brie . . ."

"*Please*, Nora. He'll ruin everything, I just know it. And I need this. I *really* need this."

At the pleading look I gave her, she shook her head with a groan. "I'm seriously going to regret this, but . . . Fine. I will."

I jumped up from the couch with a little squeal, excited for the future for the first time in days. "Thank you, bestie! You won't regret it!"

"I already am," she called as I hurried from the room to begin packing.

The event was two days away, but I needed that much time to plan out my wardrobe. Not that I would be wearing the clothes for long, if the weekend went the way I hoped.

CHAPTER 11

BRIELLE

I didn't know what I was expecting the campsite to look like, but definitely not like *this*.

The main building was a huge, three-story structure even bigger than the Rivers' mansion. It was fashioned out of logs, but that was the only rustic thing about it. Behind the structure, I spotted several strategically-spaced private cabins, one of which was mine for the weekend.

Vi had reserved it for me after receiving the go-ahead from her brother, albeit a very reluctant go-ahead. Before I'd left this morning, Kolton had pulled me aside and given a stern lecture as if I were a teenage girl going to her first co-ed sleepover. I'd listened intently, agreeing to leave if I at all felt unsafe.

As I took in the breathtaking mountains covered in white that bordered the acres of land dotted with cabins and trees, I pulled out my phone to send an obligatory safe-arrival text to Nora. Jagger would have found out hours ago that I'd left during his morning run, but I hadn't received any calls or texts from him. Not surprising. He never had before, so why would he start now?

Pushing him firmly to the back of my mind, I parked my car in the carefully-shoveled lot that already contained a couple hundred vehicles and got out with my suitcase and purse in hand. Apparently, I could expect to see a few hundred unmated werewolves from around the world this weekend, but probably more. There weren't enough rooms for them all in the main building and cabins, but that was the point. They came to hook up, so by the end of today, most would be paired up—and many would pair up several times, some in groups greater than two.

The possibilities excited me, and I practically skipped across the parking lot toward the main building. I'd always been a social butterfly and had never shied away from large crowds. The bigger the better, and with the full moon still weeks away, I didn't have to worry about wolfing out.

When I entered the lobby, I was immediately greeted by several unfamiliar males. *Hot* ones. From their spots around the open space sporting several lounge areas, they quickly looked me over, most of them with clear interest. I flashed them my dimples and was rewarded with hungry looks.

Yep. This weekend was just what I needed. My self-esteem had taken a nosedive lately, but my time here was sure to rectify that.

After visiting the reception desk to check in, I exited through a side door and followed the path toward my cabin. Most of the guests were still settling in, and after the long car drive, I wanted to take a leisurely bath before the evening fun began. I'd glimpsed a huge ballroom beyond the main lobby area where I assumed the guests would be mingling tonight. If the vibes were anything like the clubs I'd been to when I was human, I'd have no problem hooking up with a guy or two.

I'd never hooked up with more than one at a time before, but if Vi was right about the orgies they had here, I was down for trying something new. My main goal this weekend was to put my troubles behind me and rediscover myself. And if I found a potential mate in the process, all the better.

The cabin reserved for me was both cozy and luxurious, and I had no problems settling in. Several bath salts and perfumes were waiting for me in the bathroom, yet another reminder of why I was here—to engage in a primal mating dance with one goal in mind.

Sex.

I became aroused just thinking about what awaited me in a few hours, and my biological clock ticked double-time.

"Find a mate first, have babies second," I chastised my reflection in the mirror, even as I pictured my flat belly round with child. Maybe Vi was right and all this close proximity to eager virile males would push me into heat. I'd be knocked up in no time, if I was anywhere near as fertile as her and Nora.

Trying to contain my giddiness before I combusted, I sank into the scented bath and allowed the hot water to melt away the tension I'd been carrying in my body for the past few weeks. *Months*, actually. The morning runs and training had started to help with the tension, but it had returned tenfold when Jagger had put a sudden end to our sessions.

I hadn't been completely honest with Nora about how his recent behavior was affecting me. It hurt. *Physically* hurt that he'd stopped training me for no apparent reason and was obviously trying to distance himself from me.

I replayed our last session in my head for the umpteenth time, torturing myself by recalling every single detail. My fear at being rendered immobile, my victory at breaking free, my concern at the pain he was in, my impulsive act at wiping the blood from his face.

And then it had all gone sideways. He'd stopped me from tumbling backward into the creek. He'd grasped the nape of my neck in a way that had startled me, but not in a bad way. Electricity had shot through me, and I'd become hyper aware of how my body fit against his.

And then he'd looked at my mouth. *Hungrily.*

I hadn't imagined it. I *know* I hadn't. Countless males had looked at me that way before.

There was no mistaking it.

Jagger had wanted to kiss me.

But then he'd abruptly let go and started to shift. *Shift.* I'd never seen him act so . . . so *untethered.* And his voice. It had been half feral and—if I didn't know any better—filled with fear.

But that didn't make any sense. Jagger was never afraid, and he certainly didn't go feral over an almost kiss. Then again, I'd never actually seen him take an interest in females, let alone kiss them.

With a groan, I struggled to push the infuriating male from my thoughts once more so I could focus on the evening before me. At least the males here wouldn't confuse the hell out of me. Whether they were looking for a mate or just a good time, any interest in me would boil down to the same thing.

Sex.

I was going to have *sex* tonight. Lots of it. And my hurt feelings over Jagger's strange behavior weren't allowed to interfere.

A few hours later, I was primped to perfection and entering the crowded ballroom in a tight black dress. The thin material clung to me like a second skin, dipping dangerously low in front and riding high on my thighs. One inch higher and I'd be flashing the room my matching panties.

But it only took me a few seconds to realize that I was actually overdressed.

Although the large space looked and sounded like a human nightclub with its flashing colorful lights that cut through the darkness and blaring provocative music, that's where the similarities ended. Right away, my senses were overwhelmed by the pheromones heavy in the air. But that wasn't the only scent. Sweat, arousal, and cum equally filled my nose, and one look around the room explained why.

Most of the guests were naked. *Butt* naked. And although many of them were in the room's center dancing and grinding against each other, an equal number were humping like rabbits around the perimeter.

In plain sight.

I gawked at the giant orgy like a creeper, my mouth slightly askew. "You're most definitely not in Kansas anymore, Toto," I whispered to myself, struggling to swallow when I heard more than one guest reach climax with a lusty groan.

Despite my extroverted nature, I almost chickened out. Almost ran back to my cabin with my tail between my legs to pack my bags and jet out of this kinky sex fest. I was all for sexual exploration, but this was *way* out of my comfort zone. As yet another guest screamed in pleasure, I started to turn around. But before I could make my escape, I bumped into a solid wall of muscle.

"Whoa, easy there," a male voice said, grabbing my arm as I stumbled.

"Sorry," I sheepishly replied and glanced up at the handsome, brown-eyed male.

"Brielle?" he said, and I blinked at him in surprise.

"Theo, right? We met at Reid and Desirae's wedding a few weeks ago."

"Yeah, yeah. Fancy meeting you here," he said, flashing me a megawatt grin, one that slipped a moment later as he glanced around and added, "Is your bodyguard with you?"

"Bodyguard? Oh! You mean Jagger." I laughed a bit awkwardly. "No, he isn't here. Sorry about that, by the way. I would have gone home with you that night, but . . ."

When I finished with an apologetic shrug, his smile returned in full force. "So, you're here alone?"

"Yep."

"Me too. Maybe we can keep each other company."

Which was code for sex, of course.

Returning his smile, I nodded and replied, "I'd like that."

All the invitation he needed. Grabbing my hand, he led me toward the dance floor writhing with sweaty bodies. Some of them were scantily clad, but most wore nothing. Theo was bare chested but at least had pants on. Probably not for long, though.

As we joined the throng and started swaying to the beat, he immediately slipped behind me and pulled my body flush against his. I allowed the hold, raising my hands to pull his head closer, a clear invitation that I was open for more.

Not wasting a second, he lowered his head to kiss my bare shoulder—in the exact same spot where Jagger had nipped it a few weeks ago. The memory immediately crowded into my thoughts, and when Theo slid one of his hands up to cup my breast through my dress, I imagined Jagger's hand there instead.

What the hell?

Shocked that my brain had so readily gone there, I tried to push his image away. But as Theo started kneading the flesh, I couldn't stop picturing Jagger in his place. Within seconds, warmth pooled between my legs. Not in reaction to Theo, but at the mere thought of *Jagger* touching me like this.

To my great annoyance, a breathy moan escaped my lips. The eager male behind me reacted by sliding his hand inside my dress to play with my hardened nipple. Pleasure zinged through me and settled low in my belly, making me arch against him. As my backside pushed into his hard arousal, he groaned and rocked against me.

I closed my eyes, my mind made up that the frustrating male who kept pushing me away was the one now grinding against me. More pleasure spiked through me, and when he slid his free hand under the hem of my dress to touch me through my underwear, he found me already drenched with arousal.

Groaning again, he rubbed my clit and nipple in tandem, continuing to grind against me as he did. My body became one huge bundle of oversensitive nerves, beyond giddy that the mysterious male who'd used his hands to train and protect me was now using them to pleasure me. Completely forgetting the audience around us, I gave in to the high and opened my legs a little wider. He immediately took advantage and pushed aside my underwear to touch my bare clit. I bucked against his fingers, whimpering his name as I felt my climax start to build.

"Interesting," he chuckled against my bare shoulder. "I'm not used to females thinking about other males while I pleasure them, but it's actually kind of hot. He's second in command to the largest pack in America, after all. If you want to pretend I'm him while I penetrate you, I can work with that."

At that, my eyes popped open, along with the delusional bubble I'd wrapped myself in. Still rubbing my clit, Theo released my nipple so he could pull his dick from his pants. Realizing what he was about to do as he hiked up the back of my dress, sudden unease filled me, along with a stinging slap of reality.

I didn't want this. Rather, I didn't want this with *Theo*, a perfect stranger who didn't know a thing about me. I didn't even know his last name.

That wouldn't have bothered me in the past, but as he prepared to stick his dick inside me, I suddenly couldn't stand the thought of being intimate with him.

Not like this. Not right now. Not *ever*.

"Theo," I said, beginning to pull away.

"It's okay, baby," he crooned in my ear, gripping me tightly between my legs to anchor me in place. "I'll make all your fantasies come true."

A cry left me, my pleasure quickly morphing into fear as he positioned himself at my entrance and tried to jam his cock inside. I froze for a moment, paralyzed by my fear, then remembered my training. Lowering my arms, I swiftly jabbed an elbow into his gut.

Just as a surprised "*Ooph!*" left him, an earth-shattering roar cleaved the air. It cut through the moans and screams and pounding music, settling deep into my bones. Something inside me, an awareness I didn't know I possessed, immediately recognized the sound. I twisted around to find a tall figure dressed entirely in black standing in the ballroom's entrance, and all the blood swiftly drained from my face.

Jagger. It was *Jagger*.

He was seething mad, his eyes a scary bright red.

And they were locked on the male still holding me against him.

CHAPTER 12

BRIELLE

"She's *MINE!*"

It happened so fast that the bellowed statement didn't register right away. One second, Jagger was standing in the ballroom's entrance, and the next, storming like a freight train toward Theo. The male holding me finally let go, and with a growl, met Jagger head on. Screams and protested shouts lit up the dance floor as the two males collided and began to fight like possessed demons.

I'd seen werewolves fight before, but not like *this*. Theo was juiced up on testosterone, whereas Jagger actually looked like a raging demon from the fiery pits of hell.

Within seconds, it became painfully obvious who the stronger male was. Both landed vicious blows on each other, but even though he was still in human form, Jagger was more powerful by far. As he hit Theo so hard that he stumbled and nearly fell, the guests on the dance floor shuffled back to give them room. One glance and it was clear that they'd formed a ring around the fighting pair. Not for protection, but to watch the match like it was a spectator sport.

Torn by what to do, I took a step toward the fight, only to be hauled back by another male. Jagger's head suddenly snapped in our direction, his blazing red eyes locking on the male who'd grabbed my arm. Theo took advantage and rushed Jagger, cocking his fist back to punch him squarely on the jaw.

I opened my mouth to warn Jagger, but before I could, he whipped up a hand and caught Theo's fist midswing. One savage twist later and Theo was howling in pain. As he curled forward, cradling his broken wrist, Jagger gripped him by the throat in a vicious hold and yanked him close.

"You will never, *ever* touch my mate again," Jagger growled in the face of the defeated male.

My jaw practically fell to the floor. Did he just . . .

Did he just say *mate?*

Dumbfounded that he would say such a thing, I almost didn't see the move coming in time. Just like he'd done with the human orderly at my parents' house, he brought his other hand up to grip Theo's head.

Realizing what he was about to do, I snapped out of my shock to cry, "Jagger, *no!* Don't kill him."

He froze, a split second away from breaking Theo's neck, from *killing* him. But he didn't let go. Didn't back down.

My words weren't enough. I could see the truth of it in the murderous way he continued to glare at Theo.

Without thought, I rushed forward to rest my hand on one of his arms. This close, I could feel the hot fury pouring off him. Feel the tremor of barely-restrained rage just beneath his skin. His arm flexed beneath my touch, making the muscles feel like ropes of steel. He didn't turn to me, but I somehow knew I had his full attention.

Opening my mouth before I lost my chance, I spoke as calmly as I could, "This is my fault, not his. Please don't punish him for my actions."

It was the truth. I'd all but served myself to Theo on a gold platter, and he'd been so doped up on pheromones that he hadn't realized I'd changed my mind. I didn't blame him for how far things went. I blamed myself for not knowing what I wanted.

Jagger didn't move a muscle for several painfully long moments. Neither did Theo. His testosterone trip had reached a grisly end, and it was clear that he knew how close he was to death. Still touching Jagger's arm, I felt the moment something shifted in him.

He abruptly let go of Theo, only to get in his face and snarl, "If you come near her again, I'll rip off your head."

Theo's throat spasmed, and he quickly nodded before lowering his head deferentially.

Jagger continued to stare at him as if reconsidering his decision to spare his life, then suddenly turned to me. Overwhelmed by the full might of his red gaze, I didn't see the move coming until it was too late.

A gasp left me as he threw my body over his shoulder cave-man style and strode toward the exit. Everyone gave him a wide berth, their gazes carefully fixed on anything but me. I couldn't blame them. He was barely in control, and I knew they'd seen his blood red eyes.

Only a hybrid werewolf with a demonic spirit familiar could make their eyes glow red like that.

No one here stood a chance against him in a fight. Including me.

As he stormed from the ballroom, some of my shock faded, allowing room for other emotions. They flushed hotly through me, making my face heat with embarrassment. He'd crashed the gala and was now carrying me away like I was an insubordinate *child*. I'd never felt so humiliated in my entire life.

Feeling tears sting my eyes, I said through clenched teeth, "Put me down, Jagger." He completely ignored me, passing through the lobby at a fast clip. "I need to collect my things." Silence. "*Jagger.*"

Something in my voice must have finally gotten through to him, because he started to slow. Feet away from exiting the front doors, he stopped and lowered me to my feet. The second my heels touched the ground, I spun around and stormed through the lobby, retracing his steps. As I neared the ballroom again, I heard a warning growl rumble from him, but I ignored it.

At the last second, I veered left and made for the side door that led to my cabin. Jagger followed in my wake, his presence like a malevolent specter about to attack at the slightest provocation. My only comfort was knowing that he wouldn't attack *me*. Just anyone who dared come near me.

Sudden anger chased my humiliation away, and I wrenched open the door so hard that it smacked against the wall, shattering the glass. Too enraged to feel bad about it, I stepped over the mess, making a mental note to pay for it later.

Jagger didn't comment, silent as a tomb as he closely trailed me down the shoveled path. It had begun to lightly snow, but the cold flakes melted the second they connected with my flushed skin. When I reached my cabin, I expected Jagger to wait outside while I packed my things, but he came in right behind me and shut the door with a loud bang.

I finally whirled toward him, my fury spilling over. "What the hell was that back there? You almost *killed* a male for touching me and then *lied* about me being your mate. What is *wrong* with you?"

I was practically screaming in his face, tears of rage streaming down my cheeks, but he didn't say a word.

Completely losing it, I shoved his chest and shouted, "I'm sick of you treating me like a *child*, Jagger. I have every right to find a mate. Hell, I can have sex with whoever I want to, including Theo. I can engage in a freaking *orgy* if I feel like it. But you screwed it all up and scared everyone away like you always do. I hope you're happy, because I most definitely am not. I'm *miserable*, and it's all your fault!"

When he still didn't speak, I shoved his chest again. And again.

And again. It was like striking a brick wall, and my inability to move him even an inch made me angrier by the second.

Just as I was about to tear into him with words again, he finally reacted. One swift move, and he had me pinned against the door with my arms locked above my head. I gasped and struggled to break free, but his much larger body had thoroughly trapped me. Glaring daggers up at his glowing-red eyes, I hissed, "How dare—"

Before I could finish, his mouth crashed into mine.

Just like that, everything screeched to a halt. I stopped struggling. Stopped *breathing*. Every inch of me was shocked senseless.

Jagger. *Jagger* was kissing me. Well, if you could call what he was doing a kiss.

The press of his lips was anything but soft. It was hard. Bruising. *Punishing*.

He tightly gripped my wrists, using his body to render mine completely immobile. I waited for panic to fill me, for fear to take me hostage. Instead, my body burst awake like a firework, and a breathy whimper escaped me.

Jagger swallowed the sound, kissing me harder, harder, *harder*. My lips parted under the assault, and he delved his tongue inside my mouth. The second it touched mine, he jerked away from me and stumbled back.

Without him there to hold me up, my arms fell limply to my sides and I weakly slumped against the door. Struggling to catch my breath, I peeled my eyes open to find him standing in the room's center with his hands tightly balled into fists, his chest heaving and his eyes squeezed shut. He stayed like that for a full minute. Then two. With the taste of him still dancing on my tongue, I stayed where I was, in too much shock to break the silence.

After another solid minute, he slowly reopened his eyes. I

immediately saw that they'd returned to their blue-gray color, but I saw something else too. Something that made the fireworks still sparking in my body turn into pinpricks of ice.

He looked devastated. Like he'd just made the worst mistake of his life.

And then he did something that instantly made me feel like a piece of dirt. He raised one of his fisted hands and wiped his mouth— our *kiss*—onto the back of it.

The pinpricks of ice went straight for my heart, and I visibly flinched as they impaled the vulnerable organ. Jagger didn't notice. He'd already turned away from me to begin packing my things. I let him, in too much pain to move or speak.

But when he dropped some clothing onto the bed and said, "Get dressed," my hurt quickly morphed into anger once more.

"Make me," I snottily replied. Okay, not my best comeback, but I could still feel the pressure of his mouth on mine and his taste on my tongue. My brain wasn't fully back online yet.

He paused in his packing but didn't glance my way. After a tense moment of silence, he grabbed the clothing and stuffed it into my bag. A petty sense of victory filled me, but it faded a few minutes later when he finished packing the suitcase and strode toward the door with purpose. I immediately knew what he was planning, noting too late that he'd packed my purse as well. Still leaning against the door, I crossed my arms over my chest and stood my ground.

No way was he going to—

In one smooth move, he grabbed my arm and somehow managed to exit the cabin with me in tow while carrying my suitcase. Once outside, I tried to jerk my arm free, but his fingers were clamped around my bicep like iron shackles.

"Jagger, I swear," I said in a deathly quiet voice as he forced me down the path toward the parking lot. "If you don't let go of me in two seconds, I'm going to scream bloody murder."

His hand on my arm immediately vanished. But when he kept going with my suitcase, I stomped after him with an annoyed growl.

"I can't drive back without my keys," I called as he swiftly pulled away, his legs so much longer than mine. "Jagger. *Jagger.*"

Without slowing, he finally replied, "You're riding with me. I'll send someone to pick up your car."

I stopped dead in my tracks. Feeling my anger swiftly reach a tipping point once more, I snapped, "Like *hell* I am. I'll just stay here."

Before I could make good on my threat, he abruptly whirled and stormed toward me. A startled squeak lodged in my throat, but I managed to stand my ground instead of run like I really wanted to do. Prepared to fight like a feral beast if he tried to throw me over his shoulder again, I wasn't ready when he stopped directly in front of me and said in an eerily soft voice, "You either come with me willingly, or I'll tie you up and stuff you in the trunk."

My mouth fell open. Seeing the truth of his words in his piercing gaze, all I managed to get out was, "You wouldn't dare."

His gaze hardened. "Try me."

Knowing that I'd lost, a feeling of helplessness stole over me. Still, I refused to look away, wanting him to see the truth of *my* words when I slowly said, "I hate you."

He stared at me a moment more, his expression unreadable. Then he turned to walk away again with my suitcase, but not before I heard him mutter, "Good."

CHAPTER 13

JAGGER

As I drove away from the campsite with Brielle in the seat beside me, I knew three things with certainty.

One: She was absolutely furious with me.

Two: I was hopelessly addicted to her taste.

And three: I desperately wanted to taste her again.

I'd screwed up big time on so many levels, but all I could feel was relief that she was unharmed, that no one had claimed her or even had sex with her, and that she was safely under my protection once more. When I'd found out where she'd gone, I'd nearly lost my mind. Onyx had gone crazy at the thought of her being with other males, and it had taken me over an hour to wrestle him under control. Seeing that male in the ballroom all over her with his dick out, I'd almost let Onyx loose.

The bastard had touched her. *Touched* her.

He deserved to suffer. To be torn to shreds. To rue the day he'd ever laid a hand on my mate.

It had taken every last drop of self control not to exact my revenge. If it wasn't for her, he'd be dead right now. The urge to kill him was still pulsing through my veins, the image of them together still sharp in my mind. His hand had been between her legs. He'd been *pleasuring* her. A second more and his dick would have been inside her. Hell, she still *smelled* of him.

That murderous feeling rose up again, rushing hotly through my system. I gripped the steering wheel so hard that it audibly cracked beneath my palms. Surprisingly, Onyx was no longer fueling my rage. He'd actually been rather subdued ever since I'd kissed Brielle. To him, I'd finally begun the process of marking her as mine, and I could feel how pleased that made him.

That hadn't been my intention, though.

I'd wanted to *punish* her for the wicked things she'd said. I made her miserable? Well, the feeling was mutual. My life had been a living hell ever since she'd walked into it. Everything she did was a distraction, and this latest stunt she'd pulled had finally pushed me over the edge.

But when I'd brutally kissed her, I hadn't expected her to go pliant against me. I hadn't expected her to *whimper* against my mouth. She hadn't been cowed by the kiss in the slightest.

Hell, she'd *enjoyed* it.

The realization had made every molecule in my body explode awake, and before I could stop myself, I'd thrust my tongue into her mouth to taste her. Onyx had howled with satisfaction, and I'd inwardly howled along with him, instantly becoming addicted to her exotic flavor. A second more, and I wouldn't have been able to control the need to explore every inch of her mouth with my eager tongue. Even now, I struggled with the desire to taste her again. To dominate her body with mine and feel her melt against me.

But doing so would be a terrible mistake. I'd broken my promise to keep my distance from her again, and I could already feel the consequences for doing so. The invisible bond between us had roared awake, an incessant thrum beneath my skin that grew more persistent with each passing second I was near her.

Sitting beside her for the next several hours was going to be the worst kind of hell, and not because she was spitting mad at me. Her anger actually gave me something to think about besides that blasted kiss. I was very much aware that she was a free spirit and didn't like being bossed around, but once I'd seen her with that male on the dance floor, I didn't care.

She was coming home with me whether she wanted to or not. Until she was safe, I couldn't think. Couldn't sleep. Couldn't eat. Nothing made sense while she was away, and I would rather she hate me than exist without her.

Deep down, I knew these feelings stemmed from our soulmate bond. But as they continued to pulse through me, it was getting harder and harder to differentiate between the bond's pull and my own feelings.

An hour into the trip, the weather turned. Wind and sleet pounded at the Porsche, and I was forced to slow. But I kept driving, determined to make it back home without any stops. Another half hour ticked by, and the sleet turned into a maelstrom of snow. The storm screamed at us through the windows, but I kept going, refusing to let a little blizzard—

"Jagger!"

I saw the semi-truck in the rearview mirror just in the nick of time and sharply veered toward the shoulder before it could plow into us. The Porsche hit a patch of ice, and I lost control, unable to brake or steer. As we spun around, Brielle screamed, and I threw an arm out to brace her for the inevitable collision. Seconds later, we struck what felt like a guard rail, and the Porsche jolted to a dead stop.

I was unbuckling my seatbelt and reaching for Brielle a moment later. "Any injuries?" I asked, running my hands down her arms.

She straightened with a groan and lifted a hand to touch her right temple. "Yes. I just hit my head on the window." When her fingers came away wet with blood, I gently grasped her neck and turned her face toward me. She stiffened under my touch but didn't pull away, her lashes fluttering as she recovered from the blow.

"The wound is superficial," I said after a thorough inspection, watching the cut slowly heal before gently wiping the blood away. "You should be fully healed in a few more minutes."

As her emerald eyes met mine, I suddenly realized how close our faces were. One small move and our lips would touch. Her gaze darted down to my mouth, letting me know that she was thinking the same thing. Just like that, the air inside the Porsche crackled with tension, and the desire to kiss her sizzled through me.

My hold on her neck tightened, my hand circling her vulnerable throat like a necklace. Her pulse jumped beneath my thumb, and when I realized the reaction wasn't fear, my own started to race.

In no time, every inch of me hummed with need. It became hard to breathe. Hard to *think*. My thumb stretched up to her jaw, guiding her lips closer to mine. As her warm breath feathered across my skin, the air between us became supercharged, whipping my need into a frenzy.

In response to my unraveling control, Onyx surged upward and tried to force the connection. My hand spasmed on her throat, and I almost gave in. Almost claimed her mouth in a heated kiss that I knew, just *knew* I wouldn't be able to pull away from this time.

"Stop."

The command was weak, and Onyx knew it. He pushed harder, his sole focus on making me claim my mate.

"I said *stop*," I barked and threw myself back. As I violently collided with the driver side door, Brielle gaped at me like I'd grown two heads. Her hand fluttered up to her neck, and it was then that I noticed the faint print I'd left behind on her delicate flesh.

The sight was like a punch to the face, and I was out of the car in a flash, shame pressing down on me so hard that I nearly crashed to my knees. The storm tore at my clothing as I slogged through the snow to check out the accident. The semi-truck was nowhere in sight, and the dark road was empty, save for us. I welcomed the blizzard's fury, using the distraction to wrestle my wolf familiar under control once more.

Comfort mate, he growled, clearly pissed at me for not giving in.

"You *hurt* her," I roared into the wind, instantly recalling the marks I'd left on her throat.

Not hurt. Aroused, he challenged, refusing to take responsibility for what had happened. Not that I should be surprised. To him, marks were good. The more, the better. He didn't understand how they could be bad.

Knowing that arguing with him was pointless, I focused on the bent guard rail and Porsche. One glance and I knew we weren't driving away from here anytime soon. Cursing under my breath, I pulled out my phone to shoot Kolton a text. When it failed to send, I tried calling with the same result.

Pausing for a few minutes to think, I finally accepted the only possible conclusion and rounded the car to inform Brielle.

"The Porsche is totaled, and the cell signal's down," I said upon reentering the vehicle. "We'll have to wait until the storm passes to call for help."

She didn't respond, her gaze trained out the front windshield. I glanced at her neck, relieved that the marks were no longer visible. They were still there, though. Still imprinted in both our minds.

I opened my mouth to say something, to explain, to *apologize*. Before I could, she blurted, "I'm not staying here all night with you."

Hurt lanced through me, but I ignored the feeling. I had no right to feel it, and she had every right to still be mad at me. Swallowing past the tightness in my throat, I replied, "There's a hotel a few miles from here."

A frown pulled at her mouth. "How do you know?"

"It's my job as second in command to know Midnight Pack territory," I explained, then hesitated before adding, "I also lived in the Buffalo area for a while after my old pack rejected me. Hotel dumpsters were one of my go-tos for food."

Her eyes briefly met mine before flitting away again. "Oh," was all she said. She opened her mouth to say more, then seemed to change her mind and slowly closed it.

Locking away the painful memory, I continued, "If you're up for the walk, we could stay at the hotel tonight, but I suggest you change first. People might ask questions if you show up in high heels and a barely-there dress during a snowstorm."

She snorted. "Barely there? If you didn't notice, I was overdressed at the gala. No one bothered to tell me that the dress code was *nude*."

I suppressed a snort of my own, forcing my gaze to remain on her face and not the sinful little black dress she wore. "No one should have told you about the gala in the first place."

Too late, I realized my mistake.

Her eyes narrowed, and I knew she was about to give me a tongue-lashing. Sure enough, she turned to me and snapped, "Why? Because you were afraid someone would claim me as their mate and I would no longer be under your thumb?"

I stared at her, utterly lost for words.

Seeing that I wasn't going to reply, she faced forward again with a short sigh. "Forget it. As angry as I am with you right now, going to the gala was a mistake and so was letting Theo touch me. I was actually trying to stop him right before you arrived all bent out of shape."

I stilled. "You tried to stop him?"

She stiffened at the change in my tone, throwing me a wary glance. "He wasn't *forcing* himself on me, Jagger. His brain—well, and his dick—just hadn't received the message yet that I'd changed my mind."

"That's no excuse," I bit out, my rage returning in full force. "He needs to pay for his lapse in judgement."

"Well, maybe I need to pay too for stringing him along," she shot back, then heatedly added, "And while we're slinging around judgement, maybe *you* should pay too. I've been kissed numerous times over the years, but *none* of the guys wiped off the kiss afterward as if it *disgusted* them."

At that, all of my rage vanished in an instant. "Brielle," I started, but words failed me yet again.

Comfort mate. Comfort mate! Onyx howled at me, picking up on Brielle's distress.

I hesitated, and it cost me.

"You know what?" Brielle said with a small laugh, yet I didn't miss the sudden tears glistening in her eyes. "I think I'm up for that walk after all. I have a lot of pent-up energy to burn off."

Not waiting for me to reply, she unbuckled her seatbelt and lifted her hips off the seat to shimmy her dress up. Before I knew it, the dress was over her head, and she was sitting in nothing but a pair of lacy black panties and matching bra.

Blood immediately rushed to my groin, and I quickly tore my gaze from her shapely form to glare at her. "What are you doing?"

She blinked at me as if confused. "You told me to change." Tossing the dress aside, she twisted in her seat to reach her suitcase in the back. The move brought her backside parallel with my face, and my rebellious eyes couldn't help but notice that the taut flesh was covered in nothing but a tiny thong.

Struggling and failing to swallow, I squeezed my eyes shut and waited for the tortuous moment to pass. Clothing rustled, her tropical scent bombarding me from all sides. I stopped breathing, focusing my efforts on getting rid of the boner in my pants before she noticed.

After several long moments, the rustling stopped and she said, "You can look now."

I cautiously peeled open my eyes, allowing myself to breathe again when I found her in jeans, boots, and a leather jacket.

"Jeez, you must think I'm hideous," she muttered, blinking as if she was about to start crying.

"I don't," I quickly said, scrambling to say something before she burst into tears. "I think you're extremely beautiful. I just didn't—"

Sudden laughter sputtered out of her, gaining in volume by the second. "Oh, man," she wheezed, waving a hand at me. "You should see your *face*." More laughter, then, "Don't worry. I'm not offended. I just wanted to see if you were completely immune to me, and guess what? You're not."

I stared at her, slowly realizing that this had been a test. No. A *punishment*. I'd punished her with that kiss, so . . .

She'd punished me back.

I stared and stared, not knowing what to do with this unexpected power reversal. She'd punished me back. She'd punished me *back*.

"Um, hello?" She waved a hand in front of my face, forcing me to snap out of my daze. "My door won't open, so I'll have to use yours. If you don't want me to crawl over you, then you might want to—"

She started to move toward me, and I burst into action, exiting the vehicle in one second flat.

CHAPTER 14

BRIELLE

It was official. I no longer recognized myself.

For one, the three mile trudge through a freaking blizzard had barely fazed me. As a human, I would have been a basket case and complained the entire way.

For another, I wasn't bothered by the fact that Jagger had collared my throat in a chokehold. The move had been entirely domineering, not to mention possessive. There was no denying he'd wanted to kiss me again, and yet something had prevented him from doing so. As maddening as that was, just knowing that he'd *wanted* to was enough to soothe some of my earlier hurt—yet another reason why I didn't recognize myself.

Jagger Montgomery was a walking red flag. His hot and cold attitude toward me bordered on emotional abuse. Past human me wouldn't have touched him with a ten foot pole, let alone wanted him to kiss me again. We were total opposites and had nothing in common. He barely even *spoke* to me. This infatuation I had with him was illogical and not like me at all. And yet . . .

His reaction to me undressing in the car had been anything but disgust. I'd seen the flash of heat in his eyes before he'd squeezed them shut like a shy school boy. He wasn't immune to me. In fact, he thought I was beautiful. *Extremely* beautiful. Which meant that I'd probably misunderstood his reaction to our kiss at the cabin.

Something was definitely bothering him, though. He'd been

desperate to stop himself from kissing me in the car. So desperate that he'd briefly cut off my air.

Past human me would have freaked out and tried to call the cops. I didn't tolerate violent, controlling guys. Jagger was capable of extreme violence, and despite the defensive training he'd given me, there was no way I could stop him if he wanted to hurt me. I'd seen him snap a man's neck like it was a *toothpick*.

And yet, when he touched me, I didn't feel unsafe—even when the same hand that had killed a man had been wrapped around my throat. In fact, I felt the opposite, which didn't make any sense.

Something about Jagger drew me in like a moth to a flame, and I was going to get burned—*badly*—if I kept letting him play with my emotions. The mysterious male might intrigue me, but I needed to protect my heart before he broke it into a million pieces.

Becoming a werewolf had definitely changed many things about me. I loved being outside now, I wanted to settle down and start a family of my own, and I apparently had a new kink for being strangled.

But even though being dominated by an emotionally unavailable male with too many secrets to count heavily turned me on, I still *hated* when people made life decisions for me. And the minute we'd entered the hotel, Jagger had turned into his bossy tyrant self once more.

"One room, please," he told the receptionist without even consulting with me first.

"Um, I'd actually like my own," I said, my tone firm and decisive.

I thought that would be the end of it, but Jagger shocked the hell out of me by saying, "I know you're still mad at me, honey, but there's no need for us to stay in separate rooms."

I nearly swallowed my tongue, flabbergasted that he'd just called me *honey*. Struggling to recover, I got into character myself and saucily replied, "Well, you refuse to have sex with me, *honey*, so why would I want to share a room with you?"

Jagger coughed, and there was no mistaking the darkening of his cheeks. He was embarrassed. *Really* embarrassed. I fought back a vindictive smile.

Stuck in the middle of a lovers' quarrel, the receptionist looked rather uncomfortable herself. Clearing her throat delicately, she said, "I'm sorry, but we actually only have one room available at this time. All flights were cancelled due to the weather, and our rooms filled up fast. Do you want it?"

"Yes," Jagger replied without hesitation, and I barely suppressed the urge to stomp on his foot.

The second the receptionist handed us our key cards, I grabbed mine and stormed off. Ignoring my obvious need for space, Jagger caught up with me and quietly growled, "You talk too much."

"And you talk too little. In fact, I've had better conversations with a *wall*," I snarked back, sweeping right past the elevator to take the stairs instead. No way was I going to get stuck in an elevator with *him*. "Seriously, Jagger. You act like it's torture to be around me."

"It is. I'll probably get demoted from second in command after this."

When he made it sound like this whole thing was *my* fault, my temperature rose once more, and I yanked open the stairwell door to stomp up the stairs. "Then why did you follow me to the gala? And why the *hell* did you insist on us staying in one room?"

"Because it's not safe for you to be alone."

"Why? Because of what happened to me at Thanksgiving?"

"Exactly."

"Bull. The full moon is weeks away and that remaining hunter has made no effort to pursue me. You just get off on making my life *miserable.*"

"I think you're doing that just fine all on your own."

At that, I whirled so I could glare down at him. "What is *that* supposed to mean?"

Not batting an eye, he said, "You visited your human family before you were ready, and you participated in a mating event you weren't prepared for. Both ended in disaster even before I showed up. You're trying to force things that can't be forced."

Heat flooded my cheeks, and I snapped back, "How *dare* you. You don't know a thing about me."

His lips thinned, and I expected that to be the end of our conversation. I whirled around again, but before I could make it two steps, he said, "I know that your favorite color is magenta."

I stopped again, wholly unprepared to hear him say that.

"I know that you love to accessorize and own more shoes and purses than your closet can hold," he went on, flipping my world upside down with each word. "I know that you hate cooked carrots. I know that your dimples appear when you're both happy and mad. I know that you're opinionated, free spirited, and don't like to be told what to do. I know that you care and feel deeply. I know that you're fiercely loyal to your friends and family, and it breaks your heart that your parents and brothers haven't accepted the new you.

"I know you, Brielle," he continued. "And if you're miserable with your new life, then I know you'll do something about it. All I'm asking is that you do it the *right* way. The safe way."

He stopped talking then, but I could still hear his words loud and clear in my head. When I failed to respond, he brushed past me, pausing at the second floor landing to hold open the door. Moving on autopilot, I joined him and exited the stairwell, my mind a jumble of chaotic thoughts. As we entered our room, I was still so preoccupied that I didn't even notice there was only one bed.

"I'll sleep on the floor," Jagger said, and I nodded without comment, heading into the bathroom to prepare for bed as best I could. I'd left my suitcase in the car, and normally, I'd struggle to fall asleep without my nightly regimen. But when I exited the bathroom minutes later and found Jagger laying on the floor near the door, fully clothed with his eyes closed and an arm propped under his head for a pillow, I suddenly didn't care about my routine.

Hesitating for a moment, I crossed over to the queen-sized bed and pulled the top comforter off, along with a pillow. Then I padded across the room and placed them beside Jagger. As I turned to retrace my steps, I heard him quietly say, "Thank you."

"You're welcome," I murmured back, tugging off my boots before slipping into bed fully clothed. I turned off the light, and the room plunged into darkness. Seconds later, my night vision adjusted, and I peeked over at the door to see that Jagger now had the pillow under his head with the blanket over him.

Satisfied, I let my eyes drift shut.

Within minutes, I was fast asleep.

The pressure of fingers on my throat startled me awake, and I jerked open my eyes with a gasp.

"Shhh," a male voice rumbled in my ear, lightening the pressure on my throat so he could stroke his thumb up the vulnerable length. "You're safe."

With his voice deeper and huskier than usual, my muddled brain struggled to piece together who it belonged to. But as his familiar earthy cedarwood musk wafted over me, my panic faded.

"Jagger, what are you—?"

"Shhh," he rumbled again, his large body a looming shadow beside me on the bed. With his mouth near my ear, I couldn't see his face. When I turned to look at him, he nipped the shell of my ear with a stern, "No."

I froze, my eyes widening in shock. What the hell was happening? This was *so* unlike him. Before I could ask, he tipped my chin up with his thumb and lowered his head toward my neck. Then, with no warning whatsoever, he slowly licked up the column of my throat.

The unexpected sensation drew another gasp from me, and when I tried to turn my head again, he nipped at my throat with a quiet growl.

"Settle, mate," he said, and my eyes practically bugged out of their sockets.

"Mate?" I squeaked, unable to keep silent any longer. "Seriously, Jagger. What the hell are you—?"

My mouth froze in a startled O as the hand on my neck suddenly delved beneath the covers and into my jeans. It happened so fast that I didn't have time to think about how insane this was. All I could do was react to the feeling of his fingers slipping inside my panties to touch my clit. My body exploded awake at the contact, and I arched off the mattress with a strangled cry.

"Oh, God. Oh, *God.*"

He sharply nipped at my neck again to silence me, then licked the sting away when I obediently clamped my mouth shut.

Insane. This was *insane.* The car crash had given me less whiplash than this male.

But as he started to rub my clit in tight circles, I lost the ability to care. Pleasure jolted through my body, leaving me shaking and breathless, and I was on the edge of orgasm within seconds. I waited for my common sense to kick back in, but it didn't. I had *no* desire to stop this from happening. In fact, I wanted it to happen. I *desperately* wanted it to. I'd never wanted anything more in my entire life.

Shocked by how badly I wanted this, all I could do was grip the sheets for dear life and keep my moans of pleasure at bay. When my legs began to stiffen, the tension in my body about to snap, his fingers bore down on my clit, swirling faster and faster.

The intensity was too much for me, and my entire body erupted in pleasure. I cried out again, my head falling back as wave after wave of ecstasy crashed over me. Jagger licked my neck again, his fingers prolonging the orgasm with languid circles against my spasming pussy.

"Such a good girl," he rumbled against my neck. "My pretty, pretty girl."

I basked in his praise, my body humming blissfully as I slowly came down. When I relaxed into the mattress, my breathing growing steady, he licked my neck again and removed his hand from my pants. The second he did, he abruptly exploded upright on the bed with a bellowing roar.

Startled, I jerked open my eyes to find him tightly gripping his head. When he bellowed again and violently shook his head, worry filled me, and I called out his name. He didn't react, lost to whatever had taken hold of him. I sat up and reached for him, but the second I touched his arm, he grabbed my shoulders and slammed me back to the mattress.

Still recovering from the forceful move, I failed to comprehend his words as he shouted, "What did he do?"

"H-he?" I sputtered out.

"What did he *do*, Brielle?" Jagger repeated, giving my shoulders a shake.

"I don't . . . Y-you touched me."

Fear lit up his blue-gray eyes. "Did he hurt you?"

"What? No. You . . . you *pleasured* me."

At that, he yanked his hands off me as if he'd been burned. "That wasn't me," he said, horror overtaking his expression. "That wasn't *me*."

I gaped at him, certain that I'd just witnessed a man lose his mind. "I don't understand. We're the only two people here. Of *course* it was you."

"No," he said and shook his head, the horror on his face slowly morphing into anger. Into *rage*. "There's one other person here. One other *being*."

When I just stared at him, my brain refusing to connect the dots, he spat out a word. A *name*. One that turned my insides to ice.

"*Onyx*."

CHAPTER 15

BRIELLE

Jagger stood in the room's center, still as stone except for the slight tremor shaking his hands.

I knew he was silently communicating with his wolf familiar, and although his expression didn't change, I knew his emotions were everywhere. They were so intense that I could practically feel them, especially the anger. It was like an anvil repeatedly striking my chest.

"Why did he do it?" I asked, unable to bear the deafening silence a moment longer.

I'd been shocked and confused to learn that Jagger hadn't been the one touching me—not consciously, anyway. I knew from talks with Nora that the spirit entity residing inside a hybrid could take over their host's human form, even speak through them. I'd seen it for myself on more than one occasion, but I'd never thought Onyx would *hijack* Jagger's unconscious body for the sole purpose of pleasuring me.

Still, try as I might, I couldn't seem to feel any anger toward him.

Onyx was a part of Jagger, and if the wolf familiar wanted to pleasure me, then there was a good chance that Jagger wanted to pleasure me too. But Jagger clearly wasn't okay with what had happened, and that made me wonder if he ever intended to pursue me in that way himself.

After several more tense moments, he finally crossed to a nearby chair and sat down with a defeated sigh. Bowing his head, he ran a hand over his closely cropped hair before saying, "He saw how upset you've been today and wanted to comfort you. His idea of comfort is . . . well . . ." He threw up a hand in frustration instead of finishing the sentence.

Oh. *Oh.* Onyx had touched me to make me feel better. But he'd obviously wanted me to think that *Jagger* had been the one doing it, not him.

Fiddling with one of my bracelets, I tentatively asked, "Does Onyx want me to be your mate?"

Jagger stilled, then slowly lifted his head. When our eyes met, it felt like all of the oxygen left the room. Even before he answered, I knew what he was going to say. "Yes."

Something fluttered in my chest, making my heart begin to race. But one look at Jagger's pained expression, and the feeling swiftly died. "But *you* don't," I whispered, barely able to get the words out.

He opened his mouth, then closed it and looked away.

An ache replaced the fluttery feeling, a tightness that made it impossible to breathe. Even though he was only a few feet from me, he suddenly felt miles and miles away. I'd been right, then. He might be attracted to me and tempted to steal a kiss, but he didn't . . . he didn't *want* me. Not as his mate.

I shouldn't feel as hurt as I did. He'd been a pain in my butt for over a year and had ignored me for the majority of that time. But I suddenly felt *gutted*, like he'd stabbed a knife into my stomach and yanked all my innards out.

"Is it because I'm not a hybrid?" I blurted, unwilling to let this go so easily. To hell with my pride. I needed to know why I wasn't good enough for him.

"What?" His gaze snapped back to mine. "No, of course not."

"Is it because I'm willful? Because I *talk* too much?"

"*No*," he said more forcefully, anger bleeding into his tone. "This has nothing to do with your character, Brielle. I admire those things about you."

Surprise flickered through me, but I nudged it aside to press, "Then why? Why am I not good enough for you?"

"Brielle, stop. This isn't about you."

I ignored his warning, unable to stop now that we'd come this far. I had to know. I *needed* to. "Then why have you spent the past year watching me like a hawk? Why interfere with my life and learn so much about me? Why almost *kill* a guy for touching me?"

"Brielle, stop."

"Why train me? Why protect me?" I went on, my voice gaining in volume with each word. "Why look after my wolf when I shift?"

"*Brielle.*"

"Why push me away over and over only to pull me close again?" I cried. "Why *kiss* me? Why, Jagger? Just tell me *why.*"

He exploded off his seat and roared, "Because you're my *soulmate!*"

I almost fell over backward on the bed, entirely unprepared to hear those words leave his mouth. As I stared at him, shocked to my very core, instant regret filled his gaze.

"I'm sorry," he said, lifting both hands to grip his nape. "I shouldn't have . . . You weren't supposed to know. But this trip. This *blasted* trip . . ."

Understanding slowly trickled in, and my stomach dropped. "Wait. You were going to *keep* this from me?"

When he didn't respond, I stood to my feet, surprised that my body even let me. A tremble in my hands had quickly spread to the rest of me. Even my *teeth* were chattering.

Seeing the truth in his gaze despite his silence, a chill crept up my spine. Balling my hands into fists, I said, "How long have you known?"

Hearing the dangerous edge to my voice, Jagger stiffened, then lowered his arms. "Brielle . . ."

"How *long?*"

The question snapped through the air like a whip, and Jagger noticeably flinched. Just when I thought he wouldn't answer, a sigh fled him and he replied, "Since before your first shift."

I froze. *Everything* froze as I quickly did the math. That was . . . that was over a *year* ago. He really hadn't planned to tell me, then, which could only mean one thing . . .

He didn't want the bond. He'd *rejected* it.

The room suddenly tilted, and I was falling, falling, falling.

As I landed hard on the floor, Jagger lunged for me, but I yanked up a hand and barked, "*No.* Don't touch me."

He immediately halted, his face deeply etched with worry as I pushed myself into a sitting position. "Brielle," he started, but I was suddenly done, the information I'd just received already more than my brain could handle.

"No," I said, cutting him off. "Not right now. I just . . . I need some time to process this. Please just go."

Something squeezed my chest. Something *painful.* It came on so suddenly that I gasped and placed my hand over my chest, certain I was having a heart attack.

"*Brielle.*"

Jagger was beside me in an instant. But the moment I felt his hands on me, I lost it.

"No!" I screamed, shoving his hands away. "Go. Just GO!"

The pain in my chest intensified, and I curled forward with a strangled cry. Jagger reached for me again but stopped himself from touching me.

When he didn't leave, I forced myself to straighten so I could look him dead in the eye and growl, "I swear, Jagger, if you don't go right now, I will *never* speak to you again."

He held my gaze for several moments, the pain I still felt in my chest mirrored in his eyes. Finally, he stood and turned for the door.

The second it closed behind him, I curled into a ball on the floor and let myself shatter into a million pieces.

He didn't want me. He didn't want me. He didn't want me.

I repeated the words in my head the entire way back to the Rivers' estate, forcing myself to accept the truth.

I had a soulmate. We were destined for each other by *fate*. And he didn't want me.

But every time I repeated the words, the ache in my chest grew worse. It was suffocating, a great and terrible weight that barely allowed me to breathe. The only way I could survive the pain and hours-long drive across New York was by curling up in the backseat and pretending to sleep. I knew it was pathetic, but I was in too much agony to care.

The snowstorm had stopped by mid morning, but it had taken until late afternoon for the plows to clear the roads. Kolton and Griff had arrived with the truck soon after that, and Jagger had helped them hitch up the Porsche to be towed.

The ride back was spent mostly in silence, but I knew the three males were still communicating. They'd been friends—*brothers*—for over two decades and shared an exceptionally strong bond. I could tell by the tension in the truck that they were worried about my catatonic state, but none of them questioned me when I curled up on the seat and stayed that way the entire trip back.

As we neared Lake Placid, Griff leaned forward and quietly said to Jagger in the front passenger seat, "Does she know?"

Silence greeted his words. I kept my eyes closed, still pretending to sleep. After a long moment, I heard Jagger murmur, "She knows."

They could have been talking about anything, but I knew, just *knew* they were talking about the soulmate bond. Which meant that Jagger had told them about it. Which meant that they too had kept it from me. And if *they* knew about it, their wives probably did too.

My *best friend* had known that Jagger was my soulmate. And that. *That.* Made my shredded heart shatter all over again.

They'd known. They'd *all* known. And they hadn't said a thing.

CHAPTER 16

JAGGER

"You need to talk to her."

The words were delivered quietly, but they struck my eardrums like a clashing cymbal. From my horizontal position beneath the newly-repaired Porsche, I continued to tinker with the undercarriage without comment, hoping Kolton would get the message and drop it.

No such luck.

"Brielle has barely spoken to any of us all week. She feels betrayed and rightfully so. We kept the bond a secret like you asked, and although I respected your decision not to tell her, it's now affecting her health and yours. Neither of you are eating or sleeping, and that's something I can't ignore. Believe me, I've tried. I know just how daunting it is to discover you have a fated mate. But once the soulmate bond strengthens, you only have two choices."

At that, I stopped tinkering and lowered my wrench. "And what are those?"

"Accept or reject the bond. Keeping your distance from Brielle won't work anymore. You need to confront this head on and make a choice, one that you clearly communicate with her so there's no confusion. You owe that to yourself and to her, as well as to Midnight Pack. Your turmoil over the bond has made you question my authority, and we both know how dangerous that is. I consider you my brother, but if this behavior continues, I'll have no choice but to discipline you accordingly."

I knew all this already, but hearing it out loud hit me like a ton of bricks. If I didn't get my head screwed on straight soon, I could lose my second in command position. Even worse, I could get banished from Midnight Pack. Just the thought sent panic roaring through me, and I quickly set down the wrench before it slipped from my trembling fingers.

Before I could respond to Kolton's dire words, a distressed cry reached my ears. "Please don't, Brielle. *Please!*"

I was out from under the Porsche in a flash, following closely on Kolton's heels as he strode from the garage to see what the problem was. At the sight of Brielle heading toward us with two huge suitcases in hand, I stopped dead. Kolton, however, brushed past her and hurried toward his waddling wife.

"Nora, it's not safe for you out here. You could fall," he said and tried to scoop her up.

"I'm not going to fall," she replied, waving him away so she could continue waddling after her best friend. "Brie, I'm sorry. I'm *so* sorry for not telling you. It was torture keeping this a secret from you, but I promised not to say anything. I know you're mad, but—"

"I'm not mad," Brielle interrupted, sweeping past me as if I wasn't there. "I'm hurt."

Sudden pain twisted my insides, stealing the breath from my lungs. It was Brielle. Her hurt. Her pain. I'd been feeling it ever since that fateful night at the hotel. Our interactions that day had encouraged the soulmate bond to strengthen, and I could now feel her emotions as a result.

This past week, I'd felt nothing but pain. Hers. Mine. At this point, I couldn't tell who it was coming from anymore. I'd tried to stay busy, tried to distract myself from feeling it. I'd thrown myself into fixing the Porsche, remaining out here for hours at a time to avoid being near her. I'd even started using the apartment above the garage, barely stepping foot inside the main house unless absolutely necessary.

But there was no escaping the pain. We were both suffering, both struggling under the bond's incessant pull. Despite trying to avoid her at all costs, I'd noticed how thin she'd become in just one week. I'd lost weight myself, along with days of sleep.

Kolton was right. Keeping my distance from Brielle wasn't working anymore. I needed to speak with her. But as she stopped behind her car to load the suitcases into the trunk, it was painfully clear she didn't want to speak, *especially* not with me.

Still, I couldn't help but ask, "Where are you going?"

She grabbed the second suitcase and slung it into the trunk, ignoring me completely.

Panic tightened my chest, and I stepped toward her before I could stop myself. "Brielle—"

A powerful arm blocked my path, and I barely suppressed a growl as Kolton wordlessly commanded me to back down. His eyes flashed in warning, and Onyx stirred, responding to my tension.

Stop mate.

I didn't respond, too busy trying not to show my teeth at Kolton in challenge. With his stern gaze still pinning me in place, he said to Brielle, "I respect your need for space, but we still need to know where you're going for your own safety."

She slammed the trunk shut with a loud bang before replying, "Mrs. Bailey has graciously allowed me to stay with her for a while. She's been lonely ever since Desirae moved out and was all too willing to accommodate me when I asked her."

Each word she spoke was like a blow to the face.

"For how long?" Kolton calmly asked, even as he noted the way my arms had begun to shake.

"Until I can safely live on my own. Once I have better control of my wolf, I want to start over someplace new. New apartment. New job. Somewhere no one knows me."

Nora gasped. When she swayed on her feet, Kolton whirled to catch her.

I stayed where I was, feeling my own world begin to dangerously tilt. Brielle took in her best friend's reaction with a sad expression, then quickly wiped a tear away and turned toward the driver side door.

Onyx went wild, howling, *Stop mate. Stop mate. Stop mate.*

I clenched my hands into tight fists, forcing myself to hold still. To not react. But when she opened the door, I completely lost it. Exploding forward, I grabbed her hand and whirled her around. Her eyes flew wide, but she didn't respond when I bit out, "You're not going anywhere."

"*Jagger,*" Kolton barked, but I ignored him, spurred on by the desperate need to make her stay.

Gripping her hand so tightly that our fingers practically fused together, I hissed out a single word, one laced with intent. With *command.* The magic within me stirred, obediently coming to my aid. It slithered through my insides, following my instructions through the spell I'd just uttered. My palm began to heat, and I looked down just as the large snake tattooed on my forearm started to move. Its head undulated over the back of my hand before sliding toward Brielle's.

Right before it could make contact with her skin, a violent force plowed into me. My hand was ripped from hers, and I snarled my fury. As I hit the concrete floor of the garage, I blindly struck out, my fist connecting with flesh. I heard a pained grunt, and then my own face was being pummelled.

"Are you *insane?*" a voice roared, right before another punch caught me squarely on the jaw. I blocked a third one and lashed out again, but my punch went wide. "You almost *killed* her!"

At that, everything in me turned to ice. I tried to draw air into my lungs and failed. As I struggled, hands gripped my arms and hauled me upright. Before I could fully catch my balance, those same hands fisted my shirt and yanked me close.

"Don't you *ever* try that again," Kolton said in my face, his voice dangerously low. "You're hurting, I get that. But if you harm Brielle, I will end you, do you hear me?"

Shame sliced through my insides, but I managed to lower my head in submission and say, "Yes, Alpha."

"Good, then fix this. *Now.*" He let go of me with a firm shove, then turned to scoop Nora into his arms. As he stalked from the garage, she opened her mouth in protest. One look at the misery on my face and she closed it again, her expression more than clear.

Make this right.

I nodded, even though I had no idea how. What I'd almost done was unforgivable, yet another reminder of why I had to end this somehow. But the thought of officially rejecting my soulmate sent more pain through me than my body could handle.

As Kolton and Nora disappeared from sight, I finally turned back to Brielle. The second our eyes met, I knew she was aware of what I'd almost done. She stared at me in disbelief, hurt and betrayal pulsing through our bond and into me.

"You tried to *bind* me to you?" she said, a tremor shaking her voice. "Even though I have no magic of my own, and it could have killed me?"

Shame sliced through me once more. "I wasn't thinking clearly. I just didn't want you to leave."

"Why?"

"Because you're my soulmate."

Right away, I knew it was the wrong thing to say. Her eyes narrowed, and she snapped, "That doesn't give you the right to *trap* me here."

"Brielle—"

"No! It's clear you don't want me as your mate. You lost the right to have a say in my life the second you rejected our bond. I'm not yours, Jagger. I don't *belong* to you."

Tears glistened in her eyes, and I took a step toward her. She immediately stepped back with a warning growl, one that I heeded. When silence stretched between us, she shook her head with a tired sigh and turned to leave again.

My heart started to pound, faster and faster until I thought it would explode from my chest. Desperate to stop her, I burst out, "I can't control Onyx around you."

Brielle froze, her hand on the car door. Instant regret filled me, but there was no taking back the words I'd rashly confessed, words I'd never dared say aloud before.

When I didn't say more, she slowly turned to face me. I tried to wipe my expression clean, but I knew that hiding my emotions from her was pointless. The same way I could feel her emotions now, she could feel mine.

It was awful knowing that someone could peer into me so easily when I'd spent my entire life keeping everyone at arm's length. At least she couldn't read my thoughts. But as she took a moment to study me, I could tell that was *exactly* what she wanted to do.

Studying me for another beat, she finally said, "Why?"

I rubbed a hand over my mouth, wishing I could rip it off. Such a simple question, one she deserved an answer to, but doing so would mean stripping myself bare. She had no idea, *no* idea how hard this was for me. I hadn't become Midnight Pack's second in command simply because I was one of Kolton's closest friends. I'd proven my loyalty and strength countless times over the years. I'd earned the position through trials, blood, and sheer force of will. Being Kolton's right hand meant everything to me. It was so much more than a job. It was my life. My *purpose.*

Answering Brielle's question could undo all of that in an instant. The truth would leave me vulnerable. *Weak.* And if she sought revenge for rejecting our bond . . .

She could utterly destroy me.

Still, after all that I'd put her through, she deserved an explanation. It was the very least I could do. So when doubt started to cloud her expression, I forced myself to speak. To *condemn* myself one word at a time.

"Onyx isn't like the other familiars."

I knew the demonic spirit was listening, but he didn't discourage me from revealing our secret to Brielle. In fact, it almost felt like he wanted me to. His unexpected certainty gave me the fortitude to keep going, and I was suddenly spilling the whole story.

"I'm sure Nora told you that my old pack kicked me out when I was five," I said. When she nodded, I continued, "What I didn't tell her—or anyone else, for that matter—is that Onyx was completely feral back then. When he first tried to force the shift on me, my parents and pack alpha thought it was *me* that had gone feral. They tried beating me into submission for a while, but when that didn't work, they had no choice but to shun me."

Brielle's hand flew to her mouth, her eyes wide with shock. Needing to get this out before I lost my nerve, I kept going before she could say anything.

"I was lucky, actually. Most packs didn't know about hybrids back then, and when I started to shift without the aid of a full moon, they could have easily killed me to protect the rest of the pack. In all honesty, they probably should have. I spent weeks on my own after that, and Onyx rode me hard the entire time. During my time in Buffalo, I became known as the Wild Boy, and there were several instances where I almost bit and scratched humans. If Anthony Rivers hadn't shown up when he did, God only knows what would have happened."

Pausing for a beat, I prepared myself to share the hardest part. The part that still haunted my every waking and sleeping moment.

After a few calming breaths, I finally said, "I didn't realize that Onyx wasn't normal until many years later. Even though I grew up with Kolton, Griff, and Vi, I'd assumed their familiars were as equally hard to manage. But when I experienced my first rut at the age of seventeen, I knew something was wrong."

"Rut?" she questioned, reminding me that werewolf life was still fairly new to her.

"A period of heightened sexual arousal that male werewolves experience on occasion. Not as often as females go into heat, thankfully. But during that time, males feel an incessant urge to seek out females for breeding. It's all they can think about, and they'll fight anyone who stands in the way of their goal."

When I stopped again, Brielle quietly said, "What happened?"

I hesitated, instinct screaming at me not to tell her—to *protect* her from the truth. But she needed to know, to understand why I couldn't accept our soulmate bond. So I plowed ahead and without mercy replied, "I lost control of Onyx during my rut and nearly forced myself on an unwilling female."

Brielle's complexion paled, but I wasn't finished.

"I was at the Mate Gala when it happened. I'd gone there to look for a mate. Instead, I badly injured two males and utterly terrified an omega female. Although a male in rut is often volatile, what I did crossed the line. I practically *destroyed* the place like a feral animal.

"From that moment on," I continued, "I understood one thing with perfect clarity: Onyx can't be reasoned with. He's not rational or logical. He's a primal beast ruled by instinct, and somewhere along the way, those instincts merged with my own. His wants became mine, and a part of me *wanted* to dominate that female against her wishes. When I realized that, I swore to never pursue a female again. Onyx is too dangerous. *I* am too dangerous. I can't control him around you because I can't control *myself*. That's why I need to reject the bond. Not because I don't want you, but because I can't have you. This has to end before it's too late, before I lose all control and try to force myself on you too."

My words had become impassioned, each cutting me deeply as I unveiled the darkest part of myself. None but the female I'd wronged ten years ago had seen this side of me. I hadn't told a soul about that day, not even Kolton. But now Brielle knew. The beautiful female that fate had mistakenly chosen for me knew that I was nothing more than a feral beast.

She stared and stared at me, her red lips slightly parted as she digested the information I'd thrown at her. I prepared myself for what was to come, expecting her face to twist in disgust at any moment, not to mention fear. I'd just confessed that I was as unhinged as my wolf familiar. That I wanted to dominate her. That I wanted to give in to my primal instincts, even if that meant forcing myself on her.

I waited for the inevitable, knowing that she would want nothing to do with me after this. I was a monster, and monsters couldn't have someone like her. She'd already lost her humanity and old life. She'd *died* in my arms. I couldn't take anything else from her. Rejecting the bond would be agony, but if I didn't . . .

I'd utterly ruin her.

With that sobering thought in mind, I braced myself for the painful process of unraveling the bond. Intention was key, whereas words meant little. I could say that I wanted to reject it, but if I didn't *mean* it, the bond wouldn't fade. Which was why I needed her to start the process. Once I felt how much she loathed and hated me, I could finally let her go.

She continued to stare at me, but the emotions I needed her to feel didn't filter through our bond. Desperate for this torture to end, I bluntly said, "I need you to reject me, Brielle. That's the only way we're going to feel better."

Two deep dimples appeared around her mouth, the only warning she gave before snapping, "*Feel* better? You think rejecting you will make me *feel* better? I'm devastated, Jagger. Devastated by your story, but even more devastated that you're willing to throw away our soulmate bond because of something that happened a *decade* ago."

Incredulous that she could be so naive, I snapped back, "I punished you with a *kiss*. I left a *handprint* on your neck. Onyx took control while I slept and touched you without *either* of our consent. You don't find that problematic?"

"Not really, no. I wasn't exactly resisting. In fact, I freaking *enjoyed* it. And you know what else? When Theo was touching me on that dance floor, I was thinking about you the entire time. I was envisioning *you* touching me, just like when Onyx used you to touch me. I wanted it. I really, really wanted it. What happened in your past is awful, and you probably thought that telling me would scare me away, but I don't feel unsafe around you. Besides, you *didn't* force yourself on that omega."

"But I *wanted* to!" I roared, getting in her face.

"But you *didn't!*" she roared back, holding her ground.

My hand shot up and caught her throat, eliciting a gasp from her. "You feel that?" I seethed, tightening my grip. "Every inch of me wants to dominate you right now. Onyx feels the same, and if I let my control slip even a little, we'll take you hard right here in this garage."

She shivered, and my grip tightened even more, a thrill of excitement shooting straight to my groin.

Take mate. Dominate mate, Onyx urged, equally excited to have her at my mercy. It would be easy, *so* easy to give in.

I opened my mouth to tell her so, needing her to know just how dangerous I was. "One slip and I'll consume you, Brielle. You have no idea how deep that desire goes. *I* don't even know. I'll take and take until I'm satiated. Problem is, I'm insatiable. Once I let the beast out, it's over. I'll devour you, and I won't stop, even if you beg me to. I'll mark you, claim you, mate you, *breed* you. And if you don't submit to me, I'll make you."

Our faces were so close that her fluttery breaths gusted across my mouth. Her pulse beat rapidly against my thumb, but it wasn't from fear. She was turned on. I could *feel* her desire.

Time to kill it before I did something that couldn't be undone.

"Is that what you want, Brielle? To have your free will snatched away? To be at my mercy without a say in what happens? I know you. You're not a submissive omega and would hate to be treated like one. But I wouldn't care. I would treat you like one anyway. I'd force your compliance no matter how much you objected, making your life miserable. And that's why I can't have you. That's why you need to reject me. So do it. Do it now. *Reject* me."

"Stop telling me what to *do!*" she shouted and shoved my chest.

When I didn't let go of her throat, she brought her leg up to knee me in the groin.

I blocked the strike and had her pinned against the side of her car in a flash. When I felt her struggle against me, the instinct to subdue her, to *dominate* raced through my blood. Onyx howled in excitement, his own instincts bolstering mine. Like a man possessed, I lowered my head and kissed her hard, pouring all of my frustration, anger, and pain into it. She fought to push me back, but that only made me kiss her harder.

Still gripping her throat, I forced her chin up to deepen the kiss, using my tongue to pry her lips open. Once I was inside, I didn't hesitate to take what I wanted. What I'd been *craving* ever since our first kiss at the cabin. The second I tasted her again, need roared through me, and I ground my pelvis against hers with a feral growl.

She cried out as I savagely rocked against her, but I couldn't tell if it was a fearful cry or one of pleasure. I didn't stop to check, lost to the nirvana flooding my body. I'd never felt pleasure this intense before, not even during my first rut. It was incredible, so consuming that I almost let my control slip. Thoughts of her naked and writhing beneath me on the concrete floor nearly undid me. Onyx picked up on my thoughts and blasted his excitement through our connection.

Claim mate, claim mate, claim mate.

I rocked faster, my tenuous grip on control hanging on by a thread. My hips kept time with the thrusts of my tongue, and I gorged myself on Brielle's addicting taste and soft body. My hard erection fit perfectly between her thighs, and even with our clothes still on, the delicious friction tightened my balls. I chased the high, almost forgetting why I was doing this.

To punish her. To show her how terrifying I was. How *dangerous*. She shouldn't want this with me. Shouldn't want to be my soulmate. I would only hurt her. Would only *ruin* her.

But as my thrusts grew frantic, the exquisite tension in my body about to explode, I couldn't help but think that *she* was ruining *me*.

She suddenly stiffened against me with a strangled cry, and when I realized that she was orgasming, my own climax barrelled through me. I jerked against her with a groan, ejaculating in my pants. She gasped into my mouth, her rapid breaths in sync with mine as we shot sky high. I continued to rock against her, prolonging the pleasure for as long as I could. When her body went pliant against mine, I slowed, my grip on her throat easing.

Only after the high started to fade did I realize what a terrible mistake I'd just made. She wasn't cowed in the least. There wasn't an ounce of fear coming from her.

It didn't make sense. I'd just subdued her. Just initiated physical intimacy without her consent. She should be livid. She should *hate* me.

But that's not how she felt. She felt . . . relieved.

Suddenly, *I* was the one doused in fear. It wasn't supposed to end like this. Nothing about this was right. I must have broken her. Must have gripped her throat too tightly and robbed her brain of too much oxygen. She wasn't thinking straight, and that made this so much harder.

Still, I forced myself to repeat my words from earlier, needing her to do what I couldn't. "Reject me, Brielle."

With our bodies and mouths still flush together, she breathed against my lips, "No."

Frustrated by her stubbornness, I pulled my mouth away from hers to say, "I won't let this happen again. I *can't*."

She was silent for a beat, then tipped her face up to look me in the eye. "Then let me go."

I blinked down at her, struggling to understand. "What?"

"Let me leave and don't try to follow me this time."

Panic gripped my chest. "But this is your home. You *belong* here."

Sadness filled her emerald eyes. "No, I don't. Not anymore. I can't be here if you won't pursue me. It hurts too much. *Everything* hurts. But maybe with time—a *lot* of time—I'll get over you and we can be friends."

As soon as she said the words, I knew that could never happen. We could never just be friends, not after this. And I would never, *ever* get over her.

Even so, I knew that I couldn't stop her from going, not this time. For both our sakes, I had to let her go.

The second I had the thought, Onyx went crazy. He thrashed inside of me, desperate to gain control so he could make her stay. I stiffened, gritting my teeth as I fought to keep him at bay. My hold on Brielle's throat tightened once more, and her eyes widened.

With a curse, I jerked myself back, forcing my hand to release her. "Go."

Onyx snarled and cried, throwing himself against the cage my body kept him in. I shoved him down, feeling my limbs begin to shake under the strain.

"Jagger," Brielle said, taking a step toward me.

"I said GO!" I thundered, and she finally cringed back. Finally balked at the feral look in my eyes. I didn't hide it. She needed to see. Needed to know just how unpredictable I could become around her.

Dangerous. I'm dangerous. See it. SEE IT, my eyes told her.

She hesitated for a moment longer, but when I bared my teeth at her in silent warning, she relented. Onyx howled and howled as she turned and slipped inside her car, shutting the door. When the engine started and she backed out of the garage, it took all of my strength not to stop her. For a split second that lasted an eternity, our eyes met and held through the windshield.

One last chance to change my mind. One last chance I couldn't take.

I wiped my expression clean, and her own fell. She looked away, and I did too, forcing my gaze not to follow her as she drove through the roundabout and left the property.

When I could no longer hear her car, I turned and picked up the wrench I'd dropped earlier. I started to put it away, then paused, staring at my pristine Porsche for several long moments. My hold on the wrench tightened. Without a word, I raised the tool and brought it down on the hood. Over and over, I struck the gray metal, taking my devastation out on it. My *pain*. By the time I was done, it was a mangled wreck.

Just like my broken heart.

CHAPTER 17

BRIELLE

I had the nightmare again.

Only this time, it wasn't just my family watching me shift. Nora, Vi, Kolton, and Griff were there, the circle of friends who'd become my *new* family. As they peered down at me, another form joined them, darkly mysterious and wholly familiar.

Jagger watched me struggle, his expression impassive. I tried calling out to him for help, but all that came out was a pitiful whine. He stayed where he was, letting me struggle alone.

When the painful transformation was over, I expected my new family members to protect my parents and brothers from my wolf. Instead, they turned their backs and walked away. I cried out to them but they were already gone. Desperate, I turned to Jagger, but he just stared at me with that neutral expression, then silently left without a backward glance.

Betrayed, *rejected*, I howled in agony. When I was finished, my human family was gone as well. I was in a silver cage, and the burly orderlies were staring down at me.

"Don't be alarmed, Miss Lacroix," they said in unison. "This is your new home."

Home?

I'd been abandoned by everyone I cared about. All I had left was this miserable cage and a wolf I could barely control.

Sadness and pain consumed me, and I cried and cried, curling into a ball of utter defeat.

As the dream faded, a heart-wrenching sob reached my ears. I opened my eyes, realizing a second later that the sound came from me. I touched my face, and my fingers came away wet with tears. Sighing, I curled up into a tighter ball on the mattress and buried my head beneath the comforter.

It had been over a week since I'd left the Rivers' estate, and each day that passed became harder to endure. Nightmares plagued the fitful bouts of sleep I managed to get, and forcing myself out of bed every morning was like climbing Mount Everest. The pain of betrayal and rejection from being kept in the dark about the soulmate bond was nothing compared to the dark hole I'd fallen into.

So much for reinventing myself and starting fresh. Every time I received a text or phone call from one of the many people who'd hurt me, I sank even lower into the black pit of depression. I ignored them all, my grief still too raw. I couldn't work, couldn't eat, couldn't even brush my hair. My pitiful state of being stemmed mainly from one source, though.

Jagger hadn't tried to contact me even once.

He'd let me go, and that realization had completely shut me down.

I should feel relieved. *Grateful.* He was no longer bossing me around. No longer treating me like a child. I could go where I pleased and do what I wanted, exactly what I'd been wishing for. I could search for a mate who would *actually* pursue me. I could follow my dreams and start a family of my own. The sky was the limit, and no one was holding me back.

Except that someone *was.* Me.

Now that Jagger had let me go, I couldn't seem to care about any of that. None of those dreams mattered. I didn't *want* them anymore. The only thing I wanted was—

With a groan, I burrowed even deeper under the covers. How the hell had I let this happen to me? For years, I'd been confident in who I was, bold and self-sufficient. No one could stand in my way, especially not a *guy*. They were a dime a dozen. Pretty to look at and exciting to sleep with, but not worth getting my heart broken over. But with only a few words and a couple of kisses, Jagger had managed to tie me into knots. Now, I was a sopping mess of emotions and couldn't think about anything but *him*.

"Curse you, Jagger Montgomery," I growled, but the words came out as a pathetic whimper. Curse his stoic handsome face for drawing me in. Curse his gorgeous muscled body for turning me on. Curse his intense blue-gray eyes for making me feel like I was the only female in existence. Curse his serious mouth for saying too little and kissing with a passion I'd never experienced before. Curse his wicked hands for making me crave a little pain with my pleasure. Curse his bloody honor for choosing to protect me over his own desires.

It was the last one I hated the most. *He* had decided to protect me. *He* had decided my future. *Our* future. Without even asking what *I* wanted.

Anger stirred in my blood, but it fizzled out seconds later. I was too tired, too depressed to feel it for long anymore. Sadness took its place, and I let it suck me back into that black pit of nothingness.

An hour or so later, I heard a knock at the bedroom door. When I ignored it, the door opened and someone bustled inside.

"Merry Christmas, dear!" sang Mrs. Bailey, the Rivers' former nanny. "Now, I don't want to hear any of that nonsense about not being hungry today. I've been cooking all morning and need you to help me eat it all. First up is my famous steak and eggs breakfast!"

When I didn't respond, she set the breakfast tray down on the nightstand and whipped back my bed covers.

I groaned in protest, but with a few persistent tugs, I was sitting against the headboard with the tray in my lap. Even though she was twice my age and half my height, it wasn't hard for her to wrangle me into position. I was as weak as a newborn calf and had grown skeletal thin after another week of barely eating.

Mrs. Bailey took one look at the tank top and shorts that now hung loosely on my frame and clucked her tongue sadly. "I know you're grieving, dear. It took me a long time to recover after my husband died a few years back. But you're young and have your whole life ahead of you. I'd hate to see you throw it all away for a male who won't pursue you. I've known Jagger since he was a little boy, but he's always been a troubled soul. If he refuses to claim the beautiful female fate chose for him, then I know many males who would gladly take his place. I know Buck has had his eye on you. He's a strapping fellow and would make a wonderful husband. If I were twenty years younger, I'd snatch him up in a heartbeat."

I didn't respond, too busy trying not to gag at the smell of steak wafting up my nose. The boisterous, busybody woman was right, of course. Even though she tended to gossip and had probably told the entire two-hundred-strong pack by now that Jagger and I were soulmates, I knew she was genuinely worried about me. I'd be worried too, if I didn't feel so dead inside.

The invisible bond tying me and Jagger together was most definitely still active. After our night at the hotel, it had taken me a while to realize that I could feel his emotions. I usually felt enough emotions for ten people, but his emotions were different. They were sharp, like needles penetrating my flesh. For the past year, a big part of me had thought he didn't *have* emotions, so it was shocking to discover that he felt things intensely. He was just good at hiding it, unlike me.

I couldn't feel him now and hadn't been able to all week, but it was probably because of the physical distance between us—not because our bond had started to fade. I might have left, but I hadn't rejected him. Despite how miserable I was, I couldn't get that time we'd spent in the garage out of my mind.

His shocking confession. His breath-stealing passion. The explosive *orgasm* we'd shared.

He might have an untamable dark side, but it didn't scare me. It intrigued me. *Excited* me. He'd always been mysterious, but knowing about this side of him only amplified his enigmatic personality. I wanted to know more. I wanted to *experience* it. Knowing what he wanted to do to me didn't terrify me in the least.

I was a free spirit and didn't like to be told what to do, but in the bedroom? Tie me up, Daddy.

But he was obviously still traumatized by what had happened ten years ago. He didn't want to hurt me. Didn't want *Onyx* to hurt me. And yet I could feel how much he desired me. If the way he'd frantically dry-humped me hadn't clued me in, then the lust pulsating through our bond certainly would.

He wanted me. *Wanted* me. But he wouldn't let himself have me because of some misguided notion of protecting me. What if I didn't *want* to be protected?

"Oh! Griff came by and dropped these off earlier," Mrs. Bailey said, breaking through my thoughts. She hurried from the room and reentered seconds later with an armful of wrapped presents. "I know how awful it feels to find out that the people you love have been keeping secrets from you. I spent the last seven years grieving the loss of our former alpha female, only to find out that she's still alive. I felt betrayed, but you know what? Kolton and Vi thought they were doing the right thing. I'm sure they hated keeping you in the dark about the soulmate bond, Brielle, but don't forget that they still love you."

"I know," I whispered, fighting back sudden tears as she situated the presents on the bed. A quick look at the labels confirmed that they'd *all* sent me presents. Nora, Kolton, Vi, Griff, Mrs. Rivers, Melanie, and . . . and Jagger.

I snatched up the small gold box without thinking, then realized what I'd just done and dropped it.

"Oh, my poor dear," Mrs. Bailey sighed, clucking her tongue again. "You're in love with him."

I jerked startled eyes up to hers. "Wh-what? No, I'm just . . . I didn't expect him to get me a present, is all. He didn't last year, and—"

As the middle-aged woman stared at me with a knowing expression, I swallowed the last of my protests, feeling a desperate need to burrow under the covers again. It didn't matter what I said. She wasn't buying it.

Not one to let silence stretch, Mrs. Bailey spoke again before things could become uncomfortable. "Now don't stay in this room all day, dear. I expect you to be showered, dressed, and looking your best before company arrives in a few hours. I hope you don't mind, but I also invited Buck. He's all alone this Christmas, and we lone wolves have to stick together, right? Now eat before your eggs get cold. I want to see that plate licked clean."

She swept from the room before I could respond, muttering to herself as she closed the door behind her. I gaped at the closed door for a solid minute, still trying to digest the woman's unfiltered words.

In love? With *Jagger*?

I couldn't possibly be in love with him. Love didn't *hurt* this bad. Could it?

Sighing, I set the breakfast tray on the bed beside me and reached for the present labeled "From Nora." Unwrapping the large box, I opened it to find an expensive designer purse inside, one that I'd been eyeing for months. Normally, I'd be grinning ear to ear from receiving a gift like this, but sadness filled me instead. Noticing something else in the box wrapped in tissue paper, I pulled it out and carefully unwrapped it. Inside was a photo encased in a gold frame, and when I saw that the picture was of *us* during our college years, smiling and carefree, tears blurred my vision.

A note slipped free, and I picked it up to read, *Miss you, bestie. All my love, Nora.*

My lip quivered, and a tear plopped onto the card. Gently wiping it off, I set the gifts aside and reached for the one from Vi. By the time I was done opening all the presents, exhaustion pulled at my limbs. I nudged everything aside and curled up on the bed again, but as I slid a hand beneath my pillow, my fingers bumped against something hard. I grasped the object and pulled it out, then immediately wished I hadn't.

It was the little gold box from Jagger. As I stared at it, my hand started to tremble. I almost chickened out and set it aside unopened, but with a resigned sigh, I dug a nail beneath the shiny wrapping paper and popped it open. Removing it, I dubiously eyed the perfectly square box like it was about to bite me. After a lengthy moment, I carefully opened the lid to reveal its contents.

Inside was a thin gold chain nestled on black velvet. Attached to the chain was a little wolf figurine. Its head was tilted back, and it was . . . it was howling at the moon.

A tiny note was tucked under the lid, and I opened it with shaking fingers to reveal two words.

I'm sorry.

My throat clamped shut, making it impossible to breathe.

He might as well have reached through the note and put me in a chokehold. A strangled sound left me, and uncontrollable tears squeezed from my eyes. As I struggled to draw in air, sudden anger gripped me, and I threw the box across the room with a furious cry. Silent sobs shook me, then gasping loud ones.

I cried and cried, knowing with certainty now that it was over. Jagger had officially rejected our soulmate bond, and he was *never* going to come for me.

CHAPTER 18

BRIELLE

I couldn't do it. Couldn't *pretend* to be my usual flamboyant self.

The second the guests started to arrive, I knew I had to bail before they saw what a wretched mess I'd become. As Mrs. Bailey exuberantly greeted the Midnight Pack members she'd invited to Christmas dinner, I tried slipping past them undetected. Right before I could make my escape, a familiar broad form filled the doorway, and my heart sank.

The male looked extra handsome with his beard neatly trimmed and his brown hair carefully tied back in a low ponytail. Used to seeing him in flannel shirts and jeans, I was surprised that he'd dressed up for the occasion in a light blue collared shirt and dark slacks.

Deep down, I knew that he'd dressed up for me. There was a spark of hope in his brown eyes, hope that he could pursue me now that Jagger was out of the picture. As Midnight Pack's cleanup guy took in the rest of me, I was suddenly aware of how painfully thin I looked in my green sweater dress and black tights.

"Hi, Buck," I greeted him, needing his eyes to stop staring at the visible outline of my ribs through the thin sweater material.

"Brielle," he greeted back, glancing up at my face again with a troubled expression. "I'm sorry you've had such a rough month."

"Thanks," I replied, certain now that Mrs. Bailey had told him everything. Unable to bear the pity in his eyes, I leaned forward to give him a hug and instantly regretted it. The hard planes of his body were all wrong. The wolf in me recoiled, instinctively knowing that he wasn't the male I should be hugging.

Before he could return my hug, I stepped back with a tight-lipped smile. "It's really good to see you, Buck, but I have to go. I'm sorry."

The observant male saw far more than I wanted him to in that awkward moment. He'd never been able to properly pursue me on account of Jagger always getting in the way, but he knew me well enough to know that I wasn't myself. Taking me in for another beat, that spark of hope in his eyes faded. With a small nod, he replied, "I understand. Merry Christmas, Brielle."

Relief trembled through me. "Merry Christmas, Buck."

When he stepped aside, I quickly slipped out the front door, grateful that he'd let me go so easily. That he'd *known* I didn't want to be pursued. Not by him. Not right now. Not ever. And if the jagged pieces of my heart were any indication, I never wanted to be pursued by another male for the rest of my life.

With no destination in mind, I got into my car and took off. It had been a week since I'd left the house, and despite how lethargic I felt, being outside gave me a small boost of energy. The sky and roads were free of snow, and I used the opportunity to clear some of the cobwebs from my head. I drove and drove, cracking a window so the brisk air could cleanse my cloudy senses. I hadn't felt much like a werewolf the past couple of weeks. With my appetite gone and heightened senses dulled, I'd almost felt like a human again. Well, a *depressed* human.

My wolfy instincts had gone dormant. I hadn't even experienced hot flashes this month. It was like my wolf had fallen into depression as well. I could barely feel her, and even with the cold wind teasing my hair, she didn't encourage me to lift my nose and breathe it in. Nothing excited her—excited *me*—anymore. The world was colorless, and it had painted me in shades of lifeless gray.

I continued driving, trying to escape the yawning pit that called my name. But it was relentless. *Ruthless*. It didn't care how miserable I was, how frantic to start fresh and move on with my life. It wanted me to wallow in my misery, to *suffer*. I was helpless against it, unable to drag myself out.

Trapped. I was *trapped*.

Panic filled me, and I drove even faster. Escape. I had to *escape* before the pit swallowed me whole, before it consumed me completely. Before it *killed* me. I was running out of time, more aware than ever of my mortality. I'd escaped death a year ago, but it wanted me back. I could feel it in my bones, its chilling breath on my neck.

Death was coming for me, and my time was almost up.

Fear trickled in, pushing aside some of the fog I'd been living in. Death could claim me at any moment, and I was alone. On *Christmas*. What the hell was I *doing* out here?

Spurred on by the fear slowly leaking through my body, I veered onto the nearest exit ramp, needing to make things right before it was too late. My hurt and pain didn't matter right now. If I didn't say my piece, I'd regret it for the rest of my life—however long that might be.

Two hours later, I was pulling up to a familiar house, one that I'd spent my entire childhood in. Refusing to let my pain get the better of me, I left my car and headed toward the house. Before I'd even cleared the sidewalk, the front door burst open and four figures filed out.

"Brielle!"

At the sound of my mom's frantic voice, I hurried forward with a whimper. The second her arms wrapped around me, all of my doubts disappeared, and I desperately hugged her back. Moments later, another pair of arms encircled me, then another and another. Realizing that not only my mom and brothers were hugging me, but my dad too, I full out ugly cried.

"I missed you guys s-so much," I sobbed, barely able to stand under the weight of my relief. They still cared about me. Still *loved* me.

It still hurt that they didn't believe I was a werewolf and hadn't stopped my dad from calling the psych ward on me, but all that mattered right now was this. Being welcomed back with open arms. Not being *alone* anymore.

My nightmares were unfounded. They hadn't turned their backs on me. I was still one of them.

"We were so worried," my mom responded with a sob of her own. "After what happened at Thanksgiving, we feared you'd never come back to us."

"I'm so sorry," I whispered. "I'll never ghost you like that again."

"It's okay, sweetheart. You're here. We're *all* here, safe and sound."

"Well, mostly," Sawyer said from above me. "Ellie's nothing but skin and bones."

"Am not," I said with a loud sniffle, even though it was true.

"We've *all* lost weight and sleep over what happened, even Dad. *Especially* Dad," Zeke cut in.

At that, I pulled back a little. Sure enough, as everyone's faces came into view, I saw how thin and haggard they all looked. My dad was the worst, though. He looked haunted.

When our eyes met, his expression fell, and he croaked, "I'm so sorry, Brielle. I had no idea. *No* idea they would treat you like that. I can't express how ashamed I am for what happened. I only wanted to protect you, but I hurt you instead. Please. *Please* forgive me."

"Oh, Daddy, I forgive you," I choked out and reached for him. As he pulled me into a bear hug, I released some of my misery, letting it fall in droves down my cheeks. We stayed like that for a long time, making up for a year's worth of absence.

"There's something else," he finally said, pulling back to look at me. "We . . . we believe you. At least, we're *trying* to. It's the very least we can do after everything we—*I*—put you through."

More tears fell, and I wiped them away before whispering, "Thank you." Knowing they deserved an explanation for what *really* happened that night, I quickly filled them in. When I mentioned supernatural hunters, they all shared a dubious glance, but they didn't dismiss my words. They were listening. They were *accepting* who I was now, albeit reluctantly. I could work with that.

"So let me get this straight," Zeke said when I finished telling them all that I knew. "There are humans out there who *hunt* werewolves?"

"And other supernaturals, yes."

Sawyer's eyes practically bugged out of his head. "*Other* supernaturals? What else is there? Goblins?"

I lightly punched his arm. "No, dummy. Goblins don't exist. But there are witches and vampires. Oh, and hybrids. I've been living with a bunch of them this past year. They're my pack."

"That's so weird," he muttered, and I punched his arm again, hard enough that he rubbed it with a sound of protest.

"They don't seem to be taking very good care of you," my dad said, frowning as he looked me up and down.

"They take *very* good care of me," I rebutted, feeling the need to defend my new family. "I'm just . . . grieving the loss of something. I'll explain everything to you, but maybe we should head inside first. You all look *freezing*."

"Oh, thank *heavens*. I can't feel my face anymore," my mom replied and beelined for the house. Zeke and Sawyer laughed and followed after her, but Dad lagged behind to walk beside me at a more sedate pace.

"So, this werewolf business . . ." he haltingly began. "Does it come on once a month, kind of like your period?"

"Daaaad," I protested, yet a laugh escaped me, the first one I'd heard in weeks.

As I began to explain how shifting worked for regular werewolves, he held open the front door for me. When I stepped over the threshold, I winced as something sharp stung my side. I glanced down, expecting to find a loose nail protruding from the doorframe. Just as I caught sight of something shiny sticking out of the lock hole, a terrible screeching noise filled the air. I covered my sensitive ears, but the sound cut straight through, so piercing that it felt like knives were stabbing my brain.

I screamed, the agony rendering me immobile within seconds. Shouts reached my ears, but they were muffled as if I was underwater, as if my ears were filled with blood. My legs buckled, and Dad caught me, carrying me into the house. The sound followed me inside, slicing my eardrums into bloody ribbons.

"Make it stop, make it stop!" I cried, curling into a tight ball when he placed me on the couch.

"Make *what* stop?" he yelled, but I was in too much pain to respond.

The noise pierced me over and over, making it impossible to move, to think, to *breathe*. Migraines were nothing compared to this level of agony, and with no end in sight, all I could do was writhe on the couch and scream my lungs raw.

After what felt like an eternity of enduring a sound straight from hell, it suddenly switched off.

I stopped screaming but continued to violently shake, the phantom sound of that awful noise still clamoring through my skull. Hands touched me, and I cringed back, my senses extra sensitive.

"It's off," I heard Zeke distantly say over the ringing in my ears.

"She's bleeding," Sawyer said, and his concern was enough to force my eyes open.

I slowly uncovered my ears and found my trembling hands red with blood. A towel wrapped around them, and I watched my mom wipe them clean. "What," I rasped, then swallowed and tried again. "What *was* that?"

"I think it was some kind of high-pitched frequency device," Zeke replied, showing me what looked like a tiny camera or sensor—one that was now in pieces as if he'd stomped on it. "It was embedded in the doorframe, so small that I almost didn't see it. I've been contracted to install a few sound devices over the years, mostly for pest control reasons, but none of them were this high-tech. I swear we didn't do this, Brie."

"I know," I said and tried to sit up. Dad helped me while Mom continued to clean the blood from my hands and ears. When the room stopped spinning, I added, "It has to be the supernatural hunters. They must have installed it while you were away from the house, sometime after their failed attempt to secure me."

Dad's face leached of all color. "Then this was a trap meant to incapacitate you until they could come get you again. You need to leave, Brielle. *Now.*"

Alarm trickled through me, but I didn't move, my senses still recovering from the high-pitched sound waves. "B-but what about you guys?"

"They don't care about us. They only attacked us when we stood in their way. *You* are the one they want," my dad vehemently said. "Return to your pack, Brielle. They're better equipped to protect you."

I stared at the man who'd raised me, shocked that he'd said such a thing. This past month had definitely taken a toll on him if he was freely willing to admit he could no longer protect me. My whole life, he'd been my steady rock, but now . . .

We lived in different worlds. Mine was dangerous, and if I stayed here much longer, they could get seriously injured this time—or worse.

Knowing I had to leave for not only my sake but theirs, I struggled to stand from the couch. All four of them reached out to help me up, and I fought back tears of gratitude. Pausing to look at each of them, I said, "I love you all. Keep each other safe."

"We love you too, sweetheart," my mom whispered, pulling me in for a quick hug before gently nudging me toward the door.

I listened to her urging and turned to leave, but when I hesitated in the doorway, casting one last look at my human family, my dad gave me a tearful smile and said, "Don't worry, Brielle. You're always welcome inside these walls."

My tears spilled over, and I returned his smile with a tremulous one of my own. Bolstered by his words, words I'd desperately needed to hear, I left my childhood home and hurried out into the encroaching night.

CHAPTER 19

BRIELLE

I was halfway to Lake Placid when the pain hit.

Within seconds, it became hard to drive. Within minutes, impossible. I glanced up at the moon, certain it wasn't supposed to be full for at *least* four more days. It shined down on me intensely, but not so intense that I should feel its powerful pull to shift.

Another agonizing heatwave pounded through my body, and I doubled over with a groan, nearly losing sight of the road. The pain was coming more frequently, each wave sharper than the last. At this rate, I'd be transformed into my wolf within the next half hour.

Helplessness filled me. I couldn't believe this was happening. *Again.* All the stress of this past month must have brought it on, but if I didn't stop the transition process, I was probably going to die.

When I could breathe again, I fumbled in my purse for my phone and quickly dialed a number. I did it automatically, my only thought on getting help before it was too late. My shredded pride didn't matter. All that mattered was halting this before my wolf killed me.

On the second ring, a voice flooded the speaker, one that exacerbated my pain yet somehow soothed it too. "Where are you? Mrs. Bailey said you left the house hours ago."

Ignoring Jagger's commanding tone, I replied, "An hour out. But I'm not going to make it."

"What do you mean? What happened?"

I quickly explained about the visit to my parents and the hidden frequency device, finishing with, "The stress must have been too much because I'm shifting again, and—*Oh, God*," I cried out, gripping the steering wheel so hard that it cracked. "I can't . . . I can't keep driving. I have to pull over. The pain. It's . . . Oh, this *sucks!*"

"Brielle. *Brielle.* Just breathe. I'm coming to get you, but you need to hold on until then. Where are you exactly?"

"I'm . . . I'm . . ."

"Turn on tracking for your phone. Give me access to your location."

I did, restlessly squirming in my seat as sharp pulses rocketed through my body. The urge to be on all fours hit me hard, and I hunched over the steering wheel again.

"Okay, I see where you are. Take the next right," Jagger said.

I obeyed, my breaths coming in short spurts. He continued to guide me, taking me down a dirt road that led to a sprawling farm.

"Where . . . where am I going?" I panted, gritting my teeth when I hit a pothole.

"There's an abandoned barn half a mile from the farmhouse. The owners are pack members and always visit family for Christmas, so they shouldn't be there. Barricade yourself inside the barn and wait for me."

"I don't know . . . if I can wait . . . an hour."

"Do *not* shift, Brielle, do you hear me?" he snapped. "Get to the barn and search for something that could contain your wolf. Ropes, chains, an old harness."

"Those won't," I gasped out, "contain her."

"Not for long, but hopefully until I get there. If the worst happens, we need to protect the populace from your wolf."

Not that I would even survive the transformation, but if I did, I sure as hell didn't want to attack any humans. Knowing my wolf, she would probably kill and eat them. Shuddering at the thought, I turned onto the private drive leading to the farmhouse and started searching for the barn. I'd barely made it to the house when a glaring obstacle blocked my path, forcing me to stop.

"What is it?" Jagger asked when I swore under my breath.

Another wave of heat spiked through me, and I groaned out, "Road isn't . . . plowed."

Jagger bit out a curse of his own. "Then you'll have to break into the house. It's not ideal, but the owners will understand."

"No way. My wolf would *destroy* it." I could still vividly remember when Melanie had shifted for the first time and had chased me through the Rivers' mansion, destroying everything that stood in her way.

"We'll compensate them for any losses. But it's safer for your wolf to be surrounded by four walls than— Brielle, what are you doing?"

I didn't answer, puffing loudly as I left the car behind and began to struggle through the knee-deep snow.

"*Brielle.*"

"It's not . . . that far . . . away."

"Brielle, stop this instant. Every second you spend outdoors encourages your wolf to emerge. You won't make it to the barn. Brielle? *Brielle!*"

I ended the call, done being told what to do and determined to prove him wrong. I could endure a half mile hike through the snow. I'd done it before and knew I could do it now. I *had* to. Lives depended on it, including my own.

After only a few yards, though, the pain became so intense that I lost my footing and face-planted into the snow. Writhing in agony on the ground for several minutes, I dragged myself upright again and plowed on. As I trudged forward like a mindless zombie, slipping and falling countless times along the way, I finally spotted the abandoned, weather-beaten structure on the horizon. It was secluded and backed by miles and miles of woods, which was exactly what I needed right now.

I picked up speed, but after only a handful of feet, crippling pain rocked my body. I fell again with a strangled cry, landing on all fours in the snow. The position immediately awakened something inside me, something instinctual. *Primal.* A tremble violently shook me, and I gasped as something besides pain flooded my body. It flushed hotly through me and vanished, so swiftly that I blinked in confusion. Another second and I was groaning in agony once more, my limbs struggling to hold me up.

I stayed like this for an unknown length of time, panting and shaking through wave after wave of scorching pain. Every time I tried to stand up, my body gave out on me. Finally, I resorted to crawling through the snow like the animal I was slowly succumbing to. Only a few yards away from the barn, the pain overwhelmed me and I collapsed, unable to continue.

Uncontrollable whimpers and cries left me as I fought to remain in my human form. Every time a fresh wave of heat blasted through me, I expected my bones to begin breaking, but they didn't. My world was searing pain, and all I could do was cling to consciousness, desperately praying that it would end soon before it killed me.

I was on the verge of passing out when I finally heard approaching footsteps. Not one pair, but *several.* I prepared to defend myself but couldn't even lift my head. As my night vision cut through the darkness, it allowed me to focus on the three figures heading my way. I immediately recognized their faces and whimpered in relief.

Expecting Jagger to bodily hold me together like last time, I was surprised when all three males stopped dead in their tracks a few yards from me, their eyes noticeably widening.

"What?" I weakly said, confused when Jagger's nostrils flared. "Am I . . . am I shifting?"

Griff made a choking noise, but when he opened his mouth to speak, Kolton shot him a look that clearly meant *shut up*. The blond male closed his mouth with an audible click.

After a lengthy moment, Jagger stiffly replied, "No, Brielle, you're not shifting."

I gaped at him, more confused than ever. As if to contradict his words, another heatwave blasted through me. I groaned and writhed through the pain, dimly aware that Kolton and Griff had started to back up. Jagger looked like a statue made out of marble, staring at me like I was his worst nightmare come to life.

When I could speak again, I bit out in frustration, "Then what the hell *is* this?"

Jagger swallowed, his throat bobbing sharply. "You're in heat."

Everything stilled. Even my pain subsided as I tried to process his words. I was in heat? After sixteen months of waiting, I was *finally* becoming a regular female werewolf?

But why now when I was at my lowest? At my *weakest*? I'd been anticipating my first heat for over a year, but to have it come *now* was nothing short of cruel.

Two of the three males who could help me were already mated, and the third—my *soulmate*—had officially rejected me. I couldn't get any more pathetic than this.

As if to taunt me in my moment of abject misery, a sudden pulse went through me. Not pain, but *arousal*. Heat flared between my legs, so hot and intense that I couldn't hold back a moan. The second the sound of pleasure left my mouth, Jagger fell to his knees in the snow. I lifted my gaze to his face and found it twisted in agony.

"Go to her, brother," Kolton quietly said to him, still retreating as if he knew how volatile this situation had just become. "She needs you."

A desperate look filled Jagger's eyes. "I can't."

His voice was deep. Guttural. *Feral.*

My body responded viscerally to the sound, flaring so hotly that a scream slipped past my clenched teeth. The snow around me sizzled, rapidly evaporating the longer my overheated body was pressed against it.

"She's suffering, Jag," Griff said, his expression one of sympathy even as he took another step back.

"I *know*," Jagger hissed, his chest heaving while he watched me. "I can feel it. I can feel *everything*."

"That's good. It means the bond is still intact."

"It's *not* good," Jagger roared at the blond male. "This shouldn't be happening. *None* of this should be happening."

Even though the words were directed at Griff, each one struck me like arrows to the heart.

As if he could feel the sudden pain lighting up my chest, Jagger flinched and reached up to rub the spot directly over his heart.

When tense silence settled over the clearing, Griff shook his head and said, "Fine. If you won't help her, then I will."

He took a step forward. *One* step. And all hell broke loose.

Jagger exploded off the ground with a bellow and charged Griff. In a flash, Kolton was between them and shoved Jagger back, snapping, "Stop and *think* for a moment, Jagger. Griff was only trying to force your hand. He would never betray you or Vi that way."

Undeterred, Jagger surged forward again, only to be shoved back once more. Normally strong enough to hold his own against Kolton, concern filled me at how easily Jagger was put in his place. Studying him a moment longer, it finally dawned on me why. He'd lost even more weight, the lines of his body sharper from losing muscle mass. Realizing that he'd been weakened by our bond, guilt twisted my insides.

"Let him through, Kol," Griff said, bouncing on the balls of his feet. "I've been wanting to smack him around all week for letting Brielle go."

Jagger snarled at him, and Griff flashed his teeth in a taunting grin.

"*Enough!*" Kolton barked, using his alpha voice. If I wasn't already on the ground, I would have lowered my head in submission. Jagger and Griff, however, continued to glare at each other. Noting their resistance, Kolton sternly added, "This fight is not happening. The pheromones have you both on edge, and it's the only reason I'm letting this slide. Griff, go back to the truck. Jagger, I'm giving you one last chance to fix this. Either take care of Brielle or take her to a male who will."

Ah, hell, he did *not* just order my fated mate to hand me over to another male if he couldn't do the deed. If my face wasn't already flushed, it would be turning beet red right now. Not from embarrassment but *humiliation*. I didn't think I could get any more pathetic, but apparently, I could.

As Griff and Kolton turned to leave, I set aside my humiliation long enough to say, "The supernatural hunters could be at my parents'. I'm worried."

Kolton paused to nod and reply, "We'll make sure your human family is safe. And if the hunters are there, we'll take care of them."

I gave him a wobbly smile, already feeling ten times better despite the pain still wreaking havoc on my body. "Thank you. Be careful."

He tipped his chin in acknowledgement, then gave Jagger one

last stern look before turning to leave again. When it was just me and the male who'd rejected me, I became keenly aware of my awful predicament. *Our* predicament. Jagger might have washed his hands of me, but because I'd called him, he was now stuck with me.

Feeling wretchedly self-conscious, I blurted, "They didn't have to come. It's Christmas, and I feel bad that they left the festivities for this."

Now several yards away from me, Jagger breathed in and out for a lengthy beat before replying, "You're pack, Brielle. Family. They wanted to come, and I couldn't exactly take off by myself anyway."

Another heatwave blasted through me, and I bit my lip hard enough to draw blood. When I was able to form sentences again, I gasped out, "Why not?"

"My Porsche is in the shop," he said in a strained voice, looking everywhere but at me.

"Why? I thought you'd . . . you'd fixed it."

He was silent for a long moment, the only movement the rapid rise and fall of his chest. Then, "I destroyed it after you left."

My eyes widened in surprise. He destroyed his fancy car? Because of *me?* Not knowing how to take that bit of news, I decided to change the subject. "You don't have to stay here. Now that I know I'm just in heat, I can deal with it alone. I've practiced self care for many years."

He made a noise in the back of his throat, but it definitely wasn't a laugh at my joke. I tried to pick up his emotions through our supposedly still-intact bond, but the turmoil raging through my body was all I could feel.

"That won't be enough," he finally said, still not looking at me. "A female's first heat is extremely potent, and without a male to ease her suffering, the pain will become unbearable."

I scrunched up my nose. "That sounds so sexist."

153

He made another noise, and this time, I *swore* it was a snort.

"Did you just laugh?"

"No. Nothing about this situation is amusing."

"I agree, but laughing is far better than crying. I've been crying nonstop for the past two weeks and am beyond sick of it."

At my blunt confession, he finally looked at me. The second his blue-gray eyes met mine, a feeling of shame stabbed my chest. I blinked, realizing that the emotion was his.

"Forget I said that. I wasn't trying to make you feel guilty," I said. The shame continued to prick my chest, and after several moments, I couldn't bear it anymore. Couldn't bear the *pity* in his eyes. Gritting my teeth, I gathered the last of my strength and struggled to stand. I didn't know where I would go, only that I needed to get away from here. From *him*.

If I was going to be in excruciating, unbearable pain soon, then I at least wanted to suffer with some of my dignity intact.

But the second my feet were under me, agony cut through my insides like a bonesaw. It felt like my body was being ripped in *half*. I took a step forward anyway, determined to grin and bear it, but the pain was too much.

The last thing I saw was Jagger lunging toward me before the world went dark.

CHAPTER 20

JAGGER

The second she was in my arms, I knew it was over.

Scenting her heat for the past several minutes had been torture, but the agony of separating myself from her this past week had destroyed me. Onyx had been inconsolable, and we'd both spiraled into a deep state of depression. Even Mrs. Bailey's daily updates on Brielle's wellbeing hadn't made me feel any better. But now that she was in my arms, my reasons for staying away didn't matter anymore.

Feeling her warmth. Hearing her breathe. Knowing that she was safe and secure. I couldn't live without this. This was *everything*, and I wouldn't let anyone separate us again.

Including myself.

She wasn't unconscious for long, stirring awake with a groan as I carried her into the abandoned barn and secured the door. Her eyes opened, and when she realized where I'd taken her, panic fluttered through our bond.

"Jagger, no," she moaned, weakly squirming in my arms. "You don't want this."

I firmed my grip on her, refusing to let go. "This was never about not wanting you, Brielle."

"But you rejected me."

"To *protect* you."

"Then you should leave. I don't want guilt sex."

"*Guilt* sex?"

"Yeah, where you help me with my heat simply because you feel bad for making my life hell. But I'm not interested in a one-time thing with you, Jagger. If you want to protect me from yourself, then don't have sex with me out of guilt. That will only make this ten times worse."

"But you need me right now, more than you need my protection."

She barked a laugh that sounded more like a sob. "I've *needed* you for the past couple of weeks. Hell, for the past *year*."

At her confession, my legs almost gave out on me. Struggling to keep it together, I continued searching for an acceptable spot to set her down. "Your need stems from the soulmate bond. Its very purpose is to create a pull that encourages two souls to become one. But fate shouldn't have chosen you for me. Soulmates are supposed to complete each other, to be each other's safe space, but I can't be that for you. I'll only ever hurt you."

"Jagger, put me down." I glanced down to find her emerald eyes flashing up at me in anger. "*Now.*"

Despite how thin and frail she felt, her voice was steady. *Strong.* Every molecule in my body demanded I keep her close, but I forced myself to gently set her down anyway. When her feet hit the dusty floor, she immediately hunched over, eliciting a pained groan. Fresh pheromones wafted into the air, and I reached for her again, unable to help myself.

"*No,*" she said, shoving my hands away with surprising strength. The action caused her to stagger sideways, but she caught herself on a wooden support beam. Pausing a moment to catch her breath, she finally straightened and looked me dead in the eye before saying, "You think a predestined *bond* is controlling how I feel? Well, you're wrong. Sure, I initially felt a pull toward you, but since then, I've gotten to know you. To *understand* you.

"Family means everything to you. Your loyalty and devotion belong to them. You'll give your *life* for them," she continued, her words picking me apart piece by piece. "You're grateful to the Rivers family for accepting you when no one else would, but a part of you is terrified they'll reject you like your old pack did. Because of that fear, you won't let anything jeopardize your place in Midnight Pack, including a soulmate bond. You would rather give up your own dreams than risk losing the family that found you.

"That sacrifice is noble. *Honorable* even," she went on, her voice impassioned. "But I won't accept it. I want a mate and family of my own, and although you swore never to pursue a female again, I know you want the same things. You want *me*. It's why you've been protecting me all this time, why you've been watching and following me. So *have* me, Jagger. Stop punishing yourself and take what you want. Stop *protecting* me from yourself. I don't want or need to be protected. I know you, and even with an untamable wolf inside you, I *know* you won't hurt me."

My very soul felt exposed, mercilessly flayed open as she dug into the deepest darkest parts of me and dragged them out into the light. Feeling raw and vulnerable, I took a step back, then another. "You don't know what you're saying." My voice came out gruff, scraping against my throat like sandpaper. "I already *have* hurt you. I *rejected* you."

"But did you really? Would we still be able to feel each other's emotions through the bond if you had? It hurt like hell when I thought you'd never come for me again, yet here you are, prepared to help me with my heat. That means something, Jagger."

"Yes, it means that I *care* about you," I snapped. "It means that I selfishly want you, even if it would destroy *everything*. I've dreamt of having a mate and family of my own for a decade, Brielle, but that dream died the moment I almost ruined a female. It would kill me if I hurt you like that. I *can't* hurt you like that."

"You won't."

"You don't *know* that!" I thundered, so loudly that I expected her to cringe back in fear. She didn't.

"Yes, I do," she said, a calm certainty filling her voice. "When you realized I was your soulmate, you were willing to sacrifice your future in order to protect me. You suffered in silence for over a year while living under the same roof as me. I can't think of any other male who would practice that kind of self-restraint."

I shook my head, unwilling to accept the version of me she saw. "I'm too unstable. Too *dangerous*."

"So am I," she tossed back. "You're not the only one with an unpredictable wolf, you know. I'm not afraid of Onyx, and I'm most certainly not afraid of you."

I began to tremble, the protective walls I'd built around my heart starting to crumble. "You shouldn't want me, Brielle. I'm broken."

At that, she let go of the beam and took a step toward me. "No, not broken," she said, her voice gentling. "Just different."

All the air left me in a rush. When she took another step, my heart started to hammer. Onyx reared up, sensing a change in the air. In *me*. His eagerness fueled my own, and blood rushed to my groin, hardening my cock within seconds.

"Come any closer, and I'll take you," I warned her, my voice both breathless and guttural.

"Good. I want you to. Even if you reject me again afterward."

Shocked that she still wanted this, wanted *me*, even after everything I'd put her through, I decided to be honest right back. "I won't. If we go through with this, I'll never let you go, even if you want me to."

"I won't want you to," she firmly said, and Onyx howled in glee. I nearly joined him, my control slipping with each encouraging word she uttered. The wildness inside me was emerging, no doubt flaring hotly through my eyes, but she didn't seem to care. "You're my soulmate, Jagger. My family. I'm safe with you."

She took another step. A final step. Then lifted her hand and placed it over my thundering heart, nothing but trust brimming in her eyes.

The decisiveness. The willingness. The *surrender* pouring through our bond and into me was the last straw.

"Screw it," I muttered and finally gave in. Finally surrendered to the desperate need to pursue my soulmate, to *take* her like I'd dreamt of doing from the very first moment I'd laid eyes on her.

Yanking her against me, I captured her mouth in a scorching kiss.

CHAPTER 21

BRIELLE

His kisses were wild. Greedy. *Possessive.*

Each one sucked the air from my lungs and left me trembling for more. He wasted no time plunging his tongue into my mouth, reacquainting himself with my taste. I wrapped my arms around his neck to pull him closer, my own hunger making me greedy. He was fully in charge of the kiss, though, his strong fingers gripping my jaw so he could thrust his tongue deeper and deeper.

When my legs weakened under the pleasurable assault, he backed me up and pinned my body against the support beam. The second I felt his hard length between my legs, a fresh heatwave roared through me. I whimpered into his mouth, and he ground himself against me, making me see stars.

It wasn't enough, though. Not this time. I wanted more of him. *All* of him. I wanted him naked against me. I wanted him *inside* me.

I started to squirm, the need to have him inside me almost painful. When I brought my hands down to unbutton his pants, he grabbed both my wrists and pinned them by my sides against the wooden beam. I continued to squirm, and he released a warning growl. When I ignored it, he bit my bottom lip. *Hard.* Tasting blood, I gasped and jerked my eyes open.

He pulled away to check on me, his own eyes burning bright yellow with unbridled desire. When I didn't cringe away from the intensity, he focused on my bleeding lip, then lowered his head to lick it clean. The action was primal. *Animal.* And completely turning me on. Heat flared hotly between my legs, drenching my panties within seconds.

Jagger stopped licking me to deeply inhale, drawing the scent of my arousal into his lungs. A groan rumbled from him, so raw and needy that my panties dampened even more.

"You bit me," I said, my voice breathless and equally needy.

"Yes," was all he said. Then, "I need to taste you."

I glanced at his mouth hovering inches from mine. "You already are."

"No, Brielle. I need to taste you here." Dropping one of my wrists, he cupped his hand between my legs in a possessive hold. I gasped again, nearly coming on the spot.

"Yes," I whimpered out, already imagining his head buried between my thighs. "Oh God, *yes.*"

So consumed with thoughts of him eating me, I wasn't prepared when he confessed, "But I've never done it before."

I nearly choked on my spit, blinking at him in utter shock. "You've never gone down on a female before?"

"No."

My jaw slowly dropped. "Are you . . . Are you a *virgin?*"

A ghost of a smile lifted his mouth. "No, but my experience with females is . . . limited. You might have to teach me a thing or two. Your likes and dislikes, etc."

Oh. *Oh.* For whatever reason, knowing he was inexperienced in the bedroom turned me on even more. He might be the more dominant one between us, but I was more sexually experienced. That realization gave me a heady sense of power.

Seeing my expression, he gave me a stern look. "I'm giving you permission to use your mouth, Brielle, nothing more. When I taste you, the only thing you'll be able to move is your lips."

I blinked at him in confusion. "What do you mean?"

"There's a steel ring on the beam above your head and an old rope I spotted while coming in here. That should keep your hands subdued while I devour you."

My legs weakened once more, not because he wanted to tie me up, but because he wanted to *devour* me. When I didn't respond right away, worry flickered through the soulmate bond.

"You can say no if you don't want this, Brielle," he said, his voice strained. "You can still put an end to this, and I'll . . . I'll walk away."

Sudden pain sliced through the bond, letting me know how much he didn't want to end this. But he didn't want to scare me either. Learning that he was into bondage play definitely caught me off guard, especially since I'd never done it before. I couldn't help but remember how it felt to be cuffed by those burly orderlies, how *helpless* those shackles had made me feel.

But as Jagger searched my face with a vulnerable expression, allowing me to see a part of him I'd never seen before, any panic I might have felt vanished. He'd always been the one to protect me, to keep me safe. Even tied up, I trusted that he would protect me. He was my soulmate, and if tying me up got him off, then I was willing to embrace a new kink.

"I want this," I finally said. Relief immediately flooded our bond. I huffed out a laugh and lifted my free wrist. "Ready when you are. But hurry up, please. I'm *dying* for an orgasm. Or two or three. Or ten."

Even through the barn's dusty gloom, I saw his cheek's darken in embarrassment. Suddenly, it all made sense, and another laugh burst from me.

"I finally understand why you blush so easily at my sex jokes. I thought you were a prude or something, but it's because you're still practically a virgin. So adorable."

He stared at me as if I'd just given him the worst insult. "Adorable?"

I flashed him my dimples. "Definitely."

"I'm second in command of the largest pack in the country. I strike fear into the hearts of men three times your size. My wolf is—"

"Yeah, yeah, you're big and scary, blah, blah, blah," I interrupted him with a cheeky grin. "Still adorable, though."

He stared at me a moment more, then leaned forward and licked one of my dimples. The gesture was so unexpected, so *sweet* that I didn't know how to react. It was like being affectionately licked by a dog. Well, if the dog was huge, hot, and horny. When I just gaped at him, he moved on to my other dimple and licked that one too. With his hand still cupped between my legs and his tongue gently caressing my skin, I was at a complete loss for words.

Who knew that Jagger had a soft side?

"Stay here," he quietly rumbled, pulling back to look at me. When I mutely nodded, he let go of me and turned to walk away. My body immediately mourned the loss of his touch, and I couldn't suppress a small whimper.

Jeez, I had it *bad* for him. The last couple of weeks might as well have never happened. A part of me—okay, a *big* part—still wished he would grovel at my feet for putting me through hell, but he would be on his knees before me soon enough, a fact that I was anticipating with relish.

Once again imagining that voracious tongue between my legs, another pulsating heatwave rocked through my core. Need consumed me, and before I could think better of it, I slipped a hand beneath the short hem of my dress and started to rub myself through my underwear.

"*Stop*," Jagger demanded in a guttural voice. I looked up, and our eyes clashed, his bright with anger. "You are *not* to touch yourself. Your pleasure is mine and mine alone."

Holy. Hell.

I wanted to be mad that he was telling me what to do, but I was so freaking turned on right now. I started to rub myself again, and he snarled, baring his teeth before coming at me like a freight train. In a flash, he grabbed my wrists and bound them together with a thick length of rope, then yanked my arms above my head. As he secured the rope to the ring attached to the wooden beam, making sure it was tightly tied, my feet almost left the ground.

I started to protest how tight it was, but he was suddenly on his knees before me, yanking my dress up to my waist and pulling my tights and panties down so roughly that they tore in half and fluttered to the concrete floor. Before I could prepare myself, he gripped my thighs and spread them wide. My feet lost contact with the ground, and the rope bit into my wrists, but only for a moment. Jagger hoisted my legs onto his shoulders, taking my full weight, then buried his face between them.

With my thighs spread wide, his tongue easily found my aching clit. The first lick nearly sent me over the edge, and I cried out, my spine arching off the beam. Encouraged by my reaction, he dug his fingers into my thighs and licked me again, swirling his tongue this time.

"Oh God, *yes!*" I screamed, pulling at my restraints as pleasure spiked through me. "Just like that. Just like that!"

He did it again, satisfaction pulsing through our bond when I released another cry of pleasure. Seconds later, his tongue was expertly roving over my clit, hitting all the right spots with ease. For an almost-virgin, he sure knew how to make my body sing.

"You taste like a rainforest," he groaned against my clit, his hot breath teasing the hypersensitive flesh.

"That's great," I panted, nearly out of my mind with need. "But the rainforest is going to die if you don't keep watering it."

Something that sounded like a laugh rumbled from him and into my clit. The vibration made my pussy flutter, and I moaned, so close to orgasm yet not close enough.

"Please don't stop," I whimpered, not above begging when there was nothing else I could do. I was wholly at his mercy, unable to use my hands or legs to make him finish what he started. "Please, Jagger. *Please.*"

More satisfaction pulsed through our bond, and he rewarded my pleas with another lick. Then another and another until my breath came in short spurts, my body buzzing with mindless pleasure. When my thighs tensed, an orgasm of epic proportions about to rip through me, Jagger abruptly pulled his tongue away.

I opened my mouth to scream my frustration, but before I could utter a sound, he bit down on my clit. *Hard.* I choked on the scream, my eyes flaring wide as pain streaked through me. A second later, the pain became immense pleasure as he began to suck on the flesh. Harder, harder, and harder as if to forcefully milk my orgasm from me.

My body couldn't cope. *I* couldn't cope.

The scream tore from my lungs as euphoria blasted through me. Wave after wave of ecstasy shot me higher and higher, higher than I'd ever been before. Jagger continued to suck on me, and I was suddenly orgasming again, emitting a strangled cry as pleasure mercilessly pounded into me.

I couldn't breathe, couldn't think, my eyes blind and ears deaf to the world around me.

He sucked and sucked, making me orgasm over and over and over. It lasted so long that I thought I would die of pleasure, that I would cease to exist, only for my soul to continue on in an endless euphoric state.

Even if I wanted it to end, I couldn't. Jagger had complete control over my body, and something about that realization excited me so much that I orgasmed again. Being dominated by him like this was utter bliss, and that surprised me most of all. I'd never been the submissive type and most *definitely* wasn't an omega, but as he continued to suck on me, I melted. Every inch of me went pliant, surrendering to him. *Submitting.*

The second he felt me wholly submit to him, Jagger pulled away with a ragged gasp. My legs left his shoulders and uselessly fell, forcing my bound wrists to carry my dead weight. Dazed and entirely blissed out, I fluttered my eyes open in confusion. It took a moment to focus, but when Jagger came into view, I found him on his feet staring down at himself with wide eyes.

Horror pulsed through our bond, but something else did too. It was powerful, so powerful that I couldn't breathe again. A sudden urge pounded through me, strong and swift. If it wasn't for the rope holding me up, I would have dropped to all fours at his feet.

"Jagger," I gasped out, struggling against my restraints. "What's wrong?"

He continued to stare at himself, then slowly lifted his hands to unbutton his pants. Not knowing what to do, I simply watched him, certain he'd turn around if he wanted privacy. I'd seen him naked plenty of times, mostly during the full moon when he'd shift to let Onyx protect me in wolf form. He had a gorgeous body, and his dick was especially nice to look at, but when he tugged down his pants and let the thick length spring free, I nearly swallowed my tongue.

"Holy . . ." I whispered, gaping at his humongous penis like a creeper. "Is that . . . Is that a . . . ?"

"A knot," he finished, then slowly lifted his head to look at me. At the stark *fear* I saw in his eyes, I forgot how to breathe again. "But that's not all."

I started to tremble all over but didn't know why, nervous energy streaking up and down my body. Swallowing roughly, I whispered, "What is it?"

His chest heaved, his own limbs beginning to shake. "I'm in rut."

CHAPTER 22

JAGGER

This was my punishment. My *judgment* for daring to pursue a female again.

And not just any female. *The* female. The only one I wanted to pursue. The one that possessed my every waking and sleeping moment. I'd given in to my instincts. I'd indulged in her, the sweet exotic taste of her still thick on my tongue.

And now, I was paying dearly for my sins, the consequences more than I was prepared to face.

Pursuing her had awakened my dormant alpha gene, a fact that filled me with dread. My instincts would be even harder to control now, especially if I was challenged in any way. Although I'd submitted to Kolton's leadership ever since we were kids, it hadn't been easy. I wasn't much less dominant than him, and with my alpha gene fully awakened, I feared for my future in the pack. Kolton didn't tolerate insubordination, nor should he. One wrong move, and he had every right to kick me out.

If that wasn't bad enough, my body was flooding with pheromones I'd tried so hard to suppress over the years. My feral instincts were already triggered by Brielle's heat, but now that I was in rut, I could feel them consuming my every thought, not to mention Onyx's.

Mark mate. Claim mate. Breed mate.

His thoughts ran on a loop through my head, and soon, mine mirrored his.

Mark mate. Claim mate. Breed mate.

I wanted all of her. Every last inch. I wanted to sink my canines into her flesh, marking her as mine. I wanted to place my scent beneath her skin, claiming her as my mate. I wanted to *breed* her, filling her with my seed.

Just the thought of spilling my sperm inside her, of *impregnating* her, made my knot swell so big that I groaned, the sound equal parts pain and pleasure. Precum shot down the length and out the slit, coating my engorged head. I glanced back up at Brielle to find her eyes glued to my cock in rapt fascination. The stiff appendage twitched, more than happy to soak up her attention.

She was still tied up to the beam, her arms above her head and her dress barely covering her thoroughly-licked pussy. Knowing how easy it would be to take her right now nearly broke the little control I had left. One move. That's all it would take. One move, and I could slake every dark suppressed desire on her supple flesh. My mouth filled with saliva as need pounded through me, the feral insatiable beast inside about to explode from my skin.

Take, take, take. Mine, mine, mine.

As I felt the beast claw its way upward and wrestle for control, I prowled toward Brielle like the wild animal I was. Her eyes widened but not with fear. No, she was *intrigued*, and that was almost my undoing. Why did she not sense the danger she was in? Why was she *looking* at me that way? Like she *wanted* me to ravage her?

This female confounded me in every way possible. One minute, she was fiercely putting me in my place, and the next, prostrating herself before me like a lamb for the slaughter. I knew she was still getting used to being a werewolf, and that included understanding how our instincts worked, but she wasn't a naive virgin either. Her sexual experience far surpassed mine, and she should know when to practice caution.

Couldn't she see that the normally distant male before her was about to take *everything*? Not just what she wanted to give but everything she didn't. Nothing would be safe from me. I was going to devour it all, every last inch of her, and then devour her again. And again. And again.

By the time I was done, there would be nothing left untouched. *Nothing*. I would ruin her so thoroughly that she'd never look at me the same again.

Deep down, that's who I was. That's what I'd kept on a tight leash ever since I'd learned just how wild that part of me could become.

She didn't stand a chance. Once it was out, I couldn't protect her from it. Everything I'd done to her so far would look like child's play compared to what that dark part of me would do.

As I approached her, an image flashed before my eyes. A *memory*. Only, the nameless female in the memory was now replaced by Brielle. She writhed beneath me, screaming in fright as I pinned her arms and legs down. Ignoring her pleas to stop, I tore off her clothes and prepared to ravage her. She was completely helpless, wholly at my mercy. I could do anything I wanted to her. *Anything*. Excitement trembled through me, but as I looked down at the fear in her emerald green eyes, that excitement switched to terror.

I blinked, and the image vanished. But looking down at her now, tied up to the beam and completely at my mercy, the terror remained. A foot away from reaching her, I forced my gaze to her bound wrists. In a flash, I freed her from the rope and took a step back.

"Run," I gritted out, the word like acid on my tongue. She lowered her arms and simply stared at me, making my desperation spill over. "I said *run*, Brielle! I can't hold it back much longer."

The shouted words didn't affect her. I prepared to shout at her again, but before I could, she said, "Then don't. Let it out."

A howl of pure torment left me. "You have no idea what you're saying, Brielle. Don't you get it? I will *consume* you, mind, body, and soul. Once I start, I won't be able to stop. I'll *ruin* you."

"Oh, Jagger," she said with a small sigh. Then took a step toward me.

"Brielle, stop. *Stop.*"

She didn't, and panic filled me, making my heart thunder so rapidly that I thought it would explode.

"I know you're scared that you'll hurt me," she began, coming so close that I could easily reach out and grab her, "but you don't need to be. Let me prove it to you."

Struggling to breathe through the pain and terror, I managed to get out, "How?"

"Like this," she said and dropped to her knees before me.

Realizing what she was planning to do, I started to say her name in warning. Too late. She reached up and grabbed the base of my swollen knot, then leaned forward and stuck the engorged head into her mouth, precum and all. Shocked to see my dick inside her, I didn't pull away. I *couldn't.* I was instantly mesmerized by the sight, rendered immobile as I watched her try to swallow more of me.

Her warm tongue slid along my slit and licked off the precum, punching all the air from my lungs. I'd told her the truth earlier about not being a virgin, but I'd never experienced the pure rapture of having a female's mouth on me before. Her lips could barely wrap around the head, but when she began to suck on me, my vision splintered.

"Brielle," I said, her name leaving me in a whimper, in a plea. Whether it was to make her stop or encourage her onward, I didn't know. My mind had emptied the second she'd taken me into her mouth.

She continued to suck on the tip, her hand moving to explore the thick length of my shaft. My knot was so engorged that her fingertips couldn't connect, and when she squeezed it, ridges formed along the length. Every time her hand slid over one of them, they swelled and hardened, giving me the most delicious high.

Despite its enormous size, she navigated my cock beautifully, proving just how experienced she was. I wanted to be jealous at the thought of her pleasuring other males like this, but what she was doing took my full concentration.

My balls began to tighten, and she reached up with her other hand to gently squeeze them. Exquisite pleasure shot through them and up the knot's length, wringing a groan from me. My legs threatened to give out, but I refused to budge, desperate to experience more.

She picked up the pace, pumping and squeezing and sucking. I watched her the entire time, still in disbelief that she was doing this. If I blinked too hard, I could very well wake up and discover this had all been a dream. Unwilling to give up this moment, I kept my eyes on her, still as stone except for the involuntary tremors rocking my body every few seconds. When I felt my thighs tense, preparing for the release building in my balls, she sucked on me harder, *milking* me. Encouraging me to come.

I wasn't ready. Didn't want this to end.

I held on, the pleasurable tension in my body growing painful as I refused to orgasm. Brielle noticed what I was doing and squeezed my shaft, nearly forcing me to ejaculate. I staved off the need, my gaze still glued to her. When her attempt to make me come didn't work, she leaned forward and swallowed more of me. Excited to see so much of myself inside her, my knot swelled even bigger, stretching the light brown skin taut. Brielle gagged on the thickness, and a chuckle rumbled from me.

She quickly retaliated and bit down. *Hard.*

I jerked at the unexpected feel of her teeth on me. It hurt, but it was the most exhilarating pain I'd ever felt. She'd bitten me. *Marked* me.

The realization sent a thrill through me so powerful that I orgasmed, spilling my release with a guttural groan. The stream jetted into her mouth, and she took it all. The sight drove my instincts wild, and I came a second time into her mouth, my breaths ragged as I watched her lap me up like a good girl.

By the time she was finished, I could barely stand, my body blissfully buzzing. Her mouth released me with a wet pop, then she lifted my shaft and licked up the dorsal vein from base to tip, swirling her tongue over the slit before finally letting go.

"Mmm," she hummed. When she licked her lips as if enjoying my taste, my cock twitched in satisfaction. "Wow. I have a big mouth, but that puppy was too big even for me."

A laugh burst from me, and she looked up in surprise.

"You laughed."

"Yes." I smirked at her. "And you bit me."

"Yes," she said with an even bigger smirk, flashing those pretty dimples at me. "How else am I supposed to claim you?"

Another thrill shot through me, and I felt myself harden once more. "You want to claim me?"

She gave me a look, one filled with challenge. "Don't you?"

Onyx howled, thrashing inside me with an excitement I equally shared. I couldn't believe this was happening. Couldn't believe she was facing down the darkest part of me with a *smile*. She was beyond brave. *Fearless.* Trusting me that I wouldn't hurt her. Even with the primal instincts raging through my body, she refused to cower or run.

She wanted this. Truly *wanted* this. And I could no longer deny her. Could no longer protect her from that dark part of me when she so clearly didn't want me to.

"Yes," I answered her, not bothering to hide the need in my voice. "More than anything, I want to claim you."

At my confession, she audibly swallowed and rose to her feet. Our eyes held for a long moment, then she nodded and whispered, "Good. Then what do you need me to do next?"

CHAPTER 23

BRIELLE

The *look* he was giving me. It was equal parts hunger, relief, and something I never thought I'd see on his face.

Adoration.

I could see it in his eyes, but I could feel it as well, pulsing through our bond so strongly that I knew something had shifted between us—something that made my knees weak and mouth dry with nervous anticipation.

Knowing that Jagger was officially an alpha now made me even *more* hot for him. I'd never been around a male werewolf in rut before and had certainly never sucked on a knot. But, despite how intimidated I'd been by his size, the need to reassure him had eclipsed everything else. I wasn't afraid of him, and I wouldn't run. Pleasuring him with my mouth had definitely gotten my message across loud and clear, but I knew he needed more than that. *Much* more.

Good thing I did, too.

I stood before him expectantly, waiting for him to take what I was freely offering. Hoping he wouldn't pull away this time. Praying he would believe, would *trust* that I wanted this with him.

God, I wanted it so badly. Wanted *him*. Fate hadn't made a mistake in destining us for each other. We were opposites in nearly every way, and yet we also wanted the same things. A mate. A family. Acceptance. Love. He was broody and quiet, and I was emotional and loud. But we worked. We *fit*. And I couldn't wait to find out how our bodies fit together.

He must have seen something in my eyes, a signal that I was ready for whatever he needed me to do, because he answered without a moment's hesitation, "I need your complete submission."

I wasn't the least bit surprised by his response, but he needed to remember who I was, even when his wolf and instincts were riding him hard. "I'm willing to wholly submit to you, Jagger, but don't forget that I'm not an omega."

He searched my face for a lengthy beat, then said, "I don't need an omega's submission. I need the submission of the free-spirited female I've come to know and care for. The female I can't stop thinking about and who I'm absolutely feral for. The female who's somehow managed to break down all my walls and burrow inside my heart. I need her submission and hers alone. I need my *mate's* submission."

Well, *that* did it. His words weren't exactly a declaration of love, but I turned to mush anyway, blinking back tears as I whispered, "That is seriously the hottest thing anyone's ever said to me."

Jagger didn't respond, but I didn't miss the slight darkening of his cheeks. Oh man, he was definitely a big softy underneath that tough exterior. How could he ever think I'd be afraid of him?

Realizing he was too embarrassed to speak, I took matters into my own hands and reached down to grasp the hem of my dress. As I slowly—*very* slowly—shimmied it upward, his eyes turned a molten yellow. When the dress was over my head, I dropped it on the dusty floor and stepped out of my heels. Only my bra was left, and he hungrily watched me unhook the back and toss it to the floor.

He took me in for an achingly long moment, staring at my curves as if seeing them for the very first time. I let him look his fill, feeling sexier than I ever had before when his gaze grew hungrier with each passing second. The air practically smoldered from the heat building between us, and I felt my hot skin prickle with anticipation.

Something electric was about to happen. Something explosive and maybe just a little bit dangerous.

An instinct pulled at me, a primal one that called not only to me but to my wolf as well. Before I knew what I was doing, I'd dropped to all fours on the ground—with my backside facing him.

He released a sharp hiss, clearly aroused by the submissive move. But when I peeked over my shoulder at him, his eyes were squeezed shut, his hands tightly fisted at his sides.

"I'm not afraid, Jagger," I gently said, knowing that he needed one final push. "You can let the beast out. I want this."

It was enough.

His eyes snapped back open and captured mine. I took in the feral light in them and shivered. It was still him, still Jagger, but this was a different version of him. A *wild* version. A version that immediately made my stomach cartwheel and heart race.

Oh God, he was going to eat me alive.

Right as I had the thought, he exploded into motion. In a flash, his shirt and pants were gone, and he was on all fours behind me. Instinctively knowing what was about to happen, I turned my head back around and braced myself, just in the nick of time. With one swift move, he mounted me from behind. Circling a hand around my throat, he entered me balls deep with a savage thrust.

My walls immediately stretched to accommodate his thick length, and I cried out, certain he'd just ripped my vagina in half. Jagger's hold on my throat tightened, cutting off the sound. Not giving me time to adjust, he pulled out of me only to thrust inside again, so brutally that I lost the ability to breathe. Over and over, he pounded into me, his ragged breaths hot on my neck as he hunched over me like an animal. Like a powerful alpha male in rut.

It was the most primal thing I'd ever experienced and a shock to my system. But it was a good shock, an *exciting* shock. He was out of control, and I felt myself falling over the edge with him, surrendering to the carnal moment and all it had to offer.

We were simply two creatures merged into one. Instinct drove our actions, and we obeyed its incessant call. Our bodies moved of their own accord, finding a rhythm that was as natural as nature itself.

We were effortless, our destination inevitable.

It felt perfect. It felt *right*.

I fell and fell, wholly submitting to the rapturous moment. Jagger continued to doggedly thrust into me with a wildness that bordered on obsession, but when I tipped my head to the side ever so slightly—a clear and unmistakable invitation—he completely lost it.

With a guttural howl, he slammed his cock into me, so deeply that he hit a nerve I didn't know existed. A sudden vibration shot through me, so wild and intense that I had no choice but to orgasm. I threw my head back and screamed as pleasure erupted inside me, blasting to every corner of my body. My battered walls mercilessly squeezed Jagger's cock, and he loosed a bellowing roar, violently jerking as his own release jetted inside me.

Mid-orgasm, he pressed his mouth to the spot between my neck and shoulder. One swift move and his canines were embedded deep in my flesh. Biting me. *Claiming* me.

Nothing about the claim was gentle. It was rough and possessive, no doubt leaving a mark that wouldn't easily fade. Which meant that his *scent* would be buried deep, so deep that no other males would dare come near me.

I was his mate now. His mate that he *chose*.

Unable to contain my excitement, another orgasm ripped through me, and I howled at the rafters above. My spasming pussy milked another orgasm from Jagger, and he groaned into my neck, his teeth still embedded in my flesh as he fell over the edge again.

I expected him to be worn out after that, but I couldn't have been more wrong. When he'd said he was insatiable, he hadn't been exaggerating.

Still coming down from my blissful high, I felt his cock engorge. Within seconds, my walls were stretching to their breaking point, his knot completely filling me up. The smooth length became ribbed, and when they rubbed against my slick walls, the delicious friction wrung a moan from me.

In a flash, his hand on my throat shot down to flick my clit. I gasped, spasming all over his knot. He was going to make me come again in no time if his fingers kept flicking me like that, especially with his ribbed knot pressing on my sensitive walls. I had a lot of stamina in the bedroom—or, in this case, the barn—and it was thrilling to discover that he did too. He showed no signs of slowing, his dick harder than ever. I didn't think it could *get* any harder—or bigger—the length filling me up so completely that it could no longer move.

As he continued to rapidly flick my clit, his canines still deep inside me, it finally dawned on me what was happening. He wasn't just mating and claiming me. He was *breeding* me. With his knot firmly holding me in place, I couldn't stop it, even if I wanted to.

Good thing I didn't want to.

Only a few short hours ago, I'd all but given up on my dreams. And now, I was *experiencing* them. All of the disappointment, humiliation, and agony of being rejected was melting away. In its place was a peace that words couldn't adequately describe. I felt like myself again, whole and content. Not only that, I felt complete in a way I'd never felt before, like my soul had finally connected with its other half.

And it had.

Jagger had finally accepted me and our soulmate bond. We were mates now. And, soon, we would have a family of our own.

Suddenly overwhelmed by all that I'd gained in such a short period of time, tears spilled down my cheeks. Another orgasm lashed through my body, and Jagger's quickly followed. I cried out from the pleasure of it, blissfully drowning in happiness. I'd thought my dream had died. That *I'd* died. Yet here I was, fully alive and one with my soulmate.

The pain I'd endured to reach this moment didn't matter anymore. I'd survived so that I could live, and oh how beautiful life was going to be now that Jagger was by my side.

He continued to breed me long into the night, the combination of my heat and his rut making us both hornier than jackrabbits. Our bodies were slick with sweat, our breathing ragged from the constant exertion. I wanted the beautiful moment to go on forever, but the weeks of restless sleep and malnourishment finally caught up to me.

I collapsed beneath him. Literally collapsed to the ground while in the throes of yet another orgasm. I whimpered out my release, too exhausted for anything more. Jagger lifted himself off me as he came hard, his knot swelling once more to rub against my raw walls. I whimpered again as pain mixed with my pleasure, my poor vagina a battered and bruised mess.

If I was still human, it would probably take me *days* to recover from this experience. Even as a werewolf, it was going to take some time before I could properly stand, let alone walk again.

Expecting Jagger to keep going despite my exhaustion, I was surprised when he gently rolled us onto our sides and pulled me back against him, both his arms cradling me in a warm cocoon. Only our heavy breathing could be heard as we laid side by side on the hard ground, still merged together by his swollen knot.

Neither of us spoke while we waited for it to soften, but I didn't mind the silence. It was comfortable. Peaceful, even. For once, there were no unspoken words between us. Nothing that needed to be said. We were in sync for the first time ever, mind, body, and soul. It felt so incredible that my eyes welled with tears once more.

Several minutes passed before I heard a noise, one that sounded a lot like . . .

"Are you purring?" I broke the silence to ask.

The vibrating sound coming from deep in his throat faded as he replied, "Yes."

Wow. Mr. Emotionally Unavailable was purring. *Purring.* Which could only mean one thing.

He was content.

As if in confirmation, Jagger buried his face in the crook of my neck where he'd claimed me to breathe in our combined scent. He started to purr again, and I melted against him with a contented sigh. Just like that, the feral beast was gone. In its place was a gentle doting male, yet another side of Jagger I'd never seen before.

A few more minutes passed before he quietly said, "Are you okay?"

His worry trickled through our bond, and I quickly replied, "Yes. More than okay."

"I didn't hurt you in any way?" he persisted, sounding so adorably concerned that a tired smile tugged at my lips.

Shifting in his arms so I could see his face, I said with utmost confidence, "No, Jagger, you didn't hurt me."

He stared at me for a long moment, then shut his eyes and breathed out, "Thank God."

As his worry started to fade, along with his knot, I shifted my hips and he slid out of me. After having him inside me for hours, I should feel relieved, but I immediately missed the intimate connection. Wanting to be closer, I rolled over and pressed my front to his, tangling our legs together for good measure. The new position sent fresh excitement through me, and Jagger instantly picked up on it.

Reaching down to cup my backside, he pressed our pelvises together and groaned, "I can't get enough of you."

"Good," I said, softly moaning when he began to rock against me. Not hard and desperate like before, but slow and gentle, no doubt for my sake.

It was so achingly sweet that I slid my hand to his jaw and kissed him, pleased when he eagerly kissed me back. The kiss became heated in no time, our teeth and tongues hungrily clashing together. Jagger rolled on top of me, preparing to enter me once more. Laying on my back like this, I could last longer. Even though my vagina was still recovering, it was more than ready to be filled and stretched by his delicious knot again.

His tip had just started to push into my entrance when a loud growl interrupted the moment. He paused, blinking down at me in surprise. More specifically, my stomach.

"You're hungry."

"Yes. For you," I replied, thrusting my hips up to make him go deeper. He grabbed my hips to stop me, and I whimpered in disappointment. "Jagger, please."

A violent shudder rocked him, his grip on my hips growing almost painful. But instead of thrusting inside me like I wanted him to, he pulled out and abruptly stood to his feet. "You need sustenance," he said, his voice gruff as he slowly backed away. "I need to take care of my mate."

Mate. He'd called me his *mate*. And this time, it was actually true. We'd completed the bond. I could feel how strong our connection had become in just a few short hours of love-making. The invisible string tying us together had felt threadbare this morning, but it was thrumming with energy now. With *power*.

Giddy all over again, fresh excitement filled me. Jagger groaned, and I noticed that his attention was fixed between my spread thighs. My pussy fluttered with a mini orgasm, turned on by his gaze alone. A feral gleam entered his eyes, the blue-gray color flaring yellow once more.

Belatedly realizing that he was wrestling with his primal nature again, I forced my legs shut with a sigh. "Fine, do what you have to do, but hurry up. I'm starved for your dick at the moment, not food."

His cheeks darkened, and I could barely stand the adorableness. Even after hours of mindless rutting and explosive orgasms, he was *still* easily embarrassed.

Unable to stop myself, I asked, "What are the chances that you got me pregnant just now?"

Jackpot.

I heard his heart loudly thump, then begin to race, so fast that I thought he would pass out. He swallowed. Swallowed again. But when he opened his mouth to speak, nothing came out.

"I want at *least* ten kids, maybe more," I went on, forcing my face to remain neutral when what I really wanted to do was grin like a fiend. I couldn't properly see his skin color in the darkness, but I imagined it was slowly turning green. "I'd want them to be besties with Nora and Vi's children, of course, so we'd need to have them soon to ensure they're around the same age. It's a good thing female werewolves are so fertile and their pregnancies only last four months. This time next year, we could already have three babies."

He stared at me so long and hard, his poor heart trilling out of control, that I couldn't stop a snort from escaping. Once it was out, I lost it and peals of laughter left me, echoing through the barn.

"Your *face*," I gasped out, clutching at my aching stomach. "You make it so easy."

His deer-in-headlights look morphed into a scowl, making me laugh harder. I pushed to my feet and teetered over to him, trying my best not to show how sore I was. He'd railed me good, so good that my body was still recovering from the savagery of it. I'd experienced my fair share of wild sex over the years, but nothing compared to what Jagger had just done to me.

He'd *owned* me. Every inch of me had been his to do with as he pleased. He'd consumed and possessed me. He'd claimed and bred me with a ferocity that should have terrified me.

And yet, I'd loved every second of it. Being ravaged by him had awakened my own feral side, the side I'd been trying so hard to ignore. It didn't feel so distant anymore, so foreign. I felt closer to it, more in tune with it. And, for the first time ever, I hadn't felt the need to control that part of me. I'd been one with it, *understood* it.

Looking at Jagger now, I realized how similar we actually were. He'd suppressed that part of himself too, afraid he wouldn't be able to control it. But maybe it wasn't about learning to control it. Maybe it was about *accepting* it. I wasn't afraid of him or his untamable wolf, and he shouldn't be either. I'd accepted him just as he was, and now that he'd accepted me, it felt like we'd been created for each other.

We fit *perfectly* together, mind, body, and soul.

Deliriously happy that we were finally, *finally* on the same page, I slid my arms around his neck and stood on tiptoe to kiss his cheek. "You're so adorable."

He grunted in annoyance but placed his hands on my hips to

draw me closer. "You talk too much."

I grinned a mile wide. "You love it."

He pulled back to look at me, taking in my happy expression for a long moment before saying, "Yes. But that's not the only thing I love."

My heart stopped, then started up again with a jolt, skipping and fluttering until I grew faint with nervous anticipation. Struggling to swallow, I breathlessly whispered, "What else do you love?"

Without taking his eyes off me, he lifted a hand to touch my cheek. "Your face."

My insides immediately melted into a warm gooey puddle. The feral side of Jagger was intoxicating but so was this unexpected soft side. Wanting to hear more, I urged, "What else?"

His mouth tipped into a faint smile. "Your big heart."

A tear escaped my control, but he caught it with his thumb, gently wiping it away. Wrestling with a sudden influx of emotions, I managed to get out, "What else?"

He paused, searching my face as if to find something. I steadily held his gaze, encouraging him to continue, desperate to hear him say the words.

Say it. Just say it, I inwardly pleaded, filled with so much anticipation that I couldn't breathe.

He pulled me a little closer, his blue-gray eyes shining with clear certainty as he said, "I love—" He suddenly frowned, his hand on my hip shifting to my waist. "Brielle, what is this?"

Caught off guard by the abrupt question, I blinked at him in confusion.

"*Brielle*," he said more urgently, pulling back to focus on the left side of my waist.

When he pressed on a particularly sensitive spot, I sucked in a surprised gasp and glanced down. I didn't see anything abnormal, the darkness inside the barn making it hard to pick out fine details. But when I reached down and felt the spot, my fingers found a small protrusion. A *hard* one, just beneath my skin and not much bigger than a grain of rice.

"What the hell?" I racked my brain, trying to figure out what it could be. Almost immediately, something jogged my memory, and my stomach twisted with dread. "Get it out."

At the sudden shift in my tone, Jagger tensed and looked up at me.

"Get it out!" I shrieked, not bothering to hide my panic. When he didn't move fast enough, I started to claw at my skin with my blunt nails, ignoring the pain as desperation filled me.

"Brielle, stop!" Jagger ordered, but I was too incensed to listen. When I continued to claw at my skin, he grabbed my wrists and halted my frantic movements.

"Let me *go*," I wailed, struggling to break free.

He crushed me against him, his powerful hold instantly rendering me immobile. I fought anyway, but it was useless.

"Jagger, please," I begged, my breaths short and erratic against his chest. "I need to get it out."

"Tell me what it is first," he replied in a voice much calmer than mine. "I don't want you to get hurt."

"I-I don't know. At my parents' house, I felt a sharp sting and thought it was a loose nail on the doorframe, then completely forgot about it after that high-frequency device switched on. Now I remember seeing what looked like a needle tip sticking out of the lock hole. I think the supernatural hunters injected something inside me."

Despite my panicked explanation, he continued to hold me. His hand slid up my spine to grip my nape, and the firm hold was somehow comforting. Feeling his steady strength through our bond, I soaked it up like a sponge, grateful when some of my panic started to fade.

"Good girl," he said, holding me a moment longer before finally letting go. I reached for my waist again, but he stilled my hands, his touch gentle this time. "Let me do it, Brielle. Please."

At his earnest expression, I felt myself surrendering. Submitting. I trusted him not to hurt me, to *protect* me, even now. When I nodded, something flooded our bond, an emotion I felt so deeply that my very soul warmed. Fresh tears filled my eyes, and I hurriedly blinked them away as Jagger knelt before me.

"I need to make a cut. Just a small one," he said, and I watched with rapt fascination as the nail on his index finger slowly lengthened, curving into a black claw. I wasn't jealous of his ability to shift at will, but it sure would be cool to do that whenever I wanted. As the sharp tip made contact with my skin, I felt him hesitate.

"It's okay, Jagger," I quietly assured him. "I trust you."

He released a shaky breath, then gripped my opposite hip to hold me steady. As he prepared to cut me, I braced for the pain to come, but it was over in a flash. I'd barely felt the sting before he was pushing the tiny object from my skin. Seconds later, the small cut healed over, leaving behind only a few drops of blood.

"You okay?" he asked, looking up at me.

I quickly nodded, my gaze glued to the bloody object he held. "What is it?"

He stood to his feet so we could both inspect it. After a moment, he said, "I think it's a tracking device. I've just never seen one this small before."

"They're *tracking* me?" I squeaked, fresh panic filling me.

"Not anymore." He pinched the device between his fingers, and it crumbled to dust. "But we should assume they're heading this way, so we need to leave. Now."

Pausing only to hurriedly don our clothes, we made our way out of the barn. Jagger opened the door, but when I tried to leave ahead of him, he blocked me with an outstretched arm.

"Wait," he murmured, staring out at the barren landscape blanketed in white. Suddenly realizing how *exposed* we'd be on the trek back to my car, I went on high alert. Jagger inhaled, and I followed his lead, scenting the air for danger. It was hard to smell anything past our intermingled pheromones, but after a long moment, he slowly lowered his arm and whispered, "Stay close."

As he slipped out into the night, I followed close on his heels, wary of any movement or shadow. He cut a path through the snow, and I placed my feet in his footsteps, trying not to make a sound. It had been hours since I'd left my parents' house, which meant that the hunters could already be here. There was no sign of them, though. All was quiet; the only sound was the soft *crunch, crunch* of our footsteps.

I was just starting to lower my guard a bit when a sudden buzzing sound broke the silence. Jagger whirled and grabbed me so fast that I yelped in surprise. His body covered mine like a shield, his arms like steel bands around me. A low growl vibrated his chest as he assessed our surroundings for the threat. The buzzing sound continued, and after another moment, I recognized it.

"It's just my phone," I said with a shaky laugh. "I must have dropped it on the way to the barn."

Jagger tightened his arms around me when I tried to pull away, then reluctantly dropped them so I could search for the device. I followed the buzzing sound and found it seconds later, lifting it into the air with a victorious wave.

"Good thing it's waterproof, or—" My words ended in a startled gasp as something jabbed into my side. Crippling pain immediately followed, and I opened my mouth to scream, but nothing came out. A second jab struck my other side, and I dropped my phone as a heavy feeling swept over me.

"Brielle!" Jagger shouted, lunging forward when I started to fall.

As he caught me, another jab struck my shoulder. It felt like a dart filled with a strong sedative, but whatever was inside didn't just make me bone tired. I whimpered as another wave of agony streaked through my veins, the sensation like fire roasting me alive from the inside.

With a furious roar, Jagger yanked the darts from my skin. I tried to stand but could no longer support my weight, helplessly sagging against him. Jagger swept me into his arms and took off running. He only made it a few yards before more darts sliced through the air, this time aimed at him. Several of them struck his back, and I cringed when our bond lit up with his pain.

He kept going, pushing past the pain in his attempt to reach my car. When several more darts struck him, he finally stumbled, and I cried out, his agony becoming mine.

"Jagger," I sobbed, my vision wavering as whatever they'd injected me with started to pull me under. I blinked the dark spots away, only for more to take their place, spots that moved and resembled the shape of humans.

No, they *were* humans.

Struggling to stay conscious, I counted at least eight of them, armed and closing in fast. When I saw them raise their weapons, I screamed Jagger's name in warning.

He whirled around with a bellowing roar, the sound no longer human but that of a savage beast. His bones began to snap, to shift, to *transform*. Within seconds, I was wrapped in the arms of a powerful creature born of nightmares, his massive body covered in black fur and standing nine feet tall.

He'd shifted into Onyx's true form, his *demonic* form, a version of him I'd never seen in person before. His regular wolf form was huge, but this was something on a whole other level. I was child-sized compared to him, but instead of feeling terrified that a monster straight out of a horror movie had me, I felt protected. *Safe.* Even knowing how feral Jagger's wolf was, I knew I wasn't in danger.

Unfortunately, the same couldn't be said for the humans surrounding us.

Onyx bellowed out another roar, the sound booming over the snowy landscape. His dagger-sized claws dug into my skin, clutching me to him possessively. I glanced up and caught a flash of his blood-red eyes, eyes that were locked on the humans who'd frozen in their tracks to gape at him.

For a split second, I thought the terror of his transformation would scare them off. What human in their right mind would take on a nine-foot-tall demon werewolf? He could shred them into bloody little pieces without even trying. He was the predator and they were the prey. Instinct *demanded* they turn tail and flee.

But, apparently, I knew nothing about the species I'd been born into. As one, the humans raised their weapons and trained them on Onyx.

"FIRE!"

Darts zipped toward the hulking beast. In a flash, he set me down and exploded forward, snow spraying in his wake. Screams and shouts rang through the night as the monstrous wolf reached the first human and tore into him. He was a headless corpse a second later, tossed aside as Onyx went after another one.

"Bring him down! Bring him down!"

Onyx roared as more shots fired and pelted his thick hide. The great beast stumbled, and I whimpered. I tried to stand, to *help* him, but the world tilted and knocked me back down. I slumped into the snow, feeling weak and helpless. Dark spots blurred my vision again, but when I struggled to blink them away, they wouldn't budge. Pain and darkness consumed me, dragging me down, down, down.

The last thing I saw before losing consciousness was Onyx hunched over, defeated yet still on his feet as the hunters shot him again and again and again.

CHAPTER 24

BRIELLE

I woke to a world full of rage.

Bellowing roars pounded my sensitive ears, but the raw fury flooding my body was what alarmed me the most. It only took me a second to realize that the anger wasn't mine but Jagger's. Our bond was buzzing with powerful emotions, each one so intense that I struggled to breathe.

Another roar shook the air, so terrifying that I knew Onyx was still in control. A loud *boom* startled my eyes open, followed by a tremor that rocked the ground beneath me.

Clearing my hazy vision, the first thing I noticed was that my green sweater dress had been replaced by what looked like a white hospital gown. I tried to stand, but my weak limbs immediately gave out on me. I collapsed to the floor again, shaking and still in pain from whatever they'd injected me with. I focused on the cold, hard surface beneath me, noting that it too was white. My eyes traveled its length but were stopped only a few feet later by a solid white wall. I quickly took in my surroundings, and my heart stopped.

I was in a cage. A *cage*.

There was no handle on the door, and the small room was windowless. It wasn't silver like the one in my dream but pure white, like a sterile lab. Still, a cage was a cage. I was trapped like an animal, and by the sounds of it, so was Jagger.

Another bellowing roar and *boom* shook the ground, this time followed by a guttural howl. "Mate! MATE!"

The call was so frantic, so *heartbreaking* that I weakly cried out Onyx's name to reassure him.

A voice immediately answered me. Not Onyx's, but an achingly familiar one. A voice that didn't boom through the air but instead filled every corner of my mind.

Brielle!

I gasped, caught off guard by how *close* he sounded, like I could reach out and touch him. "Jagger!" I answered back, so relieved to hear his voice that I forced myself upright and staggered to the door. But the second I touched the sleek white surface, a powerful jolt streaked through my body. It blasted me back, and I hit the floor, twitching uncontrollably as painful electrical currents sizzled through my veins.

BRIELLE! Jagger roared, so loudly that it sounded like he'd just shouted into my ear.

When I didn't respond, chaos ensued. The roars and booms intensified, shaking my little prison. At any moment, I expected a massive wolf to explode through the walls.

The door to my room suddenly opened, and in walked two burly men wearing full-body protective gear. Only their faces were visible behind clear blast shields. One was black with an ugly scar down his cheek, and the other had beady little eyes and a menacing expression.

I blinked, immediately recognizing the second one. He was the man who'd impersonated an orderly and tried to take me from my parents' home on Thanksgiving.

When they both reached for me, I kicked out and caught Beady Eyes right in the groin. My bare foot did little damage to his protective gear, unfortunately, and he barely even flinched. With an annoyed grunt, he retaliated by backhanding me across the face. My head snapped back, pain flaring in my cheek. Jagger bellowed my name again, his rage a wild thing in my chest. Using it to fuel my own, I lashed out again with a furious cry, only for Beady Eyes to block my strike and thrust a long stick at me.

The second the tip of it touched my skin, white hot agony streaked through me. I opened my mouth to scream, but the pain snatched my breath away. My entire body convulsed on the floor as high voltage currents wreaked havoc on my system. I'd been zapped by an electrical outlet before, but that was a pinprick compared to this.

This was pure torment. *Torture.* They were treating me like I was a wild animal that needed to be subdued, but nothing about this was humane.

While I endured the searing torture, Onyx continued to roar and fight to break free of his own cage. Jagger called to me over and over, his voice so clear in my mind that it felt like he was beside me, encouraging me to hold on. Darkness slipped over my vision, but I clung to his voice, desperate not to lose consciousness again.

I didn't know how long the torture lasted, but when Beady Eyes finally pulled the stick away, the fight in me was completely drained. Little currents of electricity continued to zap me, seizing up my limbs and leaving me gasping for air.

Reaching down a second time, the two men grabbed my arms and dragged me from the room. I didn't struggle as we left my prison behind, but I forced my heavy eyes to take in everything we passed. The floor in the hallway was also white, along with the walls. Except that they weren't walls at all but rooms. *Cages.* Dozens of them with high-tech scanners placed outside each one.

If that wasn't alarming enough, I caught sight of several more burly men in protective gear standing at attention in the hallway. As we approached, they raised their weapons. Some carried long sticks like the one Beady Eyes had prodded me with, while others held guns of varying size—probably filled with tranquilizer darts.

They were all human and obviously knew how dangerous werewolves were, so I wouldn't be surprised if some of those guns contained silver bullets. One bullet to the heart was all it would take to kill even the most powerful hybrid.

Sudden realization hit me, and I knew those guns weren't meant for me. They were for Jagger. For *Onyx*. The booms and roars were almost deafening now, and I could *feel* how close he was. Sure enough, the two men carrying me stopped beside the room next to mine. Electricity crackled and guns cocked as the dozen or so men prepared to open the door.

Afraid they were going to shoot Onyx, I opened my mouth to warn him. Before I could, Beady Eyes gripped my hair and dragged me to my feet. Pain lit up my scalp, and that was all it took to whip Jagger—and Onyx—into a fresh frenzy. They both bellowed their fury, and a loud *boom* filled my ears, the door feet away from me groaning under the impact.

The men surrounding me held their ground, their weapons trained on the door. "Now!" Beady Eyes abruptly barked, and his scarred partner slammed his hand on the scanner. The second the door unlocked, both men shoved me forward. I hit the door and stumbled inside, sprawling onto the floor as my wobbly legs gave out.

An earth-shattering roar greeted my entrance, threatening to blow out my eardrums. Something huge rushed past me and plowed into the door, but it had already slammed shut. Onyx continued to bellow his fury, mindlessly throwing himself at the door as if unaware that I was there. His black claws scrabbled against the slick floor, struggling to gain traction.

When he backed up to charge the door again, I scooted out of the way just in the nick of time. With barely any room to gain momentum, he raced forward and slammed into the thick reinforced barricade. It violently shuddered under the impact but held strong, a fact that was obviously driving Onyx insane. Only then did I see the blood smeared on the white surface and smell the stench of burnt fur and flesh.

Every time he struck the door, he was electrocuting himself. *Hurting* himself. I'd only been able to feel my own pain and Jagger's desperate rage up until now, but seeing Onyx's beautiful black fur singed and glistening with blood broke my heart. He'd been trying to get to me. To *save* me. Even now, that was all he could think about.

Save mate, save mate, save mate, he chanted over and over, backing up to ram the door again.

As he rushed forward, his claws scraping against the floor, I finally realized that he hadn't spoken out loud. Neither had Jagger. They were speaking in my *head*, a clear confirmation that we'd completed the soulmate bond.

Onyx's massive body struck the door with another resounding *boom*. More blood splattered the white surface, burnt flesh permeating the air. His frame trembled from the electrical shocks, his breathing ragged from the pain he was in, but he wouldn't stop.

Save mate, save mate, save mate.

He backed up again, and I struggled to stand, desperate to stop this somehow. Despite his immense strength, he'd been weakened from the sedative injections. He'd been darted dozens of times, and it was a wonder he was even standing right now. Not only that, Jagger and I had both lost weight the past couple of weeks. Our health affected our wolves', our bodies and psyches intricately entwined.

At any other time, Onyx might have been able to break out. But right now, he was only hurting himself, and my heart couldn't take it anymore.

"Onyx, stop," I said, swaying yet refusing to fall again as I stood to my feet.

Save mate, save mate, save mate.

He shifted his weight to his powerful hindquarters, deaf and blind to everything around him but that door. Jagger had been right. Onyx couldn't be reasoned with. Words meant little to him, which meant that the only way to get through to him was to *act*.

Just as he was about to lunge forward again, I moved to stand in the middle of the room—directly in his path. Setting my jaw, I squarely faced him and barked, *Onyx, NO*.

Mind to mind. Something he was used to. My voice was firm, filled with command. Up until now, he'd only ever submitted to Jagger, but I had to hope, had to *pray* he would recognize me. See me. *Hear* me.

Because I wasn't going anywhere.

At first, his blood-red eyes stayed fixed on the door, oblivious to the female in his path. His powerful muscles bunched, prepared to launch him forward.

I tried one last time, one last ditch effort to make him see me before he plowed me over like a stalk of corn.

ONYX!

He froze, and I held my breath, hoping, praying. After a long moment, his gaze wavered, then slowly dropped to me. Faced with the full might of those intense eyes for the first time ever, I shoved down the need to cower. He was utterly terrifying, no doubt about it. But the longer I looked at him, at the confusion and desperation in his piercing gaze, all I saw was an oversized puppy in pain.

"Mate," I said in hushed tones, out loud this time. "Mate is safe."

He stared at me for the longest time, so long that I didn't think he understood me. Then a low whine left him. It was so sad, so *pitiful* that my heart instantly melted.

"Mate is here. Mate is safe," I whispered to him, taking a small step forward. He tracked the movement, his body eerily still as he watched me approach. I took another step, then another, trusting that he wouldn't hurt me. He might be feral, but even wild animals possessed a strong instinct to protect their mate.

When I was finally standing in front of him, my head tipped back to maintain eye contact, I threw caution to the wind and reached out to touch him. His fur was stiff with blood and sweat, but that didn't stop me from stroking my hand down his arm. I did it again and again. On the fourth time, another low whine left him.

"Mate," he said in that deep guttural voice of his.

"Mate," I confirmed.

He violently shuddered, then stepped forward and folded me into his massive arms. As his body curled over mine protectively, he wedged himself into a corner and hunkered down, holding me against him.

"It's okay," I soothed every time he released a whimper, running my fingers through his matted fur. "Mate is safe."

He lowered his big head to gently lick my cheek where Beady Eyes had backhanded me, and I felt approval warm our bond. *Jagger's* approval.

Tell Onyx to shift, he spoke into my mind, his rage from earlier nowhere to be found. *Tell him I need to hold my mate.*

Tears pricked my eyes, the need to be held by him making my exhausted body ache even more. *You think he'll listen to me?* I asked, speaking to Jagger through our bond for the first time. It felt like breathing, like the most natural thing in the world.

You just talked him down from a blind rage. You treated him like a scared pup instead of a dangerous beast, Jagger replied, pride evident in his tone. *I think he'll do whatever you ask him to.*

A tear rolled down my cheek and dampened Onyx's fur, the full extent of what I'd just done hitting me. I'd reasoned with the feral creature who couldn't be tamed. *Me.* I wasn't a powerful hybrid or even an alpha, and yet he'd listened to me. He'd *trusted* me despite his pain, terror, and confusion.

The wolf in me puffed out her chest a little, pleased that a mighty beast such as Onyx had submitted to us. We both recognized the significance of that, and I felt even closer to my wolf in that moment, not to mention Onyx.

"You did so good, Onyx," I praised him softly. "You fought hard, and I'm safe now because of you." It was true for the moment, but I knew even he was aware of how dire our situation was. Still, it felt right to reassure him before asking him to relinquish control. Continuing to speak in hushed tones, I added, "But it's time to shift back now. My mate needs to hold me."

Not a request. A command. But respectively given.

He made a chuffing noise and nuzzled my neck before rumbling in my mind, *Kind mate. Lovely mate.*

Despite my pain and exhaustion, a faint smile twitched my lips.

With one final lick to the spot where Jagger had claimed me, Onyx allowed the shift to take over. His bones cracked, and his fur receded, transforming his beastly body into that of a man. The second Jagger was back in control, he wrapped me up impossibly tight, holding me closer than he ever had before. I melted into him, needing the contact as much as he did.

It was still hard to believe that only a few short weeks ago, we'd been so distant toward each other that I didn't think it possible for us to experience this kind of closeness. According to everyone who knew him, Jagger Montgomery didn't do hugs, yet here he was, squeezing me to him like his life depended on it.

Suddenly feeling guilty, I whispered, "I'm so sorry."

"For what?" he murmured against my hair, his breath warming my scalp.

"For getting us into this mess. If I'd been stronger, none of this would have happened."

His chest rose and fell as he heaved out a sigh. "You're not to blame for any of this, Brielle. If anyone's responsible, it's me. I shouldn't have kept our soulmate bond a secret from you. I should have told you the truth about who I was and let you make your own decisions. Instead of protecting you, I left you vulnerable to attack. I was a fool to believe that rejecting our bond would keep you safe, and you have no idea how sorry I am for that."

But I did know. I could *feel* how sorry he was, and the shame he felt just about broke my heart.

Not wanting him to feel like that anymore, I pressed a kiss to his heart and whispered, "I forgive you, Jagger."

His chest sharply rose and fell as he heaved another sigh, this one filled with so much relief that I felt it all the way to my toes. As the shame faded away, he gruffly whispered back, "I love you."

I blinked, certain I'd heard him wrong. "You love me?"

"Yes. So desperately that I can no longer exist without you."

Tears of joy sprang to my eyes. Just like that, the cage imprisoning us melted away. It was just him and me, two bonded souls locked in a heartfelt embrace, sharing an infinitely precious moment. Allowing my tears to fall, I responded without an ounce of doubt or hesitation, "I love you, too."

CHAPTER 25

JAGGER

I held my mate for hours, vigilantly guarding her while she slept.

Keeping her safe was all that mattered.

Despite my pain and exhaustion, I was wide awake, my instincts demanding I stay alert. The humans had wisely given her to me, but I knew it was only a matter of time before they tried to separate us again.

I had to be ready.

My strength wasn't what it should be and neither was Onyx's, but I was determined to get us out of this hellhole before they did God-knew-what with us. Based on the room alone, this was a bigger operation than most. Not much could contain Onyx, especially when he was in rage mode, so the fact that he couldn't break down that door was more than a little concerning.

I glared at its white, blood-spattered surface for the umpteenth time, willing it to open so I could unleash Onyx on the armored men I'd caught a glimpse of in the hallway. They might have bested us in a wide open field, but in tight quarters like this, we'd tear them apart within seconds.

They just needed to open that blasted *door*.

Feeling Onyx restlessly stir in response to my heated glare, I peeled my eyes off the door and dropped them to Brielle's sleeping form. All on its own, my hand lifted to grasp her honey-brown hair. Careful not to wake her, I gently fisted the wavy mass and brought it to my face. One deep whiff of her tropical-scented locks, and I felt the tension drain from my body.

No one, *no one* had ever possessed that kind of power over me. Not only me but Onyx, too. I'd thought nothing could tame his instincts, but she'd single-handedly talked him off the ledge and coaxed him into relinquishing control. I'd done nothing to make him back down. The second we'd woken up in this room and discovered Brielle was missing, the desperate need to get to her had become our sole thought and purpose.

Now that I'd claimed and mated her, now that I'd *bred* her, every instinct I possessed demanded I keep her close. I no longer felt a need to protect her from the darkest parts of me. She'd faced that part of me without fear. She'd *embraced* it. Because of her acceptance, that wild unpredictable nature didn't feel like a curse anymore. She could handle it. She *wanted* it. And that meant more to me than she could ever know.

Those instincts would always be a part of me, would always shape my thoughts and actions, but just as she didn't fear them, neither did I. Not anymore. I could feel them simmering in my veins even now, flooding my mind and body with dark urges.

But at the moment, every one of those urges wanted the same thing. To kill anyone who tried to take Brielle from me.

She was my female. My *mate*. Nothing in the world was more precious to me, and I would do anything, *anything* to keep her safe.

Continuing to let her scent soothe my inner fire, I waited for the inevitable moment when that door would open again. They'd shoot me the second I burst into action, of course, but I'd be through the door and wreaking havoc before they could subdue me. My senses were on high alert, supercharged by the danger surrounding us, not to mention the pheromones still flooding Brielle's body and mine.

I hadn't been able to breed her anywhere near long enough, and the need to do so now kept me from feeling hunger or any residual pain from the dozens of darts and electrical shocks Onyx and I had endured. The need further heightened my protective instincts as well, which helped make up for the physical strength I'd lost over the past few weeks.

Those protective instincts eclipsed even my sexual drive, making it possible to think with my head and not my dick while I waited. Once we got out of this place, I could breed my mate until every last feral instinct was finally, *finally* satiated. But not before then. Right now, all that mattered was keeping her safe, and I needed to stay focused to make that happen.

Another hour passed before Brielle stirred against me with a low moan. The slight movement was all it took to harden my cock, but I ignored the feeling, continuing to breathe in her scent to keep the fire at bay. She stirred again with another moan, and after a moment, I understood why.

The intoxicating scent of her heat flooded my nostrils, and I stopped breathing too late. My cock hardened to the point of pain, and as I felt a knot begin to form, my focus wavered. The need to rut hit me like an avalanche, but I shoved down the feeling, determined not to cave.

I could control myself. I'd been doing it for years.

But that had been before her. Before the most exquisite creature I'd ever laid eyes on walked into my life and started to tear down my walls. And now that creature was my mate, and I'd finally been allowed to lose control. To unleash my dark side and ravage her body. And even though we were currently imprisoned, having her flush against me like this was too much.

Clenching my jaw, I shifted her so that she was no longer pressed against my groin. She moaned again in her sleep and reached between us. Reached down and touched the very thing I was trying so hard to ignore. I sucked in air through my teeth and shifted her even further away, but she wrapped her hand around the throbbing appendage before I could stop her.

"Brielle," I grunted, hating to wake her but unable to endure this torture right now.

Breed mate, Onyx whined, not understanding my inner turmoil. All that mattered to him was satiating our hunger.

I ignored him, too. No way in hell would I allow myself to have sex with Brielle in this cage. I'd allow my dick to explode before I subjected either of us to that humiliation. The humans who'd captured us obviously considered us animals, and acting like one would only affirm that belief. It was bad enough that they'd seen what I could become. I wouldn't add fuel to the flame by uncontrollably rutting my mate.

Still fast asleep, Brielle began to rub against me. After hours of healing sleep, her body clearly wanted to pick up where we'd left off. This was her first heat, and her potent pheromones hadn't even remotely begun to fade. Even trapped as we were, her instincts were urging her to scratch that incessant itch, to give in to her primal nature and pursue her mate.

That thought. That *fact* nearly undid me. My female, my *mate*, was pursuing me.

I'd longed for a mate of my own for so long, and now that I finally had one, I was in danger of losing her. And it was too much.

All of this was too much. Too much. Too *much*.

Brielle! I cried through our bond, and she startled awake with a gasp.

She immediately pulled back, disorientated and confused. I let

204

her, too busy trying to drag air into my lungs. My chest felt tight. Compressed. *Squeezed.* Like something heavy was crushing it. My heart started to pound, faster and faster and faster until it hurt. Until *everything* hurt.

"Jagger. *Jagger.*"

I could hear her voice, but it sounded miles and miles away.

"Jagger, it's okay. Look at me. Just look at me." She placed her hands on my cheeks and knelt between my legs so that our faces were level. My vision tunneled, darkness threatening to consume me, but I caught a glimpse of green. It was rich and vibrant. *Emerald.* The color of my mate's eyes.

Desperate not to leave her alone, I focused on those beautiful eyes, clinging to them like a lifeline.

Breathe, Jagger. Just breathe, her lilting voice flowed through my mind. It instantly soothed my panic, coaxing the darkness to release its grip on me. The pressure on my chest started to ease, allowing me to breathe again.

When my thundering heart began to slow, I curled forward and buried my face in her neck. We stayed like that for a long time, drawing comfort from each other's scent and touch. She ran her fingers over my short hair, and the strokes were so soothing that I started to drift off.

Unwilling to fall asleep, I reluctantly lifted my head to murmur, "Sorry."

She opened her eyes to search my face. "Don't be. I'm scared too."

I immediately wanted to deny that fear had gotten the better of me, but she'd know I was lying. My days of being a lone wolf were over. I could no longer distance myself. Could no longer hide. Not from her. My thoughts were hers now, and hers were mine.

So I decided to be honest. After everything she'd been through, she deserved nothing less. "Losing you would kill me."

Tears welled in her eyes, but they didn't fall. "After everything we've been through, I don't believe this will be our end. Our pack will find us. I know they will. We just have to survive until they get here."

I didn't respond, determined to stay strong for her. We'd been here for hours, and during that time, I'd managed to think of hundreds of ways the humans could kill us. We were already sleep-deprived, malnourished, and bombarded by pheromones. The full moon was only days away, and I worried what this stress would do to Brielle and her wolf.

Despite my determination to protect her, I didn't know what we were dealing with. We could be hundreds of miles from home for all I knew. These humans had technology I was unfamiliar with, and I'd seen a lot of sophisticated traps and weaponry over the years. They meant business, and I doubted their only goal was to keep us locked up.

"What do you think they'll do to us?" Brielle asked, making me wonder if she'd picked up on my troubled thoughts.

"I don't know, but we have to be ready for anything. We can't let them separate us, or Onyx will lose it again."

She nodded, one of her cheeks dimpling as she murmured, "Guess you shouldn't have cancelled my training lessons."

"No, I shouldn't have."

At the heavy regret in my voice, her dimple disappeared. "I was only teasing, Jagger. You couldn't have known this would happen."

"But I should have been more vigilant. They set a trap for you. They implanted a *tracker*. I should have been more prepared."

"Stop that," she said with a sternness that surprised me. "I love how protective you are, but I'm the one who returned to my parents' place without telling anybody. I knew the risks but went anyway. I just . . . I truly didn't think the hunters would try to capture me again, not after you killed one of them. It's not like I'm special or anything. I mean, as far as supernaturals go, I'm practically a dud."

She said the last part lightly, but I scowled anyway. "You're not a dud. You managed to do something that no one has ever done before. You broke down my walls and tamed Onyx. You *fixed* me. Strength isn't always physical. Yours is soul deep, and I can feel it through our bond, right here." I grabbed one of her hands and pressed it to my heart. "I've never felt strong on the inside before, but I do now. Now that I have you."

She blinked at me, her mouth forming a small O. After a moment, she said in an awed whisper, "Why, Jagger Montgomery, I had no idea you were such a romantic."

Heat rushed to my face, but I managed to whisper back, "Only for you."

She grinned at me. *Grinned.* Even amidst the danger and uncertainty we faced, her inner strength shone through. Drawn to it like a bee to honey, I leaned forward to kiss her. Our lips brushed once. Only once. And I was suddenly starving.

Before I could check myself, I wrapped my free hand around her delicate throat in a possessive hold and deepened the kiss. She melted, *melted* against me, opening her mouth to allow me entrance. My tongue plunged inside to ravenously taste her, and just like that, I was drowning. Drowning in her. Desperate for more. *Always* desperate for more.

She whimpered into my mouth and returned my kisses, so eager for me that my body roared awake once more. Within seconds, we were tangled around each other, her legs straddling my waist and our hands feverishly roving over every inch of skin we could find. Her white gown landed in a heap on the floor, and I palmed her breasts before pinching one of her nipples. She arched against me with a gasp, and the action pressed her core to my swollen cock. My mind emptied, and I groaned, reaching down to cup her backside and grind her against me.

Even as I did, even as pleasure splintered my vision, I managed to pant, "We can't. I have to . . . be ready."

"You are," she panted back, rubbing her pussy against my manhood. "*Very* ready."

I groaned again, overcome with lust for her. "They could be watching."

"Let them. I don't freaking care right now."

Oh God. If *she* didn't care, then why the hell should I?

"They'll think we're animals."

She laughed. *Laughed* at my comment. Throwing her head back to release a throaty chuckle that nearly made me come. "We *are* animals," she shouted at the ceiling. "Do you hear that, you bastards? We're animals having *sex*, so come watch the show like the perverts you are!"

When she brought her face down again, she found me staring at her in awe. "That mouth," I huskily said, stretching my thumb up to skate it over her bottom lip. "That sinfully delicious *mouth*."

I kissed her again without restraint, done trying to stop this. Her energy was fueling mine, making my waning strength return. If we had a hidden audience, so be it. They'd only see two passionate creatures unwilling to let anyone dictate their actions. They might have imprisoned us, but our bodies were still free to make love.

So that's what we did.

Finding her slick entrance, I thrust inside her. As she sank on top of me with a sigh, I closed my eyes and groaned out my relief, instantly feeling better. Being surrounded by her tight warmth felt like coming home. I was transported to a safe place far from this prison, a place where only she and I existed. Her hips kept time with my thrusts, and within seconds, we were both racing toward the finish line, our mutual pleasure flooding the soulmate bond.

She came first, her walls squeezing me relentlessly as she screamed out her release. I pushed her down on top of me until we were fully one, until not even a millimeter separated us. Only then did I let my own orgasm barrel through me, loudly bellowing out my release inside her.

My knot quickly swelled and locked us together, something I couldn't control while she was still in heat. I reached down and found her clit, rubbing it until another orgasm trembled through her. Her spasming walls milked another release from me, and I jetted more sperm inside her.

After the fifth orgasm, she slumped against me and sighed, "I love you."

I gathered her close, feeling satiated in a way I'd never felt before. There was so much I still wanted to do to her, do *with* her. So much life I wanted us both to live. But if this was to be my end, at least I got to spend it with her. My soulmate. Fully and completely without any regrets.

"I love you, too," I told her, meaning the words to the deepest depths of my soul.

About an hour later, the peaceful moment was destroyed by a high-pitched whine. It blasted my eardrums, sending Onyx into a panicked frenzy.

The door burst open, and the room erupted into chaos.

CHAPTER 26

BRIELLE

If it wasn't for the frequency device throwing off his equilibrium and driving Onyx crazy, Jagger could have defeated the armored men pouring into our cell.

Even disorientated with blood trickling from his ears, he managed to injure several of them before it all came to a screeching halt.

"Stop!" one of the men barked, and Jagger immediately froze.

I didn't understand why at first, but when I managed to lift my aching head, I found several guns trained on . . .

Me.

"Submit, or we'll kill her," the man ordered Jagger, making my blood run cold. "We'll kill your mate."

Despite the pain splitting my skull from the high frequency, I could hear Onyx's whines in my head and Jagger's panic flooding our bond. I wanted to reassure them somehow, to encourage them to keep fighting, but I couldn't. I was too scared. Too *weak*. If they were threatening to kill me, then the guns currently trained on me weren't loaded with tranquilizer darts. They were loaded with bullets. *Silver* ones.

I thought I'd been ready to face death again, but now that it was staring me down, I wanted nothing more than to live. To start my future with Jagger. To build a family. I couldn't die now. I *refused* to. There had to be a way out of this mess, but it wasn't this particular moment.

Jagger needed to submit. Only . . . I didn't know if he could.

His whole body was trembling, pain and rage making his eyes flare a bright yellow. But even though he didn't show it, I could feel how utterly terrified he was. Terrified of *losing* me. Our eyes met, and in that brief moment, I knew he'd made a decision. Sorrow filled me as my strong and proud mate dropped to his knees and submitted to the humans.

Submitted for *me*.

Onyx began to howl, bewildered by Jagger's submission. Jagger didn't say a word to his familiar, gritting his teeth as he struggled to keep him at bay.

Oh, Jagger, I quietly sobbed through our bond, unable to stop my tears from falling as two men came up behind him and yanked his arms back to clamp restraints on his wrists.

Two more men did the same to me, roughly shoving my wrists into silver-coated shackles. Fresh pain lit up my body, and Onyx's howls turned to fury.

It's okay, Onyx, I managed to say through our connection, but my words were anything but convincing. Nothing about this was okay, and my own wolf began to stir in response to my stress.

No, no, no, I whimpered to her. *It's not time.*

She ignored me, her survival instinct heating up my insides. Sweat immediately dampened my skin and soaked through the hospital gown I'd put back on. The men behind me didn't notice, too busy dragging me to my feet. The high-frequency noise continued to blare, making it hard to stand as the men forced me toward the door.

I craned my neck around, feeling a little better when I saw that Jagger was right behind me. One of the men holding me shoved my shoulder, causing me to stumble into the hallway. A fierce growl rumbled through the air, and several men shouted at Jagger to back down.

He did, but his anger was palpable, further adding to the heat engulfing my body. As the men marched us down the hall, my legs threatened to give out on me. I refused to fall, knowing that Jagger needed me. He would lose it if I passed out, and I couldn't let that happen.

I'm fine, I told him, willing it to be true.

No, you're not, he said. *You're in pain, and I can sense your wolf freaking out. And if that man shoves you one more time, I'm going to kill him.*

I didn't respond, too miserable to deny how not fine I was. The piercing high frequency wouldn't let up, following us down the hall to a reinforced sliding door. One of the men placed his hand on a scanner, and the door slid open to reveal another long hallway lined with what I could only guess were more holding cells.

We passed through that hallway too, tortured by the screeching frequency the entire way. Blood was dripping from my ears and onto my white frock, dampening the fabric even more. I so desperately wanted to cover my ears, but the shackles burning my wrists kept my hands firmly behind me.

More than once, I heard a pained cry or moan come from the doors we passed. There were more prisoners like us. More *supernaturals*. What were they doing with them? What were they doing with *us*?

My wolf pushed at the constraints of my body, desperate to escape this situation before it got worse. I curled forward under the strain, and the men holding me roughly yanked on my arms.

A small cry left me, and that was all it took.

With a bellow, Jagger lunged forward and plowed into them,

using his body to knock both men down. I staggered sideways but caught myself on the wall, looking back just as a sea of armored men descended on Jagger.

"No!" I screamed, watching in horror as they tackled him to the ground and began to kick and dart and zap him. I moved forward, frantic to stop them, but an arm snagged my waist and dragged me back, back, back. Beady Eyes had me, and when I saw that he was heading for another slider door, taking me farther and farther away from Jagger, true panic set in. "Jagger!"

Realizing that they were about to separate us, Jagger bellowed out another roar, one that Onyx joined in on. The sound was deafening in its intensity, cutting through the frequency and shuddering through my bones.

"I yield!" he shouted, his gaze locked on me as Beady Eyes reached the door and slammed his palm on the scanner. The men holding him down stopped attacking but kept their weapons trained on him, ready to fight at the slightest sign of aggression. As the door slid open, Jagger said, "Keep us together, and I won't fight again."

I held my breath, certain they wouldn't listen to him. After a tense-filled moment, one of them kicked his side and barked, "Fight again, and she *dies*, animal. Got it?"

Jagger didn't so much as wince, even as I felt his pain through our bond. Anger flooded my body, but it wasn't his this time. It ripped through me so violently that my wolf went wild. She clawed at my insides, determined to defend her mate. I almost encouraged her onward, images of her tearing into the men racing through my mind.

Settle, wolf, Jagger spoke into my roiling mind, his gaze remaining steady on mine as he calmly said out loud, "Yes, sir."

The man grunted and gestured for his comrades to let him up. After Jagger was on his feet again, we passed through the door and into a lobby area. Ahead was another sliding door, only this one looked like an elevator. As the door behind us closed, the blaring high frequency finally switched off. I nearly collapsed in relief, instantly feeling better despite the silver shackles still burning my wrists and slowly poisoning me.

When the elevator doors opened moments later, I shared a quick look with Jagger. This was our escape route. Probably the only one. If we were going to get out of here, this might be the only chance we had.

"Try anything, and she gets it," Beady Eyes hissed from just behind me, poking my side with his electrical prod.

Jagger stiffened all over, fresh anger pulsing through our bond. Yet when he raised his eyes to take in the burly man, he slowly lowered them again with a small nod.

This might be our only chance, I inwardly said to him, alarmed at how quickly he submitted. This wasn't him. This wasn't him at *all*.

He didn't respond, and the electrical prod digging into my side nudged me forward. I entered the large elevator and was soon joined by Jagger and a dozen armored men. We were packed in like sardines, yet each of them managed to keep their weapons trained on me or Jagger.

Jagger, speak to me, I pleaded with him, worried that he'd given up. Onyx whined inside my mind as if he was worried too.

My wolf continued to restlessly stir, feeling claustrophobic as the steel box jolted into motion and began to ascend. At least we weren't going down. My instincts sensed that we were underground, which would make escaping that much harder. Above ground gave us a much greater chance. But Jagger seemed frozen, and I knew I couldn't escape this place without his help.

As the elevator slowed to a stop and began to open again,

desperation filled me, and I barked at him through our bond, *Jagger, don't you dare disappear on me. I need you!*

Only when the men started to file out, prodding at us to follow, did he finally reply, *I'm right here, Brielle. I won't leave you, but I can't lose you either. Be patient. Stay strong. We can get through this together.*

Realizing that he didn't plan to escape, not yet anyway, my stomach gave a sickening lurch. *But what if they're about to kill us?*

If that was their only goal, we'd be dead already. They want us for something, and we're going to find out what that something is. Then we're going to destroy them.

His voice was deadly calm and laced with so much certainty that some of my panic faded. I could be patient. It was the staying strong part that worried me. Mentally, I wasn't in too bad of shape, but my physical strength was at an all time low.

Take some of mine. Take all you need, Jagger said, clearly having heard my thoughts.

How? I asked as the men opened another slider door.

Through the soulmate bond. Emotions and thoughts aren't the only things we can share. Here, let me show you.

A sudden rush of strength filled my body, and I audibly gasped.

Beady Eyes grabbed one of my arms to forcibly guide me through the doorway, but I didn't stumble this time. I noticeably felt stronger, like I could punt-kick Beady Eyes through a wall. The urge to do it trembled through me, but I tamped down the feeling.

Jagger had sacrificed some of his strength for me. The least I could do was practice some patience.

Better? Jagger asked.

Yes, I gratefully replied, then added, *But I don't want you to weaken yourself for me. If anyone's getting out of here alive, it'll be you.*

Don't talk that way, he said, a slight edge hardening his voice. *I won't let my mate die in this hellhole.*

Before I could respond, we stepped into a massive room, and my ability to speak promptly vanished. The space was divided into at least a dozen smaller rooms sectioned off by glass walls. The rooms contained contraptions, each one more horrific than the last. Several had steel restraint chairs or tables bolted to the floor, while others had glass incubators big enough to hold a body. There were MRI machines and all manner of expensive surgical equipment, and high above on the room's far side was a large glass pane window spanning the entire wall. But it was what I saw *behind* that glass window that sent a shiver of dread down my spine.

Humans dressed in white lab coats—doctors, *scientists*—were peering down at me and Jagger.

It was the look in their eyes—clinical yet fascinated at the same time—that clued me in to what was happening here.

This was an experimentation chamber. A place to test subjects. And their current subjects were *us*.

CHAPTER 27

JAGGER

They're going to experiment on us, Jagger.

The fear in Brielle's voice was nearly my undoing. The need to protect her was already pounding through my blood, and seeing how frightened she was almost shoved me over the edge. But the guns still trained on her kept me from reacting.

One bullet. One silver bullet to the heart was all it would take to kill her. I couldn't stop them all from shooting her. Not like this. I had to wait, even if that meant allowing them to hurt her. It would gut me. It would tear out my heart and obliterate my soul, but I couldn't save her from this just yet.

Before I could soothe Brielle with false comfort, a feminine voice over a loudspeaker said, "Secure the pair in chamber one. I'll be down shortly."

The guards immediately marched us toward a glass partitioned-off room that held two chairs with restraints. The second we were inside the room and a guard began to remove my shackles, I went deathly still. So did Onyx.

As if sensing the shift in my demeanor, several of the guards cocked their guns and trained them on Brielle once more.

The man holding her arm jerked her close, resting the tip of his electrical prod against her cheek before saying, "I have it on maximum voltage. It would be a shame to burn a hole through this pretty face."

The threat had the desired effect, and I immediately backed

down. Brielle just stared at me, her green eyes wide with fright. Onyx, on the other hand, howled in frustration when the shackles fell away and I didn't react.

Settle, I rumbled to him, keeping him locked down as best I could. *It's not the right time.*

They had us by the balls, and one false move could put Brielle's life in jeopardy. As much as it killed me to submit to these evil bastards, I couldn't risk Brielle.

Two of the guards grabbed my freed arms and shoved me into one of the chairs. I continued to watch Brielle, seeing the color drain from her face as the men began to strap down my arms and legs. When they finished securing a wide strap over my chest, they stepped back and turned to Brielle.

Her panic frantically fluttered through our bond as they proceeded to unshackle her, forcing her down into the remaining chair.

Keep your eyes on me, beautiful, I said to her, pushing a dose of calm toward her through our bond. *I'm here. I'm right here, and I'm not going anywhere.*

Tears slid down her pale cheeks, but she didn't struggle as they strapped her body to the chair. Once they were finished, the man who'd threatened to hurt her stepped forward with a syringe in hand. He quickly jabbed the needle into her neck, and she released a startled yelp. Pain and weakness stole through our bond, and I jerked against my restraints with a growl. The sneering man turned to me next, another syringe appearing in his hand.

"Hold the beast's head down," he ordered a guard, who stepped forward to grab my head and press it back against the chair. Onyx went wild, and I bared my teeth at the man approaching with the menacing needle. Pausing for a moment to leer down at me, he savagely plunged the needle into my neck. "There," he said, yanking the needle out with a victorious smirk. "Let's see how tough you are now, Cujo."

Fire immediately streaked through my veins, followed by a heaviness that threatened to sap me of my remaining strength. Still, I lifted my gaze to the human male's and locked him in a fierce stare. His beady little eyes held mine for a few moments, then began to waver. I stared harder, refusing to back down. After another few moments, he couldn't hold it any longer and dropped his gaze.

Realizing I'd just bested him, he swore colorfully and whipped out his prod, jabbing it into my side. Fresh pain ripped through my body, and Brielle screamed, begging him to stop. The man just laughed and continued to pump me full of electricity, clearly bent on breaking me. I clenched my jaw, refusing to make a sound. I'd submitted for Brielle's sake, but I wouldn't give this bastard the satisfaction he so desperately wanted.

After a solid minute of this torture, a female voice snapped, "Mr. Coolidge! Stop that at once."

The man torturing me—presumably Mr. Coolidge—reluctantly switched off his electrical prod. Still leering down at me, he testily replied to the woman, "My job is to keep these animals in line, Dr. Sloane."

"You were hired to capture them and keep them from escaping, not *torture* them. Now, I need you and your men to leave this chamber so I can assess my new subjects."

Giving me one last dark look, Mr. Coolidge whirled and exited the room, followed by the other men. When they were gone, a woman pushed forward. The first thing I noticed was the wheelchair she sat in. She wheeled forward independently, her upper half working just fine. It was her legs I glimpsed through the white labcoat she wore that weren't functioning. The loose blue slacks couldn't hide how thin they were, their muscle mass depleted from lack of use.

"It's not polite to stare, you know," the woman said, and my gaze rose to her face. She was maybe a handful of years older than me, pretty with blonde hair pulled back into a low bun. Black-rimmed glasses framed her blue eyes, eyes that openly conveyed her curiosity. When I didn't respond, a faint smile tilted her lips. "Then again, I came down here to stare at you, so we'll call it even."

Another female in blue scrubs suddenly bustled inside the chamber wheeling a supply cart. Her brown eyes met mine for a brief second, then nervously flicked away.

"Give them extra fluids, Miss Tindale," Dr. Sloane said. "I can't properly assess them when they're this malnourished and dehydrated."

"Yes, Dr. Sloane," Miss Tindale hastily replied, parking her cart beside Brielle. She focused on her first, situating an IV pole near her head that already held a few bags of fluids. I tracked her every move, watching as her trembling hands prepared to inject a needle into Brielle's arm. A quiet growl left me, and the girl flinched, dropping the needle.

"For heavens' sake, pull yourself together, Miss Tindale," Dr. Sloane said with an exasperated sigh. "I know you're new here, but he's not going to scratch or bite you. At least not while he's drugged and restrained like this."

"Yes, Dr. Sloane," the girl whispered and grabbed a fresh needle from the cart.

As she prepared to inject it, Brielle said, "You don't have to do this." The girl startled again, flicking her wide eyes up to Brielle's. "I know you're scared of us," Brielle went on, her tone calm and soothing, "but we're scared too. I was human like you just last year.

The treatment we've endured here is inhumane, and we just want to go home."

The girl hesitated, drawn to Brielle's empathic nature like everyone else who met her. Her hands stopped shaking, her expression slightly softening.

"*Miss Tindale*," Dr. Sloane snapped, making the girl jump again. "Muzzle the female and get on with your work. If you can't do what needs to be done, I'll be forced to let you go."

The girl swiftly bobbed her head and placed the needle on the cart to grab something else. It had two wide straps and connecting them together was what looked like a ball made of steel. Positioning herself behind Brielle's chair, she brought the contraption down level with Brielle's mouth and pulled the straps back. The move forced Brielle's mouth open, and the steel ball settled between her teeth as the assistant tightly secured the straps behind her head.

A garbling sound left Brielle as she tried to spit out the ball, but the straps kept it firmly in place. Rage leaked through my bloodstream, the sight of her muzzled almost more than I could bear. Tightly fisting my hands, I slowly swung my gaze back to Dr. Sloane. Now that her assistant was doing her job, she'd turned her attention to me again—rather, my body. Unlike Brielle, they hadn't bothered to put clothes on me. In my shifted state, no clothing would have fitted me anyway.

The doctor's stare wasn't sexual but purely clinical as she studied my naked form. I was a specimen to her, nothing more. She focused on my legs for an extra long beat, taking in their definition, their strength. Something that looked a lot like greed sparked in her eyes, there and gone again in a blink.

"So," she said, lifting her gaze back to mine. "I'm sure you're wondering why you're here, but first, I'd like confirmation that the female is your mate and that you are indeed a werewolf hybrid."

I didn't respond, and her lips thinned.

"I'll learn what I need to know whether you answer or not, but it'll be a lot less stressful for you both if you cooperate."

"You mean less painful?" I finally spoke, seeing the truth of it in her eyes.

"Yes, less painful. I don't enjoy inflicting pain on my subjects, so if you answer my questions, I'll have fewer invasive tests to run."

"What kind of tests?"

She gave me a stern look. "I can see that you're an alpha male, but I'm the one leading this conversation, not you. Now, I'll ask you again. Is the female your mate?"

I stared at her for a long moment, my expression blank. She stared right back, her gaze unyielding. She had guts, I'd give her that, but her body was frail. When the time was right, there was nothing she could do to stop me. No matter what she knew about me, no matter what tests she performed, I would get us out of here soon enough.

"Yes," I finally replied, and her lips tilted into a pleased smile.

"I assumed so based on the amount of sex you two had on the containment level. Is she pregnant?"

All the blood drained from my face. Alarm flickered through our bond, but I didn't have any calm to share with Brielle this time.

Dr. Sloane studied us both thoughtfully before saying to me, "I know you're highly protective of your mate. You've killed two of my hired men and injured several more in your attempts to shield her from them. Our containment level was built to restrain even the strongest supernaturals, but you nearly compromised one of the chambers in your need to protect your mate. If human males were *half* that protective of their mates, maybe I'd still be married." She paused, then added, "Although I admire your efforts to keep her safe, the best way you can do that now is by cooperating. The more you resist, the more she will suffer."

I briefly glanced at Brielle, taking in the torture device they called a muzzle and the needle now embedded in her arm that was hooked up to an IV bag. The assistant was currently prepping Brielle's stomach to insert a feeding tube, and I tore my gaze away before I could witness the needle penetrate her flesh.

Struggling to remain calm, I took a moment to collect myself before replying, "I don't know."

"You don't know what?"

I fixed my gaze on Dr. Sloane and slowly enunciated, "I don't know if she's pregnant."

"No matter," she said with a slight shrug. "If she is, we can easily take care of it."

At the implication, the *threat*, my vision bled red.

Brielle garbled out a sound that resembled a sob, and I lost it. Before I could stop myself, I was fighting against my restraints and roaring, "Don't touch her! *Don't touch her!*"

Onyx immediately responded to my fury, rising up so swiftly that black fur erupted over my arms and legs. An unearthly bellow exploded from me, and Dr. Sloane's eyes widened. Not in fear but in fascination. In *excitement*.

"Miss Tindale, the sedative. The *sedative*," she yelled over my bellowing.

A loud metallic *crash* reached my ears as if the supply cart had just fallen over, followed by a panicked cry. I strained against the chest strap, only needing a few more inches of leverage. My claws shot out, scraping against the steel chair.

Save mate, save mate, save mate.

"Miss Tindale!"

The chest strap broke, and I strained forward, so close to freedom. So close to saving my mate. All I needed to do was—

Several sharp pops reported through the air, and I was suddenly on fire. I focused on the gun now in Dr. Sloane's hand, then down to the darts sticking out of my chest. With another growl, I strained against the steel bands around my arms.

Pop, pop, pop.

More darts. More fire.

My body grew impossibly heavy, and I slumped back against the chair. The last thing I heard before losing consciousness was Brielle's voice in my mind, screaming my name.

CHAPTER 28

BRIELLE

It was the worst feeling in the world being this close to Jagger but unable to reach him.

He was slumped in the chair beside mine, trussed up like a Thanksgiving turkey with tubes and wires attached all over his body. Shortly after the tranquilizer darts had forced him under, Miss Tindale had been dismissed. Dr. Sloane was clearly disappointed with her assistant and had replaced her with another. The new assistant was coldly methodical as she pulled the darts from Jagger's chest and hooked him up to an IV pole.

She'd done this before, that much was certain, and her detached demeanor snuffed out any hope I had of gaining her sympathy. A new chest strap was brought in, along with a strap for Jagger's neck. While two of the armored guards secured Jagger's upper half to the chair once more, three humans in white lab coats joined Dr. Sloane—her colleagues, by the looks of them. Her tone changed when she spoke to them, more formal and less demanding.

After a few moments of listening to them converse, it became clear she was their superior, and my hope dwindled once more. If Dr. Sloane was in charge of this operation, we had little chance of convincing any of these humans to set us free. She might be confined to a wheelchair, but every word she uttered dripped with authority.

"You saw the way he started to shift. He's the one we've been looking for," she was saying to the woman and two men standing around her.

Ever since Jagger had partially shifted, Dr. Sloane's face had been a mask of excitement. The more excited she became, the more panicked I felt. A scientist faced with an anomaly was like a kid in a candy store. I was the same with a particularly challenging math problem. The need to solve it took over, and I wouldn't stop until I had the answer.

"What about the female?" one of the men asked, briefly glancing at me. Up until now, none of the doctors had seemed to notice me. All eyes had been on Jagger's unconscious form.

At his question, Dr. Sloane finally looked at me and said, "She's his mate, that much is certain. There have been no signs of her being a hybrid, though."

"Unfortunate," the other female doctor replied.

"Yes, it is, but she could still be useful. The male is highly responsive to her and will probably cooperate best with our tests if she's near."

"But what if she's pregnant?" the other male doctor asked.

"They were mating in the barn when the men found them, and then again in their containment chamber, so chances of that are high. Once we test her estrogen levels, we'll probably find them heightened. As we've learned, female werewolves in heat are very fertile. It drives the males wild, which would explain why he's been so aggressive. If she's pregnant, his protective instincts will become even more unmanageable, so we'll have to terminate it immediately."

"No!" I tried to scream, but all that came out was a pathetic garbling sound, the steel ball in my mouth keeping my words at bay. Tears rolled down my cheeks, but the doctors barely noticed them. They continued their conversation as if I wasn't intelligent enough to understand it, as if I was merely an animal to be experimented on.

"I want to begin testing right away," Dr. Sloane went on, her gaze lifting to her colleagues once more. "We've been at this too long to waste any more time. Focus all your efforts on the male. He's the key to perfecting our formula."

Tears continued to drip down my face as the meeting ended, the doctors scattering in different directions. The two guards left the chamber and even the assistant bustled out, leaving me alone with Dr. Sloane. She pulled a tablet from a bag strapped to the back of her wheelchair, the same bag that had contained her tranquilizer gun. The woman might be physically impaired, but she didn't let that get in her way.

If I didn't hate her so much, I might actually admire her. She was pursuing her dreams unapologetically, refusing to give up despite her limitations. But she was trying to take *my* dreams away, and I wanted nothing more than to stop her by any means necessary.

I'd underestimated myself for so long, but now that someone I loved needed me, now that my *mate* needed me, I felt stronger. Maybe not physically, but I was determined to get us out of here. All eyes were on Jagger, and maybe that was to my advantage. They'd dismissed me. *Underestimated* me. And I needed it to stay that way.

"I should thank you," Dr. Sloane suddenly said. Her gaze was glued to the tablet in her hands, but the remark was directed at me— or so I assumed, since I was the only other conscious being in the room. "We've been testing on werewolves for almost a decade and never once stumbled across a hybrid. We only just learned about them last year through our source in the Supernatural Containment Agency. I'm sure you've heard of the organization?"

She flicked her eyes up to mine but looked down again as if she didn't expect me to answer.

Tapping on her tablet for a moment, she went on, "The SCA

used to partner with us in our research efforts, but that all changed when they instated a *warlock* as one of their leaders. He thought our tests weren't humane and encouraged the agency to dissolve our partnership. My team fell apart, discouraged by the lack of funding and resources. If it wasn't for my one faithful source still working in the SCA, I might have lost all hope."

She paused in her typing to rest her gaze on Jagger's unconscious form before continuing, "Once I knew of the hybrids' existence, everything changed. I immediately started campaigning, gathering investors and reinstating my team. Once we'd secured a building that suited our needs, I hired mercenaries to begin the hunt for hybrids. We already knew that New England was a hotspot for supernaturals, but our SCA source didn't have information on where exactly the hybrids lived. We were working in the dark, tapping into multiple sources that might provide leads. Mental institutions were surprisingly helpful. We picked up a few werewolves that way before intercepting the call about you."

She swung her gaze back to me. "The problem is that without further testing, we can't confirm if the werewolves are hybrids or not, so we have to collect them all. But my hired men weren't prepared to face an *actual* hybrid the night they were sent to retrieve you. After what happened, we almost lost hope of finding you again. Your current place of residence is sealed to the public, and even my SCA source couldn't locate you. I thought for sure the little trap my men rigged up at your childhood home wouldn't work, but thank goodness it did. You helped us secure our first hybrid, and I'm ever so grateful."

My throat sealed shut. She was thanking me. *Thanking* me for helping them capture Jagger. Not only that, it was becoming more and more clear that she didn't need me. I'd simply been a means to an end, a way to get what she *really* wanted.

A werewolf hybrid.

"Why?" I tried to ask around the steel ball.

She lifted an eyebrow. "Why werewolf hybrids?"

I nodded.

She studied me thoughtfully before answering, "My mother was a brilliant scientist and at the height of her career when she was diagnosed with multiple sclerosis. She was the strongest woman I knew, but the MS destroyed her body and mind, and she was forced into a care facility. When I was diagnosed with MS at the age of twenty, I swore to myself I wouldn't become her. I dedicated my life to science and finding a cure, even when my legs gave out on me.

"I kept searching until, as luck would have it, I discovered the existence of supernaturals," she went on, excitement sparking in her eyes once more. "The discovery opened up a whole new world of possibilities for me, and I put everything into finding out what makes them tick, especially werewolves. They're strong, fast healing, and immune to human disease. If I could isolate those traits and splice them with human genes, then perhaps I could find a cure not only for MS but for *all* diseases."

Some of that excitement abruptly faded, replaced with frustration.

"But when the human trials began, each and every subject reacted the same way to my serum and were transformed into werewolves. Despite my best efforts, I couldn't remove the toxin that forces werewolves into animal form during the full moon. I tried for years to no avail and had all but given up, but then I heard about hybrids and their ability to shift at will."

At the mention of hybrids, her excitement returned in full force.

"Even if I can't remove the toxin that turns them into an animal, their ability to control the transformation process changes everything.

Humans with incurable diseases would *jump* at the chance to have the kind of power a werewolf hybrid has, even if that means living with the toxin's effects. They could walk again, talk again, *think* again. Their strength would return, and they would be free to live their lives as fully as possible. This cure could save thousands, *millions*, and your mate could be a part of that. You said you were human once, so you know how groundbreaking a discovery like this would be to the human race. Certainly you understand why I have to do this."

I didn't respond, not that I could even if I wanted to—which I didn't. If she wanted my approval, my *support* for torturing werewolves, she wouldn't get it. I knew all about feeling broken and wanting to fix myself, but no cure could justify treating others like this.

Besides, there was a huge flaw to her plan. It was the celestial spirit residing *inside* a hybrid that gave them their magical abilities and superior strength, allowing them to shift whenever they wanted. Without that spirit, they were the same as any other werewolf, including their DNA.

Injecting a human with hybrid blood wouldn't transform them into a hybrid. It would simply turn them into a werewolf, the kind that shifted with the full moon every month.

Not that I would tell her that. If Dr. Sloane knew the truth, she would have no more need for me *or* Jagger. And if she no longer needed us, I heavily doubted she would just set us free. More than likely, we'd be tossed into a cage and forgotten about. Or worse— killed.

No way was I helping this woman destroy our lives more than she already had.

When all I did was stare at her coolly, she resumed tapping on her tablet, completely unfazed. After a few minutes, the wolf within me stirred, growing increasingly restless the longer we were tied down. The full moon wasn't for a couple more days, but just like last month, she didn't seem to care. Other than when Jagger had tied me up in the barn, being subdued *terrified* her, and now that he wasn't awake to comfort me, she was starting to freak out.

Within minutes, I was drenched in sweat, visibly trembling from the heatwaves pounding through my body. A buzzing noise reached my ears, and Dr. Sloane paused to fish a cellphone from her labcoat pocket.

"What is it, Dr. Fenway?" she distractedly asked, still tapping on her tablet.

"The female's heart rate and oxygen levels have increased significantly," a male voice said through the phone's speaker. "Are you sure she's not a hybrid?"

At that, Dr. Sloane's eyes snapped back to me. One look and her expression changed from disinterest to intrigue.

My stomach dropped. Crap. *Crap.* If she started testing me, my wolf was going to lose it. I could barely breathe, let alone keep a scared wolf at bay. The longer Dr. Sloane stared at me, the more she panicked. Sweat practically poured down my face as she thrashed inside me, desperate to claw her way out and escape whatever the scientist had in store for us.

I clamped my teeth down on the steel ball, swallowing a pained whimper. *Settle*, I pleaded with my wolf, with *myself*.

If I started to shift, I was done for. And what would happen to Jagger if I died? Our bond would unravel, would break. For *real* this time. How would he cope? How would *Onyx* cope?

Jagger, wake up. Wake up! I silently begged him, unable to stop more tears from falling. *I need you!*

Silence.

231

Still staring at me with renewed interest, Dr. Sloane put away her devices and grabbed the wheels of her chair to move toward me. My heart started to pound, faster and faster and faster. I couldn't stop it. Couldn't *control* it.

Jagger, please. Please, wake up! Onyx? Onyx!

Dr. Sloane pulled up beside me and watched my struggle for several moments, her eyes brightening shrewdly with each passing second. "Regular werewolves can't transform without the full moon's aid," she quietly observed, tapping her chin lightly. "Yet you are exhibiting all the signs of a werewolf about to shift. Are you a hybrid, too?"

I shook my head, and she frowned.

"Lying will only force me to take more tests. *Painful* ones. Now, answer me honestly. Are you a hybrid?"

I shook my head again. Her scowl deepened.

"Fine. If that's how you want to play this, then you give me no choice." Whirling her chair around, she barked, "Mr. Coolidge!"

My heart practically beat out of my chest when the beady-eyed man reappeared and strode back inside the glass room.

"Yes, Dr. Sloane?" he said, raking his gaze over me in a condescending manner.

"The female might be a hybrid. I need you to force her wolf out."

Terror gripped me.

"Now?" he asked in surprise.

"Now," she impatiently replied. "If she breaks free of the chair, I'll tranquilize her."

A sadistic excitement flashed in the man's eyes, and when he pulled out his electrical prod, my wolf went wild. Pain lit up my body, my bones vibrating as she desperately tried to gain control.

Jagger! JAGGER!

I was losing the battle, my control over her slipping, slipping. She was too scared. *I* was too scared. I needed to defend myself, but I couldn't do it like this. I needed *her*, and she readily answered my unspoken call, a call I could no longer keep silent.

Three steps and Mr. Coolidge was by my side. One swift move and the sharp prod was pressed to my neck.

Jagger, please!

Electricity jolted through my body, so powerful and agonizing that I couldn't hold on any longer. My wolf surged up and took control. When I felt the first bone break, the only thing I could do was scream.

CHAPTER 29

JAGGER

Agony. Desperation. *Fear.*

The powerful mix of emotions pulsating through the soulmate bond forced me awake once more. I jerked my eyes open, my instincts screaming that Brielle was in danger. Her own screams ricocheted through my mind and blasted my ears, growing in desperation with each passing second.

When I found her half-shifted in the chair beside me, her arms and legs covered in rich brown fur, panic flooded me. Onyx reared up, ripped awake by the ensuing chaos. He immediately came to my aid, infusing his strength into my muscles.

"Brielle!" I shouted over her screams, struggling to break free of my restraints. Another of her bones cracked, then another and another, painfully molding her body into that of a wolf's. Her ribcage expanded, and the strap over her chest snapped. "Brielle, *no!* Fight it!"

Blinding agony streaked through our bond, and she screamed again, her body convulsing against the chair. Onyx noticed the man electrocuting her a split second before I did. He howled in fury, and I let the sound erupt from my mouth. Unholy rage burned away the remaining sedative in my blood, filling me with a strength that surprised even me.

In one great heave, I exploded off the chair, my arms and legs partially shifting as I tore the restraints, tubes, and wires from my body. Even as I did, I watched in horror as Brielle's face transformed into her wolf's, her screams morphing into agonized howls. Unable to contain her shifting form, the muzzle snapped in two, along with her arm and leg restraints. Fully wolf now, she released a pitiful whine before tumbling off the chair and hitting the floor.

"NO!" I roared, already feeling the life drain out of her. It happened so swiftly that I couldn't move, couldn't *think*.

Her yellow wolf eyes met mine for one brief moment, then slowly rolled shut. She was dying. *Dying*. I could feel our bond flickering, feel it *fading* as her heart and breathing started to slow.

Open your eyes for me, beautiful, I pleaded with her through our weakening bond. *Brielle? Brielle!*

Save mate, save mate, save mate, Onyx whimpered, his pain melding with mine.

Helplessness flooded me, but something else did too. A feeling. A *knowing* that tugged at my very soul, an instinct ancient as time itself.

Not questioning it, I gathered all the strength raging inside me and shoved it through our bond. Shoved and shoved until it all went to *her*. To my beautiful mate. Every last drop. Realizing what I was doing, Onyx joined in, helping me speed up the process even more. The energy left me in a violent rush, so forcefully that I fell to my knees, unable to carry my weight.

Live. LIVE! I bellowed into Brielle's mind, willing my strength to save her. Soulmate bonds were powerful, the most powerful bond that existed, and I was calling on it now. *Begging* it to transfer my life force into her.

She had to live. She *had* to. I couldn't exist without her, and if that meant giving up my life so that she could live, then so be it.

I kept shoving, kept begging, giving all that I was to Brielle until darkness clouded my vision. I landed hard on the floor, my limbs growing impossibly heavy. Everything grew faint—my heartbeats, my connection with Onyx, the soulmate bond. I reached for Brielle, needing to touch her one last time. Needing to feel, to *know* she was still alive.

Before I could reach her, the last of my strength faded and the world went dark.

CHAPTER 30

BRIELLE

I only remembered flashes. Brief glimpses that felt like a dream.

Like a nightmare.

There was pain as my bones snapped. Terror as my wolf broke free of her cage. Sorrow as death rose up to claim me. I thought that would be the end. It should have been. And yet . . .

More images came to me. Memories. Shocking ones. *Horrific* ones.

Shattered glass everywhere. And blood. So much blood. It painted the white floor a garish red, pooling darkly beneath a male body. A body covered in armor with the helmet missing. The face was unrecognizable, mutilated so violently that it no longer looked human. But the electrical prod lying beside him told me everything I needed to know.

It was Mr. Coolidge. He was dead.

Bloody prints surrounded his body, and with growing horror, I realized who they belonged to.

Me.

Had I . . . had I killed him?

My mind immediately tried to reject the idea, but deep down, I knew that I had. I'd killed him. I'd killed a *human*.

My stomach heaved, but when I turned my head to throw up, nothing happened. My body wouldn't listen. It was running on autopilot. No, on *instinct*. I felt oddly detached from it yet perfectly aware of its every move, like a backseat driver unable to reach the steering wheel.

I'd felt this way before. *Many* times. Every time that I'd—

Oh, no. No! I'd shifted. I'd shifted into my *wolf*. She was racing through the dark woods at full speed, plowing through the snow and any obstacle that stood in her way. But how? I couldn't feel the pull of the full moon. This shouldn't be possible. I should be *dead* right now.

And where was Jagger? Where was my *mate*?

I quickly sifted through the horrific memories and found one of him on that same blood-spattered floor, his face ashen and still. *Too* still. Was he . . . was he—?

No. I couldn't say it. Couldn't *think* it.

He wasn't. He *couldn't*.

We have to go back! I screamed at my wolf, frantically trying to wrestle back control. How had this happened? How was I still alive, and how had my wolf escaped? Why did she *leave* him there? *How could you? How could you!?*

She ignored my screams, ignored my cries. Ignored everything except the instinct singing in her bones, demanding she keep going.

Home, home, home, it chanted, so incessantly that I knew exactly where she was headed. Not to my parents but to my *pack*, to the family that had taken me in, that had accepted and loved me unconditionally. That had kept me *safe*.

As my mind melded more and more with my wolf's, her memories of the past few hours became mine. I saw an overturned wheelchair, heard the frantic shouts of Dr. Sloane. Bullets and darts zipped through the air. More glass shattered as my wolf barreled through the lab in a desperate surge to escape. I realized then that she hadn't fled out of cowardice or fear. Leaving Jagger behind had gutted her. She would have killed *everyone* in that dreadful place in order to protect him, but she couldn't do it alone.

She needed help. She needed our *pack*.

Suddenly, I remembered receiving an influx of strength shortly after she'd taken over. I'd felt reborn, as if new life had been breathed into my lungs. The energy, the *power* had been unlike anything I'd ever felt before. It had given my wolf the strength she needed to break free of that horrible prison and the people in it. The energy had been wholly familiar, and yet it hadn't been mine. It had almost felt like . . .

Oh, no.

With a sinking heart, I finally pieced together what had happened. Jagger had sacrificed himself for me. I was alive right now because of him. Because of the bond that tied us together. He'd given me his essence. His *life*.

Oh, Jagger, I sobbed, heartbroken that he'd given up everything for me.

Before I could succumb to grief over his sacrifice, I felt a flutter. A faint pulse in my chest where our invisible bond was. It was so weak that I almost missed it, but that tiny thrum of energy sent hope soaring through me.

He was alive. My mate was *alive!*

I cried out in joy, and my wolf released the sound in a howl that echoed through the night. For the first time ever, it felt like we were in perfect sync. Her instincts had driven her to seek help, and although every mile away from Jagger was agony, I trusted her. I trusted her to save my mate.

And so I stopped fighting. Stopping trying to take back control. She knew what to do, and I *trusted* her.

Hurry, hurry, hurry, I urged her onward, knowing she wanted the exact same thing that I did. Her slim legs practically sprouted wings, carrying us through the countryside at breakneck speed. She was unstoppable, fueled by the power of my mate. The soulmate bond continued to weakly pulse, and I clung to it like a lifeline, willing Jagger to keep on living.

Please, I whispered, praying he could hear me somehow. *Please don't give up.*

The moon was high in the sky when I started to recognize sights and smells along our northwestern trek home. My wolf ran even faster, spurred on by the fact that we were almost home. When the main gates to the Rivers' family estate finally came into view, she didn't stop. She jumped right over them and kept on going, her sides heaving and breaths clouding the air as she doggedly approached the end of her mission.

We were racing across the vast front lawn when the door of the mansion burst open. The second I spotted a pregnant female with fiery red hair standing in the doorway, I burst into tears. My wolf started to cry as well, whimpering as she approached my best friend.

When we leapt onto the porch, Nora rushed forward and wrapped her arms around my wolf's neck without hesitation, loudly sobbing, "Oh, Brielle."

I cried harder, and my wolf did too, relieved to be reunited with one of our favorite people. Moments later, our relieved cries turned to cries of pain, and my wolf's legs gave out. As she collapsed onto the porch, worry shivered up my spine.

Something was wrong. Something was *very* wrong.

The energy that had carried us for the past few hours felt drained. *Empty.* That energy had been keeping us alive. Now that it was gone, we were starting to die again. I could *feel* it.

"Vi, get out here! It's Brielle!" Nora urgently yelled, kneeling beside my wolf. "It's okay, Brie. You're safe now. I'm going to help you shift back."

My wolf weakly whined, nervous yet wholly trusting our alpha female to help us. She'd saved us once from death, and I knew she could do it again. Her magic was powerful, allowing her to heal almost anything.

A familiar dark brunette joined us on the porch then, gasping when she spotted me. "She's shifted. How is she still alive?"

"I don't know, Vi," Nora grimly replied, "but she won't be for much longer if we don't help her. I need you to hold her steady while I do this."

Vi nodded and knelt beside my wolf's other side. Both females were weeks away from giving birth, but that didn't stop them from helping their friend in need. I was grateful, *so* grateful for them. I'd left, and they'd readily welcomed me back. My past feelings of betrayal felt so small now, and I wanted nothing more than to make amends. But when I tried to speak, all that came out was a pathetic whine.

"Shhh, it's okay, Brie," Nora soothed, running her hand over the fur on my face. "I'm going to fix this."

My wolf shuddered, closing her eyes as our strength continued to rapidly decline.

"*Now*, Nora," Vi said. "Her heartrate is slowing."

Sudden light burst behind our eyelids, and a wave of warmth swept over us, *through* us. "Shift, Brie," Nora quietly yet firmly ordered. "You have to *shift*."

My wolf resisted, flinching away.

Vi grabbed my wolf's shoulders, surprisingly strong as she held her down. My wolf thrashed in her grip, whimpering as the warmth intensified, growing hotter and hotter.

"Shift!" Nora barked, her quiet demeanor falling away to reveal the alpha within. Her fingers dug into my wolf's face, the magical light pulsing from them and into our body sharp and demanding like her voice. "*Shift*, Brielle!"

The command jolted through us, shoving us over the edge. One of our bones snapped, and I screamed, the sound belting from my wolf's mouth in an agonized howl. Vi and Nora worked together to hold me still, staying by my side as I painfully transitioned from wolf to my human form.

When it was finished and I lay panting on the cold porch, naked and utterly spent, they both gathered me into their arms. Tears streamed down my cheeks, and I sobbed, beyond grateful to have survived. Already, I felt my strength slowly returning. Not Jagger's this time, but mine. At the mere thought of him, my sobs grew hoarse until I could barely breathe.

Still, I began to tell them everything. About my heat and our time in the barn, about how Jagger used our soulmate bond to save me, about the fact that I *loved* him and could barely function knowing that I'd left him all alone in that godawful place. They listened without interruption, quietly offering me their support and comfort.

The second I was done, though, Vi stood up and hurried back inside the house, saying over her shoulder, "I'm calling the boys."

Apparently, Kolton and Griff had been scouring the earth ever since discovering that Jagger and I had been taken. They weren't the only ones, either. The entire *pack* was out looking for us, even Mrs. Bailey. Even my *human* family.

If that wasn't acceptance, if that wasn't *love*, I didn't know what was.

"Don't worry, Brie," Nora said, wiping the tears from my face. "We're going to get him. We're going to get your mate back."

CHAPTER 31

JAGGER

Being alive but barely existing was absolute hell.

I was in a catatonic state, but my body was wide awake, every sense acutely aware. I could smell the spilled blood surrounding me, hear the shouts and crunch of glass beneath panicked feet, feel the hands lifting me into a chair and strapping me down once more.

Needles jabbed into my skin, and I didn't react. I couldn't. I was paralyzed, and yet I could feel *everything*.

"Hurry!" Dr. Sloane barked. "He's useless to us if he dies."

Poking. Prodding. Jabbing. It felt endless. They crammed an oxygen tube down my throat, and I couldn't even choke on it.

"What about the female?" one of the other doctors questioned.

"We don't have the resources to recapture her right now," Dr. Sloane snapped. "With Mr. Coolidge dead, the mercenaries need a new field leader. I don't understand how this even happened. The female was *weak* compared to the male. She shouldn't have been able to escape our facility."

The doctors continued to speculate among themselves, but I tuned them out. Only one word stuck in my mind and remained there like a flickering candle of hope.

Escape. Brielle had *escaped*. Which meant that she was still alive.

Relief barrelled through me, and I finally allowed myself to relax. She was safe, and that was all that mattered. Darkness tugged at me, and I sank in and out of consciousness. I didn't know how much time passed, but after a while, the frantic voices and bustling around me faded.

I thought I was finally alone when a plaintive whine filled my head.

Onyx, I breathed out his name through our connection, relieved to hear him again. He whined a second time, the weak sound filled with confusion. *We saved her, boy*, I told him, and I immediately felt him settle.

Saved mate, he contentedly said.

Saved mate, I confirmed.

We lapsed into silence after that, the comfort of each other's presence enough for us both. We'd struggled to coexist for so long, but in this moment, we were one entity. One being. We'd sacrificed everything to protect Brielle, and now, we could finally rest.

It felt like days passed. Time dragged by slowly, my existence little more than tubes and wires. My breathing tube was eventually removed, but they kept an oxygen mask over my face, constantly monitoring my vitals. Numerous vials of blood were removed from my body, and after catching bits and pieces of conversation, I finally figured out what they were doing with it, with *me*.

Trying to create a permanent cure for human diseases.

Werewolves contained DNA that humans didn't, DNA that could eradicate sickness and all sorts of maladies. But there was no absolving the toxin that bound werewolves to the moon's cycle. That toxin was a disease in its own right, and the scientists experimenting on me clearly didn't want their cure to be infected with it.

Apparently, they thought *I* was the solution to this problem.

The toxin in my blood was acceptable to them, all because I had the power to shift at will. Too bad they knew nothing about hybrids. Too bad their experiments were for nothing.

They'd find out soon enough that I wasn't the solution they were looking for.

Every time they stuck me with another needle and I tried to move, my body failed me. Never in my life had I felt this weak and helpless. Despite willing all of my strength to Brielle, I'd somehow retained a sliver of it, just enough to keep me alive. I didn't know what was worse. Dying or existing in this vegetative state.

The immense strength I'd once possessed had left me, and I didn't know if it would ever come back. I hadn't tried to access it again through the soulmate bond, uncertain if Brielle still needed it. Our invisible connection was practically nonexistent, so threadbare that I struggled to feel it.

Could *she* feel it? Did she know I was still alive?

I wanted to call out to her, to hear for myself that she was okay. But wherever she was felt too far away. She was beyond my reach, a fact that brought me equal parts relief and pain. She was safe, but I'd sworn I wouldn't let anything or anyone separate us again, and I'd failed.

Miss mate, Onyx softly whined, more subdued than I'd ever felt him. He hadn't tried to gain control ever since our strength had vanished, too weak to initiate the transformation. But I could feel how sad, how miserable he was, not just because we'd been reduced to a pincushion but because Brielle was gone.

I miss her too, I told him, remembering our brief time in the barn together and how perfect it had been. I'd finally had everything I wanted, but it had been too good to be true. Fate must have finally realized that a beast like me didn't belong with a beauty like her. I was broken, now more than ever. Having a family of my own had been too much to hope for.

I would die alone, just like my birth family had wanted me to. Just like—

NO, Onyx abruptly growled. *Miss mate. Miss family. No die. No die!*

Surprised by his outburst to my morose thoughts, I didn't respond.

Must fight. Must live! he went on, so impassioned that I couldn't help but feed off that unexpected burst of energy.

Wait.

That energy hadn't existed before. It was *new*.

For the first time since I'd given my essence to Brielle, I allowed myself to think of the future again. Maybe this wasn't the end for us after all. Maybe, just maybe, I would see my beautiful mate again.

Hours later, I had enough strength to open my eyes. An hour after that, I moved my fingers and toes. I still felt weaker than a newborn pup, but every hour that passed, a little more strength infused my body. It was progress.

Even more, it was *hope*.

"Are you sure we should test the volunteers on a full moon? Maybe we should wait to administer the serum in a few days."

"He's a *hybrid*, Dr. Fenway," Dr. Sloane answered her male colleague. "Hybrids aren't affected by the full moon and neither will our test subjects. You'll see."

The man protested with another concern, but I tuned him out, focusing on the fact that only two days had gone by since Brielle had escaped. Two days of remaining perfectly still so the humans experimenting on me didn't know I'd regained mobility. Partially, anyway. I didn't know if I could break free of my restraints again, but I felt strong enough to do some damage if given the opportunity.

"I've made my decision," Dr. Sloane snapped, cutting through my thoughts again. The pair weren't directly beside me but close enough that I could easily overhear. "I've been in this wheelchair for five years, Dr. Fenway. *Five years.* I'm not giving this disease one more day of my life."

"I understand, Anita, but—"

"No, you *don't* understand," Dr. Sloane interrupted. "My body is a ticking time bomb, and every day that passes, this disease devours more of me. My vision is growing worse, and my memories have become more and more muddled. I need to test the serum *now* while I still can."

"Yes, but—"

"I'm done discussing this, Dr. Fenway. The volunteers know the risks and are willing to accept them at the chance of being cured. Get them ready, or I'll find someone who will."

A pause, then I heard the retreat of footsteps as Dr. Fenway no doubt went to do her bidding. Dr. Sloane wasn't one to be trifled with and clearly wasn't above firing anyone who got in her way. Her eagerness to test the cure would only end in failure, though. The human volunteers would shift with the full moon the second that serum hit their bloodstream.

But there was no guarantee they'd survive the transformation process. Humans with compromised DNA were at greater risk of their bodies rejecting the werewolf toxin. Brielle had been healthy, and even *she* would have died if not for Nora's healing magic.

"This is going to work. I just know it," I heard Dr. Sloane say before wheeling away. Silence fell over the lab, but I remained perfectly still. Onyx did the same, for once understanding the need for patience.

Not long after, several voices filled the lab, some I recognized and some I didn't. The human trials must be about to begin. A quick peek confirmed it, and I watched through lowered lashes as a handful of people in hospital gowns were led to glass chambers and strapped down like I was.

They looked excited. Hopeful. And probably had no idea that a cage awaited them one floor below if the test failed.

No one seemed to notice me tucked in the corner of the lab. I'd been discarded, forgotten, left to rot in this chair. My contribution to their "cure" was over, and they no longer needed me. Not even bothering to carry me down to a containment chamber, they'd simply thrown a sheet over my comatose body and walked away.

The sheet had slipped from my face, though, allowing me to observe everything.

Dr. Sloane was wheeling from chamber to chamber, offering words of encouragement to each subject. Doctors and assistants were everywhere, pushing supply carts and hooking up the volunteers to monitors. I spotted a few armored guards stationed near the exits, their weapons carefully concealed. The viewing platform overlooking the lab—the one weak spot that Brielle's wolf had used to escape—was still devoid of glass, but the mess had been swept clean.

All-in-all, the humans seemed prepared to face whatever outcome that came from these trials, but I alone knew the truth. They were playing with fire, and all hell was about to break loose.

When it did, Onyx and I would be ready.

The humans received their injections moments later. Dr. Sloane looked on, closely watching them with hope in her eyes. Seconds passed. Minutes. When nothing happened, the doctors began to restlessly stir. One of the male test subjects suddenly cried out, but it wasn't a pained cry.

"I'm cured," he excitedly proclaimed. "I'm cured!"

A few of the other subjects started to say the same thing, and the doctors cheered. I didn't move a muscle, waiting for the other shoe to drop.

It happened seconds later, starting with a surprised gasp, then an alarmed shout. "What's happening to me? What's *happening* to me?!"

A female subject screamed, terror filling her eyes as dark claws began to emerge from her fingertips. Another subject cried out in agony as their bones started to break, the transformation process swiftly overtaking them.

"Dr. Sloane! *Dr. Sloane!*" a guard yelled, rushing across the lab toward her. "We're being breached!"

Over the cries and screams of the shifting humans, I heard a distant *boom* as if something heavy had just struck a door or wall. When it happened again, a voice filled my head. *Her* voice.

Jagger!

My eyes snapped open.

Jagger, I'm here!

A hot tear rolled down my cheek.

Another distant boom reached me, and I knew then that it wasn't something. It was my alpha. My pack. My *family* had come for me, led by my beautiful mate.

Brielle, I hoarsely called back, overwhelmed to hear her voice again.

Mate! Onyx howled in glee.

Oh, thank God, Brielle sobbed, sounding so relieved that another tear escaped me.

Before I could respond, a shrill voice interrupted, shrieking, "This is all your fault!" I looked up to find Dr. Sloane wheeling toward me, her face lit with fury. "Your mate brought them here. I should have killed her when I had the chance!"

I didn't reply. Just stared at her, my expression devoid of emotion. A furious cry burst from her, and she whipped out a gun to point it at my face. A shot rang out, and I flinched. More shots fired, and I realized then that they weren't coming from her. Guards were rushing across the lab, firing at two huge forms standing on the edge of the viewing platform above.

At the sight of them, a huge grin split my face.

Dr. Sloane whipped her head around to see what had caught my eye. When she spotted Kolton and Griff in their demonic wolf forms, all color leached from her face. "No."

More figures appeared, more faces I recognized. Bill and Noah Andrews were among them, along with several other field agents from the SCA. They wasted no time firing back at the armored guards below, not just with bullets but with magic. Even more familiar faces came into view, lining up along the platform's edge.

Energy surged through me.

My pack. *Midnight Pack* had arrived.

They were all in their wolf forms, their bright yellow eyes peering down at the growing chaos below. One pair in particular caught my attention, and I locked eyes with my mate.

Onyx went wild, straining to get to her. My body violently trembled, the restraints holding me down groaning under the force.

Dr. Sloane's gun clattered to the floor, and she reached into her pocket for something else. My eyes snapped back to her as she pulled out a syringe, and I tensed, finally ready to fight. But instead of aiming it at me, she jerked up her coat sleeve and positioned the needle in the crook of her elbow.

"It won't fix you," I finally spoke to her. "Not in the way you want it to."

She looked up at me and paused, seeing the truth of it in my eyes. Pursing her lips, she said, "I don't care anymore. Anything is better than rotting away in this wheelchair for the rest of my life."

With that, she plunged the needle into her flesh.

Almost immediately, she felt the effects of the serum. Her eyes brightened, her lips parting in a surprised O. Reaching up, she removed her glasses and blinked, whispering, "I can see again." With a gasp, she reached down and touched her legs. "My strength is returning! I can . . . I can . . ."

Ignoring the chaos around us, she scooted forward in her chair and set her feet on the floor. Awkwardly, she pushed up, her thin legs trembling as they took her weight for the first time in five years. A laugh left her, and she shuffled forward a step. She took another, and that's when it happened.

"No!" she cried, collapsing into a heap on the floor. Her body started to convulse, and a scream of pure agony belted from her.

At the sound, a chill skated down my spine. I'd heard that scream before. Knew what it meant.

"Help me!" Dr. Sloane screamed, writhing on the floor as her body tried to shift. Tried and failed.

It was rejecting the toxin, and there was nothing I could do to help her.

As her body continued to rage against the serum she'd injected herself with, I finally told Onyx it was time. He didn't need to be told twice. Surging upward in excitement, he used the strength we'd been slowly building for the past two days to partially shift. My arms and legs lengthened, sprouting fur and packing on more muscle. Together, we fought to break free of our restraints, pouring all the energy we had into the effort.

An extra dose of energy suddenly shot through me. Surprised, I glanced up and spotted Brielle's wolf on the same floor as me now, her yellow eyes intently fixed on mine.

Hope that helps, she said to me through our bond.

I grinned at her a mile wide. *It most definitely does.*

With the combined strength of all three of us, I easily snapped through the restraints and tore off the oxygen mask, tubes, wires. Without taking my eyes off her, I stood and stepped forward.

Before I could pass by Dr. Sloane, she grabbed my ankle and whimpered, "Kill me."

Reluctantly, I looked down at her, taking in how small and helpless she now seemed. Sweat beaded her brow, her body continuing to convulse as it fought off the transformation.

"Kill me!" she repeated, *begged*, a scream slipping past her clenched teeth.

I stared at her a moment more, then reached down and picked up the gun she'd aimed at my head. It would be easy, *so* easy to kill her. She deserved nothing less for what she'd done to me, my mate, and countless other supernaturals. I held the gun for another few moments, then bent and pried her hand off my ankle, placing the gun in it instead.

"Do it yourself," I told her, then turned and walked away, leaving her to face the fate she'd brought on herself.

The second my eyes met Brielle's again, I picked up speed. All around us, wolves and SCA agents were fighting against armored guards. Doctors and their assistants were running around in a panic as the humans transforming into werewolves for the first time broke free of their restraints. The lab was a mess of havoc, but I ignored it all, my sole focus on the beautiful female dashing toward me in wolf form.

We met in a clash of fur and partially-shifted limbs, so forcefully that we bowled each other over and collapsed to the ground. I fiercely gathered her against me, laughing when her long tongue darted out and caught my cheek.

Mate! Onyx yipped like an overgrown pup, wagging his tail so excitedly that I let it spring out to beat against the floor.

I tightly held Brielle to me, letting the chaotic world around us fade. She was safe in my arms, exactly where she belonged. All the pain and suffering I'd endured melted away, replaced with a certainty that our future together was secure.

I could feel it in my soul. Feel it through the precious bond that was strengthening between us once more.

Brielle snuggled close and whispered through our bond, *I love you.*

I heaved out a contented sigh, whispering back, "I love you, too."

EPILOGUE

BRIELLE

I was on the edge of orgasm when a little voice from the doorway chirped, "Whatcha doin'?"

Startled, I yanked my teeth free of Jagger's neck and tried to scoot back on the counter. Standing between my legs, Jagger pulled me closer, his fingers digging into my bottom as he thrust inside me like a madman. I desperately tried to stave off the orgasm but was too turned on by his feral energy. An uncontrollable whimper burst from me, pleasure cascading through every inch of my body.

As my walls squeezed Jagger's rock-hard cock, that same little voice yelled, "Uncle Jag is wrestling with Auntie Brie again!"

Jagger jerked inside me with a low groan, his own pleasure filling our bond.

"Mellie, we're not—" I started, then gasped when another orgasm hit me. Jagger slipped a hand between us to rub my clit through my underwear, prolonging the fresh wave of ecstasy. I gave up trying to pull away and curled my legs around his waist, moaning breathlessly.

I was in the throes of another trembling orgasm when a new voice, this one deep and male, said in exasperation, "Really, Jagger? The kitchen *island*? We cook and eat there."

Realizing that our *alpha* had caught us having sex—*again*—heat flushed my face.

"I swear they're worse than me, Vi, you, and Nora combined," another male commented.

"Agreed," Kolton replied to Griff. "Good thing they're moving out today. I'm pretty sure they've *wrestled* on every surface of this house."

"Don't forget the garage," Griff muttered.

Jagger ignored their teasing, lightly kissing my neck as we came down from our blissful highs. After another moment, he pulled out and readjusted our clothing but continued to stand between my legs, languidly running his hand up and down my back.

"Is Auntie Brie okay?" the little voice who'd outed us asked in concern. "Her face is all red."

"Oh, she's more than okay," Griff snickered. "Just worn out from all the wrestling."

I opened my eyes to glare at him over Jagger's shoulder. He grinned at me like a fiend.

"What about the baby? Is she okay with the wrestling?"

Kolton glanced down at his sister in surprise. "She?"

"Yep. I had a dream last night that the new baby was a girl," Melanie said, her dark amber eyes twinkling brightly.

Jagger stilled.

"Are you sure?" I asked her, my embarrassment suddenly long gone.

"Of course," the almost eight-year-old replied with an upturned tilt of her nose. "My dreams are never wrong."

And they weren't. Her premonitions were coming more and more frequently now that her familiar's magic had started to manifest. She was an Oracle. A strong one. And surprisingly adept at her new abilities already. She'd predicted that Nora and Vi would give birth on the same snowy day in early January, and they had. Both babies had been boys, one with dark red hair and the other with blond.

Thankfully, Melanie was still clueless about the birds and the bees. Although, with her inquisitive mind, she would figure it out soon enough.

Her confirmation brought an onslaught of happy tears. "A girl," I said in a hushed whisper, my throat tight with emotion. "We're going to have a *girl*."

Girl! Onyx exuberantly howled, and I huffed a laugh.

Jagger didn't respond, but I felt an unexpected flicker of fear through our bond.

"What is it?" I asked him, leaning back to see his face.

Over the past couple of months, I'd learned to read him so much better. His expressions were still subtle, but with the help of our soulmate bond, I often knew what he was thinking before he even said anything. When I'd told him almost two months ago that I was pregnant, he hadn't said a word. But he didn't need to. I could *feel* his sheer joy through our bond. It had been one of the happiest moments of my life.

And now I was experiencing another one, overjoyed that we would be having a baby girl in just a few short months. Jagger, on the other hand, looked so green that I thought he would be sick. I searched his face, worried when I couldn't hear his thoughts.

"Jagger?" I gently pressed, wondering if this was all too much for him.

Everything in his world had changed in such a short amount of time. After recovering from his close brush with death, he'd gone from being a dominant male in the pack to an alpha. His lone wolf status had vanished as he became a soon-to-be father and a husband in only a matter of months. In typical werewolf fashion, we'd wasted no time getting hitched, my baby bump noticeably visible through my mermaid wedding dress.

The entirety of Midnight Pack had come to the wedding, but that wasn't all. I'd invited everyone I could—members of the SCA we considered friends, the royal vampire family who'd become our close allies, Reid and Desirae from Lunar Falls Pack, Griff's brother Mason from Moon Bay Pack.

And then I'd done something unheard of: I'd invited my human family.

Humans didn't attend werewolf weddings and for good reason. Doing so was like throwing rabbits into a wolf den. But I'd wanted them at my wedding so badly that Jagger had caved, promising to keep them safe. And he had. Everyone who got too close to them had received warning looks and light growls, ones that promised punishment should they overstep. No one had dared lay a hand on my brothers or parents, deferring to Jagger's newfound alphaness. Even Kolton had kept his distance.

But now that the wedding was over, it was time for even more big changes. Although Jagger was still Midnight Pack's second in command, he could no longer ignore his new alpha instincts to take charge as the leader of his own family. Staying under another alpha's roof was no longer possible, especially with a mate and baby on the way. Later today, we would be moving the last of our stuff to the property directly north of the Rivers' estate.

There was a quaint cabin-style house in the woods there surrounded by plenty of running trails, including a trail that connected to the one Jagger had frequented for the past several years. I was already in love with the place and couldn't wait to decorate it.

Kolton had been more than understanding when we'd announced our plans to move and had even bought the house for us as a wedding present. Nora, Vi, and I were sad that we wouldn't all be under the same roof anymore, but now that Griff and Vi had their baby boy, it wouldn't be long now before they too moved into their newly-built house.

Everything was changing, yet they were good changes. They excited me, but I knew that Jagger took longer to adjust to new things. He still struggled to open up sometimes, used to keeping his emotions to himself. I'd grown accustomed to using our bond to interpret his silence, but for the life of me, I couldn't decipher why the news of having a daughter made him afraid.

Jagger, speak to me, I softly urged him once more, running my fingers over the buzzed hair on his nape. *Is this all happening too fast?*

A line bisected his dark brows. "No, it's not that," he finally said, reaching up to touch the gold necklace he'd given me for Christmas— the one I wore every day and never took off. "It's just . . . What if I fail to protect her?"

At the vulnerable look on his face, my heart melted. "Oh, Jagger," I whispered. "You won't fail. You sacrificed your life to protect me, and I know you'll do the same for our daughter. And besides, you have me now. We'll protect her together."

The line between his brows slowly faded, and he whispered back, "I'm blessed to have you as my mate."

"I know," I said, flashing my dimples at him.

He leaned forward to lick one, and I burst into a fit of giggles.

"Ugh, again?" a female voice groaned. "Who caught them this time?"

"Mellie," Kolton and Griff answered Vi at the same time.

I dropped my legs from around Jagger's waist, and he finally, albeit reluctantly, pulled back. Before I could hop off the counter, he grabbed my hips and lowered me to my feet, placing a less-than-chaste kiss on my lips. For a private male, he sure wasn't shy about PDA. In fact, he was probably the worst out of the three males, to my delight. I'd thought for sure he would be a bedroom-only kind of lover, but we barely used the bed for sex—unless he felt the urge to tie me up.

"Pregnancy hormones, am I right?" Vi said, wagging her eyebrows at us as she approached with a little squirming bundle in her arms.

Noticing that she was breastfeeding on the go, Jagger averted his eyes but stayed close by, slipping behind me to rest a hand on my growing stomach.

"Yes," I agreed, reaching out to stroke Isaiah's fine blond hair. "With the amount of sperm Jagger puts inside me on a daily basis, I'd totally be pregnant if I wasn't already pregnant."

Vi snorted, and Griff loudly guffawed. Jagger didn't say a word, but I smirked when embarrassment warmed our bond.

So adorable, I crooned.

Just you wait until later, mate, he lightly growled into my mind. *There will be no one to hear you scream once we're moved into our house.*

I shivered in anticipation.

"What's so funny?" another female voice asked, and I looked over Vi's shoulder to see my best friend enter the kitchen with her own precious baby bundle and two little toddlers. Luca shot past, and his younger sister Lillian who'd just learned to walk desperately tried to keep up. As she tripped and started to fall, Kolton bent down and scooped her into his arms.

"Jagger's sperm," Griff answered Nora, grinning again when her eyes comically widened.

"What's sperm?" Melanie asked.

"Sperm is the stuff that comes out of a male when he wrestles with a female," Griff replied with a wicked smirk.

Melanie wrinkled her nose. "Like sweat?"

"Well, not exactly. You see—"

"Griffin, behave yourself," an older female voice chastised.

Charlotte pushed through the growing crowd, making for the refrigerator and completely ignoring the aroma of sex permeating her pristine kitchen. After placing three cartons of eggs, a slab of ham, and two packets of bacon on the island, she paused to eye us all shrewdly before saying, "If you're not in here to help me make breakfast, then *scoot*."

We all shared a collective look, one that spoke of so many things. Life had brought us so much turmoil lately yet even more blessings. Through the pain and heartache, we'd found connection and love. Enemies had tried to tear us apart, but we'd fought for each other and become stronger in the process.

This world I'd been thrust into was dangerous, but as I looked at each of the faces around me, I knew that I would never have to face it alone. We were a pack. A *family*. And as we all started to help with breakfast, I knew that whatever fate had in store for us, our bond would last forever.

ALSO BY BECKY MOYNIHAN

WOLVES OF MIDNIGHT
Midnight Vow
Midnight Claim
Midnight Queen
Midnight Hunt (spin-off standalone)
Midnight Bond (spin-off standalone)

A TOUCH OF VAMPIRE
Shadow Touched
Curse Touched
Fate Touched
Sun Touched (spin-off standalone)
Forever Touched (spin-off standalone)

THE ELITE TRIALS
Reactive
Adaptive
Immersive

GENESIS CRYSTAL SAGA
Dawn till Dusk
Fall of Night
Stars till Sun

ACKNOWLEDGMENTS

I can't believe the Wolves of Midnight series is over!! I'm a little sad right now, but mostly happy and so very grateful that I had the opportunity to write these characters. I love them to pieces, and they will continue to live on in my heart! This series changed my author career immensely, and I'm beyond blessed that so many readers have fallen in love with this world.

I did a poll recently, and it looks like many of you are excited about a dark academia witch/warlock series set in this same world! I plan on writing that next, so make sure you're following me for more news on that soon!

As always, thank you to my lovely beta readers for taking the time to leave me early feedback. Allie, Morgan, Kate, and Melissa, you ladies seriously rock!

To my ARC readers, thank you a million times over for making my day every time my books receive a new review. Each and every one of those reviews are like gold to me! An especially big thanks to Amy for giving me the idea for the epilogue scene. I hope you liked it!!

To ALL of my readers, thank you to the moon and back for loving my books and supporting this grateful indie author! I owe the success of this series to YOU!!

BECKY MOYNIHAN is a bestselling, award-winning author of paranormal romance and urban fantasy. Her books include the A Touch of Vampire series, Wolves of Midnight series, The Elite Trials series, and the co-written Genesis Crystal Saga.

When she's not writing, you can find Becky curled up on the couch in her North Carolina home, binge-watching shows and sipping Mountain Dew.

To stay up to date on new releases, sign up for her monthly newsletter: www.beckymoynihan.com/newsletter